Praise for

The Gondola Maker

Silver IPPY Award for Best Adult Fiction EBook
Finalist for the 2014 National Indie Excellence Award
Shortlisted for the da Vinci Eye Prize
Category finalist for the Eric Hoffer Award

"I'm a big fan of Venice, so I appreciate Laura Morelli's special knowledge of the city, the period, and the process of gondola-making. An especially compelling story."

— **Frances Mayes, author,** *Under the Tuscan Sun*

"Sixteenth-century Venice is the star of Laura Morelli's well-crafted historical novel about the heir to the city's most renowned gondola builder."

— **Publishers Weekly** S⸱⸱⸱⸱⸱ ⸱⸱⸱view

"The heir to a gondola empire ⸱ ⸱⸱⸱⸱⸱⸱ ⸱nat-ing glimpse into Renaissance Ve⸱⸱⸱

— ⸱ ⸱⸱⸱⸱⸱ ᴅook of the Month

"Laura Morelli has done her research, or perhaps she was an Italian carpenter in another life. One can literally smell and feel the grain of finely turned wood in her hands."

— **Pamela Sheldon Johns, author,**
Italian Food Artisans

"Laura Morelli's extensive research into 16th-century Venice and the art of gondola making brings history to the present."

— *Foreword Reviews*

"Romance, intrigue, family loyalty, pride and redemption set against the backdrop of Renaissance Italy."

— *Library of Clean Reads*

"Historical fiction at its best."

— *Midwest Book Review*

the Gondola Maker

Laura Morelli

Published in the United States of America by Laura Morelli.

Library of Congress Control Number 2013922567
Hardcover ISBN: 978-0989367127
Paperback ISBN: 978-0989367103

The Gondola Maker / Laura Morelli

www.lauramorelli.com

FREE DOWNLOAD

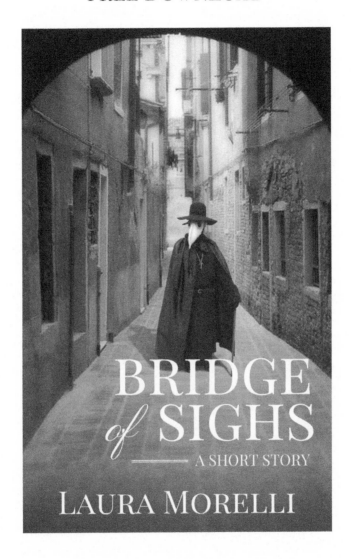

Join my Readers' Group and get a free copy
of my short story, "Bridge of Sighs."

To get started visit
www.lauramorelli.com/bridge-of-sighs

Dedicated to those
whose hearts propel their hands

Venice, 1581

Chapter 1

I chew my lower lip while I wait to see my father's gondola catch fire.

Beneath the boat, a pile of firewood is stacked so high that I find myself in the odd position of looking up at the underside of its black hull. A meticulous servant or day laborer has split the logs and arranged them into neat stacks, then pressed dried brush into the spaces between the wood, with the intention to start an impressive blaze. The gondola has been lashed to the largest logs of the pyre, yet it remains skewed at an angle. From my vantage point, I cannot help but admire the craft's flowing lines, its elegant prow reaching toward the sky as if to defy this injustice.

My father had nothing to do with the crime committed in this boat, of course. I feel certain that none of the onlookers has any idea that my father, our Republic's most renowned gondola maker, and I, a young man barely worthy of note, crafted this gondola with our own hands. Surely no one has noticed our *catanella*, the maple-leaf emblem we carve into the prow of each gondola that emerges from the Vianello workshop.

I stand in a crowd of bakers, clockmakers, tailors, housewives, fishermen, and merchants, all hungry for a fiery spectacle. I cast my eyes to what must be hundreds of individuals gathered around me. No, not one of them is thinking of my proud father or myself, even though I helped my father craft this fine boat just two years ago in our family boatyard. The only man on people's minds is the one who threw the rock that started this humiliating affair.

I hear murmuring behind me, then the crowd parts in unison. I scramble to the fringes just in time to feel the swish of a silk robe as a man strides purposefully by me, ignoring my presence as if I were a mere bird fluttering out of his path.

"The Councillor," I hear someone whisper beside me. My heart begins to pound.

Beneath the clasp that holds his garment closed, the man's chest protrudes. His brow pulsates at the temples, and flecks of gray dust his otherwise slick head of black hair that shows beneath his close-fitting cap. A perfectly straight nose and an even, thin-lipped mouth define a regal profile. Silently, the man circles the doomed boat, turning his piercing dark eyes into the depths of the pyre as if he can see through to the other side. He looks up at the great black craft, and everyone in the circle follows his gaze, shifting from foot to foot in anticipation.

The man in the silk robes completes his circumnavigation of the pyre. Finally, he addresses the crowd, which has grown silent over the course of the man's dramatic entrance. A shadow darkens his face, and his mouth forms a scowl as the deep cadence of his voice reverberates through the air:

"The Lords of our Most Excellent Council have ruled in the case brought against Bonito Banfi, boatman of Cannaregio, so that justice may be served in a manner proper and fitting to any individual who would seek to disrupt the peace and stable government of our Most Serene Republic. Accounting for the harmful scourge that irreverent boatmen bring to the peace of Our Most Excellent State, Bonito Banfi has been sentenced to ten years of service on the convict galleys."

By now all of us have heard the story of Bonito Banfi, the condemned gondolier whose boat—the same one that launched from our boatyard ramp two years ago—will burn on the pyre.

The tale has spread across the Venetian Republic for nearly ten days. As with so many crimes in our city, this one began with a family quarrel so old that no one remembers how it had started. Banfi had been making his rounds of the ferry stations when he spied his archrival, another gondolier called Paolo Squeran. Squeran owed him money, Banfi said, to settle a gambling debt. The two men commenced a shouting match, their foul words echoing across the canal waters from one gondola to the other. The verbal insults escalated and began to draw crowds of onlookers to the edge of the quay.

Banfi didn't know it, but the passenger riding behind the curtains of Squeran's gondola happened to be the French ambassador, returning to the embassy after a meeting at the Great Council. Banfi lifted a large rock that he had been carrying in his gondola just in case he happened to cross paths with Squeran. Instead of hitting Banfi's rival, however, the rock rang against the ambassador's passenger compartment. The curtains parted and the enraged ambassador emerged from his peaceful retreat to hurl insults of his own, in French, at the offending gondolier. The ambassador then ordered Squeran to ferry him directly to the Council of Ten, where he lodged a formal complaint with the body of justice-makers.

Banfi's sentence, so it has been recounted, is to serve for ten years on the convict galleys. Banfi's ankles were shackled, and he has been escorted to the state shipyard, where he will be chained to a crew of prisoners forced to row one of Our Serene Republic's sailing ships, part of a fleet that embarks each day for Crete, Corfu, Acre, and other port cities of our colonies in the eastern Mediterranean. To be sure, the convict galleys mean a sentence for Banfi that is worse than prison, perhaps even than death. A host of ills awaits him, seasickness and diarrhea the very least of his worries. All of us have heard the stories of dysentery that make you vomit blood, scurvy that causes pus-filled wounds to emerge across your thighs, and gangrene that turns your feet black. This is all on top of falling victim to whatever tribulations one's fellow prisoners might inflict under cover of darkness.

A modest state pittance will be provided to feed and clothe Banfi's wife and four small children, who watched tearfully as six of the state night-guards, the *signori di notte*, seized the gondola. Within hours, the boat was sentenced to this fiery doom. The intent, of course, is to set an example for the notoriously foul-mouthed gondoliers whom everyone in the crowd already considers the scourge of the city.

Before the pyre, I watch the man in the silk robes, himself surely one of The Ten who received the complaint lodged by the French ambassador. I see his lower lip twitch, an almost imperceptible, involuntary spasm that seems at odds with this otherwise well-composed official. It vanishes as quickly as it appears. He continues:

"Today, it is both my obligation and my privilege to oversee the public disgrace of this boat, as an example and a symbol for any boatman who would seek to act in any manner against Our Most Excellent Government. The greatest weight shall be placed against those who would seek to disrupt the peace of Our Most Serene Republic. So decreed on this four-hundred-fifty-first day of the reign of our Most Illustrious and Benevolent Prince Doge Nicolò da Ponte."

He turns and nods to a servant hanging on the edge of the crowd. I draw my breath now and watch a lean, muscular African dressed in a pair of drab breeches and a short-waisted jacket step forward into the circle. The crowd presses back to make room for the Councillor, who stands to face the prow of the boat. The servant approaches the pyre with a lit torch, which he begins to swing, igniting the wood prepared beneath it.

Small flames dance inside the pile of brush and logs. Within moments, flames climb, rapidly reaching up to lick the bottom of the great black craft. With a crackle and a whoosh, the gondola is engulfed in a blaze. I suck in my breath, but soon smoke assails my nostrils and the heat tightens the skin on my face. As the wooden planks begin to crack and char, I recognize the same malaise I have experienced at public executions—an incongruous mix of fascination and revulsion that forces me to freeze in place, incapacitated.

My feet feel glued to the cobblestones, yet I need to avert my eyes. I look beyond the pyre where the gondola now stands ablaze and cast my attention past the square and into the Grand Canal. Cargo boats, private gondolas, and public ferries traffic the great basin that extends between the Piazza San Marco and the island of San Giorgio Maggiore. What must amount to more than five hundred gondolas bob in the vast expanse of glittering water, more than I have ever seen assembled there in all of my twenty-two years on this earth. The boatmen and their passengers are gathered there for just one reason: to watch this boat burn between the great columns of justice that mark the gateway to the city. I gaze skyward now at the tall, white columns, one topped with a shimmering, gilded, winged lion, the other with Saint Theodore treading on a crocodile. These two statues are the symbols of My Great Republic, My Most Serene, my home, the city of my birth, the only place I have ever known.

Of course, this gondola-burning isn't the first public humiliation that I have witnessed on this very spot in my life, but I am certain that it will be the most memorable. Nearly every day, on the platform between the columns of justice in the *piazzetta*, the smaller square off our main Piazza San Marco, some poor wretch is clapped in the stocks for cursing in public, snitching an apple from a fruitseller, staggering drunkenly into his parish church, or committing crimes much more serious.

A few times, I have seen rapists and thieves dangling by their necks from a rope suspended between the columns. Their bodies hang for days, sometimes weeks, to decompose before our eyes, their cheeks bloated and black, their eyes bulging as if they were watching the crowd below in a frozen expression of horror. A few of my braver childhood friends hurled rocks and sticks to make their doll-like bodies swing and spin, then ran off laughing as armed guards from the nearby Doge's Palace chased them until they disappeared into the shadows of the arcades lining the square. I had never had the nerve to do it myself. My father would have seen me hanged, too.

When I was a very small boy I even saw someone—a man who had murdered eight people, they said—tied with ropes to four horses by his wrists and ankles between the columns. When slaves whipped the horses, they galloped into four different directions. The man's body exploded, and as long as I live I will never forget the sound it made, something akin to a ripe melon bursting from the inside out. I watched, frozen, as a flock of shrieking seagulls descended to fight over a feast of entrails. At the sight of it, a woman standing beside me vomited on my shoes. All of it was meant to uphold the just and civilized society of Our Great Republic of Venice, so it was explained to me.

None of those public spectacles, however gruesome, compares with this one, at least for me. My father will not leave the boatyard today. He could not bring himself to watch one of his own creations so publicly disgraced. That is because this is not just any gondola. It is one of the most perfect boats we have ever made. Although I am proud of how I shaped the prow, I know I will keep my pride to myself, as my father will not permit me to show it.

The sound of crackling fire snatches me from my thoughts, and I turn my attention back to the burning boat. It has disintegrated even faster than I could have imagined. The flaming craft remains little more than a skeleton now, like the bones of an enormous fish. Curls of black smoke rise into the gray sky. My eyes follow the black embers upward, where they seemed to take flight, dancing crazily in the haze.

The spectacle nearly over, onlookers scatter away from the square to resume their lives as if nothing of significance has happened. Their voices echo through the narrow alleyways that snake away from the Piazza San Marco. Beyond, in the wide expanse of the Grand Canal, an eerie light makes shimmering patterns on the water, and the dark gondolas crowded there begin to disperse without a sound down the smaller rivulets and watery passages that pervade our great city.

I cannot seem to move myself from the spot where I have stood transfixed. The flames of the burning boat are dying now, but the embers glow, making wavering reflections in the water. Overhead, a bird coos. I watch it hop from its perch on the stones of a building facing the square and sail gracefully to a fluttering landing. Birds begin to gather and peck at detritus left behind by the crowd. Two gray birds squabble over a crumb lodged in the crack of a cobblestone. I take one last look at the pyre and then force myself to leave the square.

The harsh stench of burning lacquer lingers in the air long after the crowd has dispersed. The smell of scorched paint stings my nostrils, yet I feel incited to inhale this aroma. It is repugnant and yet at the same time strangely comforting. I sense that my clothes and even the dark locks of hair that fall across my cheeks are impregnated with the smell. I feel my head reel and my stomach turn. Of course. I don't know why I did not recognize it before. It is my family's secret recipe for boat varnish, a special lacquer we use to protect the boat keels from the lichen that collects on them in the canals. The origins of the recipe were lost even to our own boat-making ancestors, but we continue to mix it in the jars of my father's workshop every day. The smell grips me, haunts me as I quicken my pace, eager to find my way through the narrow alleys leading back to my neighborhood in Cannaregio.

When at last I reach the fish market near home, I find that Signora Galli, the fishmonger's wife, has already set aside something for me. I approach her stall as she plunges her arm into a bucket, scooping out a writhing handful of eels trawled from the sea this morning, and plunks them on the scale.

"Tell your sister to make everyone a nice *risi e bisoto* for the midday meal," she says, wagging a pudgy finger at me. "Good for the baby."

"Thank you," I say.

It looks as if someone has dumped the entire contents of the Venetian lagoon onto a wooden table before me. From this bounty, the fishmonger's wife selects a few small fish and presses them into my satchel.

"She's a bit old to be birthing a baby, your mother," Signora Galli continues. "But a woman must accept children from God no matter when they come." She puts her hands on her hips and nods.

"*Santo Stefano*, let the poor boy go home," says Signor Galli the fishmonger, slapping his wife's backside affectionately with a rag as she accepts my coins. "He has no time for your opinions. The boy has a full day's work ahead of him in his father's boatyard."

"*Salve.*" I salute the fishmonger and his wife.

It is true, I am eager to reach home now. We are waiting for the baby.

Chapter 2

"Mamma?"

I cross the threshold into the dim warmth of our house, dropping my felt hat and satchel on the table that fills the room. My younger sister, Mariangela, is chopping onions and boiling water in an iron pot over the stone hearth fire. Now that our mother has reached the end of her pregnancy, Mariangela refuses to leave her side even for a moment. I would never admit it, of course, but I relish chores out of the house, like market-going, that my sister would normally do herself. Part of me delights in slipping temporarily from my father's view, but I do not admit that either, especially to myself.

My sister silently gestures with her chin to the adjacent room.

I peer into the bedchamber without entering. From the doorway, I soak in the stillness of the house, broken only by the dull rhythm of Mariangela's chopping. My mother lies on her side with her back to us, breathing heavily, her entire body heaving up and down under a loosely woven cloth. It's the same bed where all of us were born—me, then my brother Daniele, then Mariangela. I try to remember how many times my mother has become pregnant in between, but I've lost count.

As long as I can remember, Donatella Vetraio di Vianello has been in a constantly fluctuating state of with child or no longer with child. She has lost so many little souls, even some before my own birth twenty-two years ago. Most went to the world hereafter before they glimpsed our mother's sparkling gaze. Finally a boy came into the world but he lay ashen and still in her embrace. Months later, a stronger one pushed out of my mother's womb, his forceful cry drawing neighbors as far away as Signora Faldi's bakery some eight houses distant. That's the tale our father told us once, his eyes lighting up before a shadow overtook his face. He never recounted it again.

Only as a young child, after I noticed the tiny grave in our family plot, did I raise the question with my mother, possessing then the courage that innocence brings. His name was Primo, she told me, the first-born. My father had taken him into the boatyard within days of his birth, and my mother had had to pry the child away to feed him or put him in the cradle my father had made. She smiled, then, seeming to read my mind, and she gathered my bony shoulders and squeezed me tightly.

"What happened to him?" I asked wide-eyed.

"It was the day before his third birthday," my mother said, her voice quavering as I have never heard it before or since. "Your uncle Tino found him floating in the shallow water at the bottom of the boatyard ramp." My mother left the room then and I was left to imagine the rest.

I was not supposed to be the eldest son. Yet, here I am, the accidental heir to my father's boatyard. I suppose I consider it nothing short of a miracle that I am here at all.

On the opposite side of our bedchamber stands a wooden bed fashioned from our father's own tools, where my younger brother and I sleep. Our sister occupies a narrow cot next to our parents. Their bed now stands at an angle so that my mother can get into it without climbing over my father. This bedroom, along with the kitchen and a small gathering room, constitutes the only home I've ever known. Occasionally, when our father has taken on a new apprentice, we've set up a temporary cot in the kitchen, but it is only the five of us now, soon to be six, God willing.

Sensing my presence, Mamma turns her head toward the door, opens her eyes halfway, and gestures for me to come. I approach carefully and perch on the edge of the bed. Immediately, she presses against my back and brings her small left hand to my face. I cover it with my larger, calloused one. I favor my left hand, just like my mother. She smiles.

"I brought the fish from the market, Mamma."

"Good," she replies. She looks into my eyes, and her body softens. We are like mirror images, my mother and I, our eyes the color of the amber stones that come off the ships from the East, trapping small black insects inside their glowing orange orbs. People tell my mother and me that our eyes seem to burn with flames or shine like the sun. My mother's eyes sparkle, defying the sadness that must lie beneath. A fortuneteller in the Rialto once told my mother that she and her eldest son had descended from gypsies and were destined to wander. It made my mother laugh, and her eyes glowed even more. Today my mother's eyes are uncharacteristically dull, ringed by dark circles. I feel the weight of her unease for the new soul that grows inside her womb.

"Signora Galli sends her regards to you and the baby," I tell her, acknowledging with a glance the taut abdomen that touches my hip. "And she also scolded me for doing the shopping."

Mamma laughs, but it ends in a weak cough. "Did you see Annalisa at the market?"

"No," I say, and turn my gaze to the window to watch a gull wheeling in the sky.

Annalisa Bonfante is the girl who will be my wife. Since I was old enough to toddle around the boatyard, my parents have worked to arrange a union between their eldest son and the *ferro* maker's daughter. My father's sole concern is the future of our trade; he has insisted on ensuring this alliance to bridge our two related crafts. It took Father nearly a year to convince Bonfante that I was worthy of his daughter's hand, though, as the gruff blacksmith already had in mind the son of a master goldsmith in Rialto. My father is both skilled and persistent in his arguments. Once his mind is set, there is no changing it. My own thoughts about the engagement have never been asked.

It is not that Annalisa Bonfante is an unreasonable choice for a wife; she is a fine girl. Her skin and teeth look healthy, my mother has pointed out more than once, and my aunts take note of her broad hips. Annalisa's mother and grandmother have taught her to cook, raise hens, and embroider linens. She is nearly sixteen, ripe for marriage. She will be a good mother and bring me sons to build gondolas in our family boatyard for years to come.

I am already well aware of Annalisa's skin and teeth. Her hips, too, for that matter. Once Annalisa's father had finally agreed to his daughter's betrothal, she found a way to steal away from her market-going long enough to track me and push me behind the wall of a vegetable warehouse in Castello. For a girl, she surprised me with her nerve. In the mere moments we had together before being interrupted by a cabbage seller pulling a laden cart, she had managed to grab the ties of my shirt, press me against a stone wall, and let me taste the salt in her mouth.

Next spring I will marry Annalisa in our parish church. Every member of the boatbuilding guild will be there. We will move to a small but solid house provided by Annalisa's father. I will continue to work in my father's boatyard, and at the moment of his death, it will become my own. I will teach our sons how to season walnut and oak, fashion the keels to be virtually indestructible, and stain ten different woods with our family's own formula of lacquer that will make the craft watertight. On my own deathbed, I will pass the business on to my eldest son. It is preordained.

My mother's breathing draws me back to the present. Her eyes are closed again, and I watch her swollen girth rise and fall gently under the blanket. Her face is lined, but her hair spreads in waves across the pillow, and I remark that she is lovely. My father parades his beautiful wife at meetings of the Scuola Grande, but that is the only time I have ever seen Domenico Vianello treat her in this manner. I believe that my mamma loves Father, but at times I fail to understand why. I learned at a young age that my father's way of showing affection is through discipline. With his wife, he is particularly harsh. I have never seen Father raise a hand against her, but I read the pain of his abrasive manner in her eyes. She swallows the sting of his words and never utters anything unkind to him or about him. I have never told anyone, but I hope that at the least, Father will match my sister Mariangela, soon to be of marriageable age at fourteen, with a husband who will treat her with greater regard.

My mamma's breathing is labored, and her temple throbs. I rise and slip out of the room. I take my hat from the table, salute my sister, and step out the house. If I can reach the boatyard before the bell clangs in the tower of Santa Maria Assunta, I may avoid my father's wrath. I quicken my pace. The day is young, and there is work to be done.

Chapter 3

"Where have you been?" my father growls as he looks up from sanding a long oak plank to see me tiptoeing down the stone stairs into the boatyard, trying to avoid notice. "I promised Signor Pesaro a new gondola by December! The ribs are not even in place yet. Most of them are still stacked in the storehouse," he grumbles.

I say nothing, for the best way to respond to my father is through action, not words. I have already resolved not to mention the boat burning, and certainly not my attendance at the event, which could only serve to make my father more ill-tempered. Still, the image of the burning boat haunts me as I carry out my tasks. I head across the boatyard toward the storehouse.

In spite of its renown, the Squero Vianello, our family boatyard, is little more than a haphazard conglomeration of buildings surrounding a boat ramp. Its three structures—the workshop, the storehouse, and our home—have been standing longer than anyone remembers. The boatyard has an entrance on the landward side as well as a mooring on the canal, so we can access it from the water or from the alley. The buildings in our little compound have been restored, altered, and enlarged so many times that they resemble a jumbled assemblage of stone, metal, and wood, the work of many generations of Vianello men, each of whom has left his mark.

I lean my weight against the door of the storehouse, and it heaves open reluctantly, scraping along its metal track as it rolls to one side. I stand still for a moment while my eyes adjust to the darkness. I inhale the familiar aroma, a mixture of damp earth, seasoned wood, rusting metal, and lacquer, then I step carefully into the dust-flecked gloom. There is hardly space to walk among the piles of wood, paintbrushes, varnish, hammers, adzes, planes, axes, nails, and buckets, not to mention splintered pieces of ancient gondolas waiting for my father to breathe new life into them. The storehouse contains all the gondola-building supplies we will ever need in my lifetime. I seem to be the only one of us who perceives the disorder. If I could ever find relief from my work, I would have time to devote to reordering the varnishes, stacking the scrap wood neatly by type, or arranging the tools so that we don't spend so much time hunting for things as I am now.

Along the back wall, I find what father is looking for: *corbe*, the U-shaped ribs that will give form to the new gondola we are building for Lorenzo Pesaro. Truth be told, the fair-skinned, thin-lipped spice merchant is as pompous as he is prosperous, but that is none of our concern, Father is quick to remind my brother and me. The man has fine taste in boats as well as a large purse, and that is all that matters. Pesaro is one of the few patrons who occasionally appear unannounced to inspect the progress of the gondola they have commissioned us to craft. The ever-present possibility of an unexpected visit from a client puts Father on edge. I feel his nervous energy project itself onto me in the form of tingling bumps creeping across my arms and up the back of my neck.

"Luca!" My father's voice booms from the direction of the workshop, and I flinch. "Where are those *corbe*?"

I rifle through the stacks of wooden ribs, feeling for the right sizes. During the rare times that orders for new boats slow, my father commands us to craft *corbe* for future projects. My brother, uncle, and cousins spend countless hours pre-making these gondola ribs. You could never have too many on hand, my father says. My younger cousins cut, sand, and fasten the curved frames of oak and elm together with wooden nails, fashioning increasingly narrower and wider pieces to form, respectively, the skinny fore and aft ribs, and the sturdier members that will support the flat central keel of the boats. We stack the finished ribs in the storehouse, which makes the work in the boatyard more efficient during times when we have many commissions.

"*Arrivo!*" I emerge from the storehouse into the sunshine and begin organizing the ribs by size along the exterior wall. From the corner of my eye I catch sight of my cousin, Roberto, standing in a gondola tied to one of the posts that mark the canal-side entrance to the boatyard. A scuttle in one hand and a horsehair brush in the other, Roberto is refreshing the paint on one of the mooring posts. He salutes me with the paintbrush, bracing himself in the rocking boat with his legs spread wide and his hair falling sideways across his brow as he cocks his head to paint.

This is my favorite place to work in the boatyard. The *téza*—the hulking, shed-like structure open on its southern side to the boat ramp—is covered with a truss roof of wooden beams supported on massive brick pillars. Here we take each gondola through the final steps of its construction: varnishing, water-testing, and finally launching it in the water before our house. The ramp slopes gradually from the *téza* into the dark waters of the canal. Made partly of stones, partly of packed earth, the ramp turns to mud during the spring's rainy season, and everyone must watch his step to avoid slipping on the muck. Beyond, a cluster of mooring posts painted with red and black spirals stands just off the ramp in the water, marking the entrance to the *squero*. In the summer, we take frequent leave of our work to walk down the ramp and splash our faces with cool canal water. In the winter, we watch our breath vaporize in the damp air as we varnish boats under the shelter of the great roof.

Along the back wall of the *téza*, stacks of timber wood stand exposed to the open air, left to season sometimes for years. These raw planks of oak, ash, elm, cherry, fir, larch, and mahogany once grew as trees in the great forests of the Dolomite Mountains to the north. I, never having ventured outside Our Most Serene City, find it impossible to imagine trees so large growing in such vast quantities. The barge captains who traffic the timbers down the rivers to our boatyard describe forests as thick as grass stretching as far as the eye can see, punctuated by the craggy cliffs of the Dolomites, a sight I have tried many times to envision. My father buys timber only from two barges, whose captains he has known for years and whose lumber he has come to trust. Each autumn Father hand-selects our raw planks, avoiding pieces with knots, splintered edges, and other imperfections. Some of the planks in the storage area, I calculate, have lain there for ten years or longer, waiting to be transformed into a boat at the moment when Domenico Vianello deems it right.

The narrow sliver of water before the *téza* is not the Grand Canal, but it remains our own piece of this Most Serene City, where we witness an ever-changing pageant of watercraft. Our days are propelled by the rhythm of the boatmen who steer simple cargo rafts, flat-bottomed lagoon craft, small rowboats, dinghies, and infinite numbers of black gondolas through the waterway that borders the *squero*. A few times, I have feasted my eyes on diplomatic boats, exempt from the decree handed down from the Doge himself that boats must be painted black to avoid the sin of opulence. These ambassadorial craft are the most conspicuous, some decorated with red velvet upholstery, carving along the sides and decks, and even gilded figures and animals on the prows. Other times, private gondolas owned by men rich enough to afford the steep fines imposed for breaking the sumptuary laws pass our *squero*. These fine boats are usually rowed by two men instead of one and are also elaborately painted and gilded. Today there are the usual comings and goings of the water-seller's raft, a neighbor's unadorned gondola, and a boy in a rowboat.

"Luca!" my father's voice booms again.

I duck into the dimly lit workshop with a stack of gondola ribs draped over each forearm. Father stands with his hands on his hips, looking over the shoulder of my brother, Daniele, who is tapping a long oak plank gently with a mallet. Father looks up briefly as I enter but immediately turns his attention back to his younger son's hammering. "No! More force on the underside, like this," he instructs in his usual abrasive manner. "Give me the mallet." Domenico Vianello is a perfectionist; everyone knows it. Daniele, an acquiescent boy, watches patiently as our father demonstrates again how to maneuver the tool. Sunlight streaks into the space from the giant doors, and I am struck by the identical profiles of my father and my brother, as if both men were molded from clay by the same master, one a younger version of the other. My brother is content and good-natured, even under my father's heavy hand. Daniele is responsible for the mallet-work now, our father having long ago grown weary of my left-handed efforts that did not conform to his idea of how it should be done.

It was not always so. One of my earliest memories was overhearing a neighbor woman whisper that the gondola maker's eldest son was marked by the devil. My father must have believed it, as he did his best to undo my curse. In the boatyard, I was not allowed to pick up tools with my left hand. I lived for most of a year with my left hand tied behind my back during my hours in the boatyard, untied only at mealtime. Even now, I feel the knuckles of my left hand tingle when my father raises his voice.

It was my mother who taught me to temper my ever-present compulsion to use my sinister hand, as she herself had had to do. At the table and in our parish church, she squeezed my left hand tightly while teaching me to make the sign of the cross with my right. In public, she instructed me to sit on my left hand or keep it in my pocket; in private, she reminded me that the left hand was the "hand of the heart." At night she nursed my knuckles, bruised and swollen from where my father had struck them with a rasp each time I had reached for an implement.

I never mastered the tools with my right hand nearly as well as with my left. Eventually, Father gave up trying to force me to use my "correct" hand in the boatyard and assigned many of the duties that the eldest son might be expected to do to my brother, who is gifted with dexterity and unmarked by Satan. My uncle and cousins mercifully turned a blind eye to my affliction, and my brother loved me anyway. I did what I could to make beautiful and seaworthy boats, just like my father and grandfather. Our work carried on.

A crude wooden frame hammered into the earthen floor occupies the bulk of our workshop's interior space. No one knows how long the frame has been there; Father recalls his own grandfather using it as a basic mold for the workshop's gondolas. We still use the roughhewn mold, little more than a few pieces of lumber arched to approximate the size and proportion of a standard gondola, to begin each boat. My younger brother is practicing one of the most critical steps in the construction: attaching the long oak planks that run the entire length of the boat on the left and right of the keel and provide the fundamental integrity of the boat. I have practiced it countless times and understand instinctively why my father is so attentive at this stage; it is critical to get this part right. If the longest planks are even slightly malformed, we have to dismantle the boat and start over again. My father will not settle for anything less. Then we curve the oak planks by soaking one side with water and applying fire with a torch to the other, a deceivingly simple and particular warp that, once achieved, forms the distinctive shape of the gondola. Once the two oak planks are in place, we will begin to place the gondola ribs that I have carried from the storehouse. For a while—up to two dozen moons—the craft will resemble the carcass of a gigantic fish. Then, day by day, the gondola begins to take shape.

We do not do everything ourselves, to be sure. As every boat maker does, we send some parts of the work to specialists who carry out their own trade better than the Vianello family. The oars and oarlocks are crafted by Signor Fumagalli the oarmaker. My uncle handles the decorative carvings that adorn our standard boats, but for more elaborate commissions we hire an elderly carver who worked for my grandfather, one of the only men in Venice who still carves the elaborate swirls and flowers in the manner done in the time of my great-grandfather.

Along with my brother, my uncle, two cousins, and myself, Father employs a journeyman named Andrea, the son of a distant cousin. A grown man, Andrea is dimwitted and has not spoken a word since his parents died of the pestilence that befell our city when he was a small boy. Though completely mute, he is a genius with needle and thread. The man can sew and upholster leather, silks, and many other fabrics better than any professional. His skill is the only thing that saved him from living as an outcast in the streets. He sleeps in a spare room off the workshop and takes his meals with us or with my uncle's family. Father had to make an appeal to the confraternity for approval to have upholstery completed within the confines of our boatyard, and since then, Andrea has worked as diligently and meticulously as any member of our workshop. Andrea silently fashions any parts of the boat to be adorned with fabric or leather, from the seats to the curtained enclosures, *felze,* of our more elaborate boats.

Although I have watched boats being built since I was old enough to toddle from the house to the boatyard, I still find the gondola-making process part hard labor, part alchemy. Each gondola begins as nothing more than raw planks of wood but emerges from our boatyard transformed. Even though I am intimately familiar with each step, even though I have been present every day,

each time the men heave open the doors of the workshop and release our latest creation into the daylight for the first time, easing
the craft down the ramp and into the cool canal waters on its first
voyage, the sight of it stops me in my tracks.

Father boasts that his reputation for quality gondolas is thanks
in part to the fact that he does not allow himself to be distracted
by the same diversions of the other boatyards. Domenico does not
tolerate anyone other than his own assistants and the occasional
client into his *squero*. Ours is one of the few boatyards in the city
that is not covered with loiterers: well-meaning friends, bossy rela-
tives, curious guild members, bored boatmen, nosy neighbors. I
have seen my father chortle with disdain every time we row past
the Squero San Selvaggio on a neighboring canal, where gondoliers
congregate to play cards, tell jokes, regale each other with tall tales,
and cajole the boat makers through the workday and well into the
night. Nothing but idle fools, Father assures us. It is shameful, but
above all, no way to work.

While I carry the wooden ribs from the storehouse to the
workshop, aromas of my sister's cooking waft into the boatyard.
I salivate, thinking of the slimy, writhing handful of eels that the
fishmonger had pressed into my satchel. Mariangela, though just
a girl, is already an accomplished cook. She works alongside our
mother every day, of course, but she also inherited our grandmother's natural knack for flavor combinations, which is not the kind of
thing that can be taught but only inherently understood.

The bells ring from the tower of Santa Maria Assunta, and we
break for the midday meal. The clanging bells are the only thing
that I have ever seen stop our father in his tracks. No matter how
much work we have before us in the boatyard, the meal hour is
sacred. It is the only time when work can wait. My uncle Tino and
his two young sons disappear around the corner to their home a
hundred paces away, where I am sure my aunt has prepared cabbage
stew or something else that is less inspired than what Mariangela
has crafted for us.

My brother sits beside my father on a narrow wooden bench while Mariangela serves our plates. I notice that my sister's hair has turned blonde seemingly overnight, the result of pouring a foul-smelling concoction of white wine, saffron, urine, and lemon juice over her tresses, then sitting in our sun-filled vegetable garden until it turns a remarkable shade of gold. This small act of self-interest is the only one my sister allows herself, and we men know better than to comment on the subject.

I sit alone on the other side of the table so that I can peer into the bedroom where my mother lies, moving in and out of sleep. The onions and eels taste just as good as they smell, and I inhale the vapors swirling up from my plate. The house is silent except for the sounds of spoons scraping against the plates and our father slurping from a tankard of warm beer that Mariangela brewed over the winter in the storage cellar. No one utters a word, and the air becomes heavy with our attention trained on the doorway to the bedchamber. I steal another glimpse of the back of my mother's head, her hair tousled haphazardly over the blanket.

After the meal, we return to the *squero* to continue our work on Signor Pesaro's new gondola. While my brother and I begin to lay out the ribs to match the frame, Father sits at his workbench at the back of the shop, sketching on a piece of parchment. He fancies himself a draughtsman, and it is true that he possesses some natural skill. He draws each one of the boats he makes even though it is unnecessary—the man could build a fine gondola with his eyes closed. He does it for conceit but also because he enjoys it. Father squints his eyes and holds the drawing at arm's length. Finally, he peels the piece of parchment from the table, rolls it up in his hands, and ties it closed with a thin leather strap.

"I need for this to go to the *remer*," he remarks curtly.

I jump. "I'll take it." I scramble to my father's workbench to grab the roll, slap my hat on my head, and walk out the door before he can send one of his apprentices instead.

Chapter 4

Anton Fumagalli, the oarmaker, is the oldest person I know. To those unacquainted, his appearance is misleading: his teeth are all gone, and his lips sink into his skull like a shriveled fig. He stoops when he walks, yet his hands are strong and able, and his body, though wiry, is muscular and solid as a rock. Deep creases mark his cheeks, and he pushes back wisps of gray hair with his tanned, strong hands.

But Signor Fumagalli is more alive than most men my own age. As I scuff along the familiar paths to the oarmaker's workshop, a smile crosses my lips. I relish my visits with the *remero*. Signor Fumagalli specializes in making *fòrcole*, the rowlocks that secure the oar and allow a boatman to steer his gondola even in the narrowest and most crowded canals. Like my father, Signor Fumagalli is the undisputed master of his trade, a perfectionist who could imagine no other way to spend his days than using his hands to create a masterpiece from a humble block of wood. But the comparisons between the two men end there. Where my father behaves like a despot most of the time, Master Fumagalli possesses a generous soul. Instead of closely guarding his trade secrets, he shares his craft enthusiastically with everyone he meets. Not that anyone else on earth would have the skill to copy the master's work. His studio teems with visitors, but somehow amidst the chaotic comings and goings, Signor Fumagalli finds the discipline to craft oars and rowlocks that the inspectors hold up to their guild members as examples of the best of their trade.

As I cross the threshold of the *remero*'s studio, I see the master at his workbench, where he is inspecting a block of walnut, running his hands along the grain as if he were stroking a dog. His eyes are closed. "This is one of the best ones you've done so far," he is telling an apprentice, "but it still needs work." I watch the oarmaker run his palm down the side of the carved chunk of wood, reading it with his hand as if he were blind. His fingers explore its crevices. "Too thick on the aft side," he explains, "and more carving is needed in the lower oar position. Signor Bondi is even shorter than I am, and he will need more leverage for reversing the boat."

When the oarmaker opens his eyes I am standing before him. Immediately he drops the block on his workbench and greets me with a gaping smile, a grip on the shoulder, and a slap on the back. The *remero*'s shop is much better than ours, full of light and flecks of sawdust, with a line of worktables along the right side and designs for some of the master's *fórcole* tacked along the wall on the left. A wall of shelves houses a neatly arranged collection of handsaws, files, and scrapers. Near the front entrance, a table displays some of the master's best works. Here, divorced from their boats, they appear like strange curvilinear beings rather than boat hardware, their elegant silhouettes smoothly sanded and polished with nut oils to a high sheen.

The oarmaker's shop sits on a high embankment above the Sacca della Misericordia, the basin on the north side of Cannaregio, which affords an expansive view onto the canal and beyond to the island of Murano. Master Fumagalli counts some half-dozen apprentices in this studio he inherited from his father. These apprentices have the pleasure of watching boats pass while they work, and even glimpse naval ships in the distance headed to Corfu and Cyprus. All day, boatmen tether their gondolas at Master Fumagalli's boat ramp, waiting in line to have their oars and rowlocks repaired, waxed, replaced.

I hand over my father's design for the spice merchant's new gondola, for which he has charged Signor Fumagalli to make the rowlock and oars. The oarmaker rakes his sawdust-covered palms down the front of his leather apron and inspects the drawing through squinted eyes. My father and the oarmaker have never signed a written agreement; there is no need. Signor Fumagalli is like an extension of our family. Signor Fumagalli's grandfather was once apprenticed to my great-grandfather, but the connections between the two families go back longer than that. The oarmaker has often told me the story of hearing my first cries from our boatyard when I came into the world. This is why, he says, he considers me his nephew even though we are not related by blood. My father laments that the oarmaker has no children; otherwise I am certain that he would have already arranged to marry me off to the oarmaker's daughter instead of to Annalisa Bonfante.

"I want you to meet my newest apprentice, Samuele." Signor Fumagalli motions to a shy-looking boy of about ten years old, who is sweeping curls of beech wood beneath a worktable. "You know the Aragona family, no? Samuele is their youngest." The boy averts his eyes but nods slightly, squirming under Signor Fumagalli's grip on his shoulder.

"And this," Signor Fumagalli says to his young assistant, bowing dramatically and waving grandly toward me, "is Luca Vianello, the heir to the city's greatest gondola-making enterprise. One day Luca, along with his many sons and grandsons, will make sure that every canal in the Venetian Republic is filled with their beautiful boats!" He laughs again, his mouth a gaping crescent, and the air reeks of spoiled apples.

I shrug. "I wouldn't go as far as that. Actually I was thinking that I might apprentice myself to a glassblower instead," I joke.

"What's that you say? *Madonna mia!*" the oarmaker cries, chuckling. "A glassblower! Ha!" He screws up his face, spits on the floor, and pounds his fist on the table.

Relieved to no longer be the center of attention, the young Samuele wriggles away and quickens the pace of his sweeping.

"No!" cries Signor Fumagalli, and a serious expression crosses his face. "You will continue the legacy of your father, the greatest boat maker of the Vianello clan! A maestro, I swear it on my life. And you, my boy, you have it in your soul, too. Glass—ha! No, you work the wood like no other journeyman in the city. The three of us—you, your father, and myself—we make the most beautiful boats La Repubblica has ever known!" His voice booms through the workshop as he makes a grand gesture toward the canal beyond his studio window. Two of his apprentices exchange squelched smiles.

"A glassblower like the lovely Donatella's father," he chuckles again, and his face softens. "What would you do if you were a glassblower, eh?" Signor Fumagalli slaps me mockingly alongside my head, causing a lock of black hair to swing across my cheek.

"Well, for one thing, I wouldn't have to work for a tyrant."

"Your father? Your father! My boy, your father is the greatest gondola maker in Our Most Serene Republic!" His mouth turns into a frown. "You don't know how good your lot in life. No one else makes a boat like Domenico Vianello. As a draughtsman he's not bad either," adds Master Fumagalli parenthetically, tapping the piece of parchment with the back of his hand. "Anyway, my boy, it's your destiny. *Destino*! Do you deny it?"

"To be perfectly honest, *remer*, I might have made other plans for myself," I reply, surprising even myself with my bravado. "But I respect my father's wishes. What choice do I have?"

"Speaking of destiny," continues Signor Fumagalli, distracted now and ignoring the comment, "how is your dear mother? Any sign of the baby?"

"Not yet," I reply. Suddenly, I want to get home.

I bid farewell with a smile and begin walking back toward the family workshop. When I reach the Misericordia canal, though, I hesitate. On a whim, I turn my heel and head toward the north instead.

I know I am close when I reach the church of Sant'Alvise and begin to hear the ringing sound of hammering on metal. Members of the blacksmith's guild, including the family of Annalisa Bonfante, cluster in the streets surrounding the squat old church.

Annalisa's father is a master of the *ferro*, the comb-shaped, pronged iron prows that decorate the bows and sterns of all but our more utilitarian gondolas. The apprentices and journeymen in Master Bonfante's workshop forge standard models using templates that Signor Bonfante stamped years ago. Master Bonfante devotes himself to crafting elaborate custom *ferri* destined for ambassadorial boats and the crafts of patrician clients who can afford to pay the stiff fines for breaking the sumptuary laws.

From a distance, I glimpse the Bonfante blacksmith's foundry and its contents—tools, gates, raw metal, projects finished and half-finished—that spill out of its double doors onto the narrow walkway that borders the canal-side. Usually the door to the workshops stays flung open to let the heat escape as the men hammer copper and iron with their hulking forearms. From this jumbled dungeon of a workspace, Signor Bonfante crafts impressive decorations that are the crowning touches of each gondola that emerges from our boatyard. The *ferri* are deceivingly heavy: it takes two men to carry one, and at least three to mount it properly to the boat. When I was ten my Uncle Tino accidentally dropped one side of a *ferro* and it broke my toe; to this day I remember the pain.

While Annalisa's mother tightly manages the finances of her husband's business, Annalisa and her two sisters spend the day cooped up in the house behind the shop as if imprisoned, kept busy with washing, baking, and sewing. Rarely is one of the three girls allowed to venture out of view of the hawk-like eyes of their mother. With a fluttering in my stomach, I recall how Annalisa cornered me against the wall at the market that day, and I wonder how she had managed to escape.

Hearing the ear-splitting sound of hammering molten iron, I know that Annalisa's father and his assistants are occupied.

Avoiding the canal-side entrance to the shop, I slip down the alley leading to the back garden of the house. My pace slows and I peer through the ornate iron gate into Annalisa's courtyard. There she is, pulling breeches from a basket on the ground and hanging them on the line. I stand unnoticed for a moment, watching her. Annalisa's dress is simple but gathered around her narrow waist like a noble lady's. Her apron is tied in a neat bow, and her light brown tresses are tidily braided under her simple white sheath. Her hands work quickly and ably, repeating gestures done thousands of times as she pins a tablecloth and a shirt to the line.

I cup my hands to my lips and whistle like a bird. Annalisa spins around on her heels, a startled expression on her face. When she sees me through the bars, her face softens and she scampers to the gate, trying to keep her footsteps from being heard.

She giggles. "My mother will murder you with her bare hands if she finds the two of us here without her!"

"I live dangerously." I grin.

"What are you doing here?" she asks, gazing into my eyes.

"I had an errand in the neighborhood, so I thought I would stop by and say hello."

"Hello, then."

"Annalisa!" Her mother's voice.

"Argh," she whispers.

"It's fine. I just wanted to lay eyes on you." I start to turn, but Annalisa reaches her hands through the iron gate and firmly grips my wrists. Startled, I look into her large brown eyes.

"My mother will be at the vegetable market before the *marangona* rings tomorrow morning, and I'll be home alone. Come back then?" Her mother calls again. Annalisa's eyes search my face. "Promise?" I nod. Annalisa releases my wrists, then turns and runs into the house.

I swagger down the alley toward home, listening to the echoes lifting upward and reverberating off the stone walls. Something inside of me stirs as I think about this next meeting with Annalisa, and my mind searches for an excuse to leave the boatyard in the morning. Our brief physical encounter in the market has left me hungry for more. I wonder if that desire will ebb once we are married. I am old enough to understand that marriage seems to have the effect of dampening a man and a woman's desire for one another. I have seen it happen with my aunt and uncle, who, after fifteen years of marriage, seem more likely to kill each other than sleep in the same bed. It is true that I desire Annalisa, but if I am honest with myself, I am not sure that I desire to be married to her, to settle into the life so clearly laid out before me.

I decide to travel the quayside of the Misercordia canal, observing the variety of boats docked there as I walk: rowboats covered with tarps, several plainly outfitted gondolas, and many rafts. I recognize a particularly fancy gondola as a product of Gianlorenzo Venin, my father's archrival. I would never admit this to my father, of course, but I pause to admire the carving that the Venin brothers employ on the keels of their boats, a large emblem of a fishtailed siren with a fierce expression on her face.

"Luca! Luca!"

The sound of a familiar voice breaks my trance. Then I see my brother Daniele rowing one of our smaller boats through the canal, slicing the water in his quick approach. His chest heaves and beads of sweat line his brow.

"Luca, I've been looking for you everywhere." He turns his oar to slow the craft, then gently bumps the side of the boat on the quay. "I rowed first to the *remero*'s studio, but they said you had already left. Then I thought you might be in this part of town instead," the lanky boy continues, looking past my shoulder toward the street where Annalisa's house lies. I register panic on my brother's face. "Brother, please, come quickly!" I step into the boat.

"It's Mamma."

Chapter 5

My brother uses the *puparin*'s single oar to maneuver the boat down the narrow channel with swift and able strokes. This particular *puparin* is similar in design to, but smaller than, our family's gondolas, and is better suited to Daniele's youthful frame. We prefer taking the *puparin* over one of the gondolas because the lighter craft is easier to maneuver. Still, the boat is four times as long as the boy; yet Daniele makes rowing it look nearly as effortless as walking. His forearms, too fully developed for a boy of fifteen, propel the boat ever faster toward the family boatyard as the sun sinks below the horizon and the sky over the Grand Canal grows dim.

"The midwife looked worried," his voice wavers. I notice now that Daniele's eyes are reddened and a drop of sweat slides down his temple. The craft slices the still water, sending ripples to lap against the stone walls of buildings lining the canal. Daniele's legs rock gently back and forth, hefting the oar.

"What—why?! This morning Mamma seemed well enough." My hands grip the sides of the boat, my knuckles straining, as I lean toward my brother.

"I don't know," continues Daniele tearfully. "I heard the midwife say the baby is stuck. Oh, Luca, Mamma looks terrible! Her skin is ashen and she's not speaking." He sniffles and sputters as he rows even faster.

"For God's sake! I told Father that she was too old to have babies! Look what he has done to her!" I thunder without thinking, slapping my knees. "The woman is forty-four years old! Doesn't he have enough children?" I've said too much, even to my own brother.

I fall silent, remembering the evening when our parents had announced the news of Mamma's latest pregnancy over a bowl of vegetable stew. Mamma blushed, while our father beamed and teased her a bit before taking a bottle of Uncle Tino's best home-made wine into the boatyard to celebrate.

But I had felt nothing but disgust. I pled with Mamma to make it the last time. And now is she really going to die? I ask angrily. I do not speak out loud against my father this time, but I curse him inside my head.

"They called for Father Davide," Daniele continues, lowering his voice to a whisper as we approach the *squero*. Uncle Tino is waiting for us at the narrow dock that runs along the canal-side entrance to our house. When he spies the *puparin*, he begins to wave his hat.

"*Tutto bene! Tutto bene!*" he cries, wiping tears from his eyes. "*E arrivato il piccolino!*" The little one has arrived.

"Mamma?" pants Daniele, now breathless from making his fastest-ever crossing of the Grand Canal.

My uncle extends his arms to grab the stern of the boat as it slows. "She's sick, but she will live," he replies, offering his arm to hoist us from the boat.

"*Madonna mia*," I sigh.

We sprint down the short alley. As we cross the threshold into the dark coolness, we hear a baby crying. Father Davide, an el-derly priest who baptized all of us, is putting on a hat to match his somber black cloak. As he exits the kitchen, he says nothing but smiles wearily and squeezes my arm.

In the candlelight, I see my mother propped up in bed, pulling a newborn baby with a full head of black hair to her bare breast.

The smell of sweat and blood fills the house. I try to quiet my thundering heart as I step into the room. Daniele, still panting, follows. Mariangela looks up from where she kneels on the floor, wringing blood from a rag over a bowl of black water. My sister's face is completely drained of color; she looked exhausted, as if she has aged twenty years in one day. The midwife, a plump, pragmatic woman who has attended my mother many times, perches on the edge of the bed. She lays a gentle hand on Mamma's leg and talks quietly to her.

Mamma musters a smile as we enter the room. She looks awful, her eyes sunken and ringed with dark circles. Her lips are dry and cracked, her hair a tangled bird's nest. I have never noticed so many streaks of gray through the frizz of her tousled locks.

"It's a boy. Isn't he beautiful?" She pulls the baby from her breast and turns him so we can see our brother's face. The baby's cheeks are flushed with color, his eyes like black marbles. The skin of the baby's chest and back are nearly transparent. Web-like blue veins trail beneath the surface, and I feel as though I could almost see the baby's tiny heart beating. "Antonio," Mamma whispers.

The midwife shushes her, then addresses us. "Your mother has had a very difficult delivery. She needs her rest now."

"He's perfect, Mamma," I say, and I lean down to kiss her forehead, which feels clammy and smells sour.

My father, brother, and I set up makeshift cots in the workshop so that Mamma and the baby can rest. Mariangela and the midwife stay awake, taking turns keeping a watchful eye on Mamma and the baby. There is little we can do, and we abandon the house to the women. As I listen to my father snore gruffly, images of my mother's sunken face filled my head, and sleep will not come. After what seems hours of fitful tossing, I rise and step outside.

The only sounds in the boatyard are the shrill cheeping of a frog and the steady lapping of water against the wall. I descend the slick ramp to the canal and heave myself onto the stones. I exhale as a mixture of pent-up joy, relief, and malaise well up in my breast. I reach my hands into the cool, mossy-smelling water and bring them to my face.

Out of view of my sleeping family, I finally allow the tears to collect in my palms.

THE GUILD MEETING is already underway when my father, brother, and I slip quietly into the back pew of our guild chapel. I hear the familiar voice of Armando, the chief officer or *gastaldo* of the boat makers' guild, who, as always, insists on reading the statutes aloud from an impressively large book with a gilded cover that normally stands locked away behind an iron grate inside a niche in the chapel wall. Of course, we have all heard it before: how old you must be to be promoted from apprentice to journeyman; how much money each boat maker is expected to contribute to the communal retirement and chapel maintenance funds; how we are obliged to cede the making of *ferri* to the blacksmiths' guild; how much we would be fined if we hired a non-Venetian in our workshops.

I glance around me and wonder how many of the men assembled in the chapel could honestly say that they follow every rule to the letter. I search my mind for a time when I witnessed my father go against the guild statutes, but I can't think of one. For years he has held the position of Overseer of Apprentices, a coveted role to which his peers elected him. In this position, my father's influence extends to other boatyards, setting the same high standards that he demands in his own workshop.

"The price of a gondola shall be set by the guild," the *gastaldo* intones, and I wonder how many of the men in the chapel are even listening. Several familiar faces turn to greet us with a nod, a smile, or a silent salute. Uncharacteristically, we are late.

At dawn, Mariangela came to the boatyard to share the news that Mamma and the baby were resting peacefully. I agreed not to disturb them, even as anxious as I felt to see them for myself. My father had risen from his cot in the boatyard hours before, eager to make progress on Signor Pesaro's new gondola before we had to depart for our annual guild meeting. As pink light dawned over the canal outside the *squero*, I watched my father inspect the gradual warp of the keel by running his hand down its side. We had torched the side of the boat the day before, tweaking the warp with fire and water, but now Father grumbled to himself as he fingered the seams between the planks. I knew that my brother and I would be required to start over again.

The guild meeting adjourns, and the real business of the boat makers begins in the tavern across the square from the church portal. The men, creatures of habit, file across the cobblestones to imbibe a tankard of beer while they nurture the ties that have bound their families across generations. The tavern proprietor, Signora Bruni, serves the men their drinks, greeting each by name. My father's colleagues crowd around him, congratulating him on the birth of a new son, *piccolo* Antonio, a new heir to the *squero*.

From the sidelines, I watch my father. His thick black hair, flecked with gray, flows neatly away from his high brow, and his dark brown eyes light up as his colleagues praise and congratulate him. He is a handsome man, I admit. Instead of wearing him down, a lifetime of manual labor has kept Domenico Vianello strong and vital. He has aged well.

In the distance, I hear a church bell, then another, then a third, announcing the mealtime hour. It starts slowly, then the clanging of several dozen church bells build to a crescendo, wildly out of sync. For a quarter hour or more, the entire city sings with the cacophony of peeling bells, urging us home in dissonant voices that echo across the canals. We men begin our return to our boatyards. My father and Uncle Tino stroll down the alleys, joking and teasing one another with familiar banter. My brother, my cousins, and I hang behind the older men. We move through the haphazardly laid-out neighborhoods, which teem with small storefronts that spill over with everything from fruit to birdcages and leather belts, while boats docked along the quaysides function as shops, selling spices, dishes, rugs, and medicinal plants.

We arrive at our own boatyard, and I cut down the alley to our house, unable to wait any longer to see my mother and the baby.

As soon as I feel the cool darkness of our kitchen, I know that something is wrong. It is still. Too still. A foul smell fills the air. There is no pot boiling on the fire. There is no fire in the hearth at all.

I rush to the bedroom.

Mariangela crouches on the floor at the end of our parents' bed, her knees drawn to her chest, clutching the infant close to her body. Her face is completely blank, and she stares into space as if she does not realize I have entered the room.

I look in the bed now. My mother is there. And yet she isn't. Her frail body has sunken unnaturally into the bed, as if the mattress were trying to consume her. A shocking volume of blood soaks the sheets and spreads outward from beneath her, forming scarlet rings across the linen cover.

Daniele enters the room now and gasps in horror. "Where is the midwife?" he shouts.

"She left... She went looking for you," replies Mariangela weakly. She continues to stare forward blankly.

I rush to my mother's side and kneel to look into her face. Her fiery amber eyes are now sunken and dark, her skin ashen and completely lifeless. Her cracked lips hang open slightly. No. It can't be.

But there is no doubt about it.

My mother is gone.

Chapter 6

I row the *puparin* as fast as my arms will take me.

The sun casts spangled patterns across the vast surface of the lagoon; it is as if floating gemstones gleam and wink at me. The world is oblivious to the horror of my dead mother, her sunken face, the bloody linens. Through my tears, the gems sparkle and shine, blinding me. I row mindlessly, paying little attention to my direction.

I don't know how much time has passed when I find myself near one of the public moorings of the Lido, the elongated barrier island that protects the Venetian lagoon from the Adriatic Sea. I lash the boat to one of the posts and climb onto the docks. I wander, not needing to find my way, for Daniele and I have spent many hours on the beach at the Lido on Sunday afternoons when our father finally takes a rest from the *squero*. On those excursions, we search for shells, watch girls walk along the sandy paths, and eat the crusty bread and cured ham our mother packs for us in a cloth.

Today is different.

I wander the beach, which stands eerily deserted. I hug my arms around my ribs to ward off the wind and in an unsuccessful attempt to comfort myself. A barrage of images floats to the surface of my mind, unconnected in time and context. I am in the kitchen, no more than three years old, singing a song while my mother claps her hands and laughs. Next, tears stream down Mamma's face as she buries her own mother in a tree-lined cemetery plot on Murano. She brushes a lock of hair from her brow while stirring a large pot containing her homemade *minestra* over the fire. Splintered images emerge into focus, then fade as I shuffle through the sand.

For long stretches in between, my memory seems to go blank. Is it, I wonder, my mind's own means to protect itself from unbearable pain? I cannot begin to understand what my mother's death means for me, for my father, for my brother and sister, for the baby. It is too much. I pick up a shard of a shell and cast it with great force into the foamy surf that laps the hard-packed sand.

I imagine my mother as a girl on Murano, where my father says he first spied her walking to the vegetable market—a sheer stroke of luck—and trailed her in his rowboat. He followed the dark-haired beauty back to the studio where her father made window glass for the finest private residences in Venice. That night, our father told us, he went straight home to convince his parents to ask the glassmaker for his daughter's hand. At first, my grandfather resisted, preferring that his son marry someone in their own confraternity, or at least within the boatbuilding trades. I wonder if, given enough time, my mother might even have caught the eye of one of the patrician clients of my grandfather's glass studio, as beautiful and intelligent as she was. True to form, Domenico Vianello's persistence paid off, and the marriage was ultimately arranged between the glassmaker's daughter and the son of the gondola maker. Six months later, fifteen-year-old Donatella was carried off to the Vianello family boatyard in the family's finest gondola with a new husband some twenty years her senior, while a regatta of aunts, uncles, cousins, and family friends cheered as they processed down the Grand Canal. When my grandfather died, Domenico Vianello inherited the boatyard.

On any other day, I might stop to appreciate the beauty of the great swaths of pink and blue that streak the dusk sky on the Lido beach. Instead, I turn my back and return to the mooring where I have left the *puparin*. In a fog of despair amidst the beauty of the color-streaked sky, I row slowly back across the wide lagoon and into the familiar narrow waterways that lead to the *squero*.

By the time I reach home, the sky is black and the moon appears as a slender sliver of glowing white. I moor the boat alongside the ramp that leads into the *téza*. Sighing heavily, I climb out of the boat and walk past the workshop, biting my lip, bracing myself for what awaits me inside the house—surely a collection of grieving siblings, family, and friends—and my mother's body, again.

It is time to face it.

From the corner of my eye, I perceive light and movement, and I hesitate. It can't be; my eyes must be playing tricks on me. I approach the door of the workshop and peer inside. I can hardly believe my eyes. My father. He is hunched over Signor Pesaro's gondola. He has stripped off the great oak planks that form the curved sides of the boat, the planks that I expected our father would have us do over again to meet his standards. Now our father is re-forming them himself with a torch, little more than a bundle of marsh reeds set ablaze. The flames make wavering, dancing patterns of light and shadows against the back wall of the workshop.

"You..." I begin, incredulously. My father looks up from his task. "What are you doing? You're working? At a time like this?"

Father sighs, then stands with his shoulders back, facing me squarely. He holds the torch out to one side and makes a silent shrug with the other palm open, as if to say, "What of it?"

My jaw falls. "*Dio Mio*! All you think about is work! Your wife is dead. Everyone is in mourning. You have a new baby. And here you are in your workshop, doing what... making a boat?"

My father gestures again, this time with a bit less bravado. Dark circles ring his eyes. He sighs, then, and his shoulders heave. He turns his back to me and places the heel of one hand against the frame of the boat, as if for support. Quietly, he replies, "You'll do the same one day, Luca. There is no other way to live, you must know that."

I hesitate, then react. "To hell with your work! To hell with destiny! Mamma is dead! Things can never go back to the way they were, don't you understand? This is not the way things are supposed to be!"

I pause and attempt to quell my words, but the anger has welled up inside my breast and has nowhere else to go. "It's your fault that she is dead! Don't you understand? The burden of her death is yours alone to bear. You knew she wasn't healthy enough for another baby. The woman is... was... too old! You already have your sons, but that wasn't enough for you. You had to produce another heir for your boatyard! When I think of it I feel I will vomit!"

I pause, surprising myself with this outburst. I have never spoken out against my father in my life. Years of emotion begin to spill over—the weight of my destiny, my future laid out before me, my marriage to Annalisa Bonfante, my work. Tears well up, but I swallow hard to fight them back. I glare at my father.

"How can I live here anymore? How can I work here with you? Knowing that it was your fault? That you killed her! I feel like walking out this door right now—forever!"

Throughout this tirade, Father stands frozen, his back to me, perhaps the only way that I dare to spit out such hateful words to him. He turns to face me now, fixing his piercing eyes on his eldest son. I watch them turn black with anger as he chooses his words carefully, quietly, and matter-of-factly through pursed lips.

"Everything I have done in my life I have done for my family, not only my wife and my children but for my future grandchildren, for the continuation of my father and my grandfather's legacy, for the future of this *squero*. If—after all I have done—you feel compelled to leave, then maybe you should."

I freeze, letting my father's words sink in. I am remotely aware of my own heartbeat. It grows into a dull throb, leading down my arms and legs, through the tips of my fingers and toes. Anger that I never knew I had in me begins to well up from the depths of my soul.

Then I hear the rushing sound, as if I can hear my blood coursing through my own veins. It starts at my feet, then rises up through my legs, into the pit of my stomach, and up through my face. Finally it fills my head, deafening my ears to the world outside my body. It grows louder until it makes my scalp tingle. All the hairs on my head seem to stand on end.

And then, the rage spills over.

With a single, violent sweeping motion, I brush my father's papers, tools, and parchment off the workbench. My father recoils from the sudden rage and force of his normally sullen child, a gut reaction that makes him hunch his shoulders, draw his hands near his breast, and transform his normally proud face into a twisted, startled expression. The torch crashes to the floor.

In less than a second, the torch flame leaps from the ground. It flickers in the draft, then dances onto a nearby cloth soaked with the varnish we have been using to waterproof another gondola under restoration. The stain-soaked cloth ignites with a sound like a dragon exhaling, then flames begin to leap wildly from it. A scrap of the singed canvas rises in the draft, then drifts like an autumn leaf to a drop-cloth piled haphazardly on the floor at the back of the studio. From there, it jumps to a pile of oak scraps, and curls of smoke begin to rise from the stack of wood. Within seconds, the entire back of the workshop is ablaze.

During those few short moments which seem to progress over hours, my father and I stand transfixed at the unreal sight of the flames catching the wood and cloth on fire at the back of our workshop. Then, Domenico Vianello snaps out of his startled daze and leaps into action, pulling off his waistcoat and beating wildly at the flames. He calls for Uncle Tino, his voice growing louder and more panicked as the seconds pass and the flames grow unabated. The leaping flames make my father's frenzied face glow, and for a moment he looks demonic, his skin red and twisted in anguish, and his black eyes reflecting shimmering flames. In the distance, I hear iron locks and wooden doors scraping open, and the sound of men's frantic voices outside the boatyard.

But I can see that it is already too late.

The flames make crazy dancing patterns, and I stand transfixed for a moment as I watch my family boatyard, my destiny, my whole life, disintegrate.

I turn my back and run.

Chapter 7

Boatmen. The mere thought of them is enough to make his blood boil.

The Councillor stands at the window, gazing out onto the Grand Canal. On the quayside below, a row of private gondolas lines up at the mooring. The Councillor watches a boatman escort one of his colleagues, their meeting now adjourned, into a boat adorned with gilded birds. The man disappears behind scarlet curtains, then his boatman steers the gondola into great basin that extends between the Piazza San Marco and the island of San Giorgio Maggiore. Beyond, several dozen cargo boats, private gondolas, and public ferries traffic the canal.

Deep creases form on either side of the Councillor's thin lips. Those in the watercraft trades outnumber any other single class of Venetians. That's what makes it such a threat to peace and order when these scoundrels break the law. How many times has he preached this message to his fellow members of the Council of Ten? Besides regulating coinage and sodomy, public order is the Council's primary duty to His Most Excellent Prince. Keep boatmen under control, and the Most Serene City will run as reliably as the clock in Saint Mark's Square. He sighs. Keeping them under control is precisely the problem. Every day, the Councillor receives news of some infraction involving boatmen. A fruitseller's daughter, raped under the tarps of a cargo raft. Gondoliers paid off handsomely for illegal smuggling among the merchant ships in the lagoon. Kickbacks earned in support of the prostitution trade.

Gambling competitions that begin at the ferry stations and end in un-
restrained cursing, fistfights, or blood spilled in the canal.

Blasted. There it is again: that old familiar burning sensation that
begins somewhere below his ribs, then wells slowly, tortuously upward
into his chest. When it reaches his throat, he knows, there will be pain-
ful regurgitations and the taste of sour eggs. The left side of his mouth
twitches. The Councillor strides to his desk in the corner of the room,
his robes flapping, and slides open the drawer. With long, elegant fin-
gers, he fishes around until he locates a small paper packet with powder
in it, an ingenious blend that the pharmacist has prepared for him. He
pours the powder in his mouth and sucks on it with great force, soften-
ing the sand-like mixture on his tongue.

Boatmen. Criminals, every last one of them.

While he waits for the concoction to take effect, the Councillor
paces across the marble floor of his chamber, taking in each one of the
dozens of oil paintings suspended on the walls. These pictures never
cease to bring him pleasure, none so much as those painted by the artist
Gianluca Trevisan, a master of color and light. The Councillor stops
before a small picture of Venus and Cupid that Trevisan painted for
him some five years ago. His eyes run over the vibrant, pink flesh of the
nude Venus; he drinks in the ponderous hips and delicate hands. At
last, the Councillor feels the burning in his chest begin to calm.

His mind sufficiently distracted from the vagaries of the canal and
toward the dual pleasures of art and the flesh, the Councillor summons
his secretary.

"Baldoni!" he calls, and almost immediately, a portly man with
satin buttons from his waist to his chin enters the room and bows.

"Magnificence?"

"Today we must complete the draft contract for the latest painting
from Master Trevisan."

"You speak of the portrait of Signorina Zanchi that you have
commissioned?"

"Yes," he says, feeling the familiar hunger returning. "I am most eager for Master Trevisan to begin the picture."

"Right away, of course," the secretary says, and he retrieves the ink-well and a fresh parchment folio from the cabinet.

Chapter 8

For four days, I have hardly eaten, surviving on the occasional scrap of cabbage lodged in the crack of a cobblestone, the detritus of market day in Rialto. I have done my best to stay hidden during daylight hours, observing, waiting—for what, I cannot say. I have drunk water from public fountains, cat-napped under the shelter of an arcade or against the wall of a vacant alley. At night I have wandered, a ghost-like spectator of the dark underbelly of Our Most Serene Republic.

Over this time the burden of truth has laid itself bare inside my head. For all I know, my childhood home is destroyed. I do not even know if my family survived the fire. And if they have, who would claim me now? Not my cousins, my uncle, certainly not my father. My brother and sister might find some compassion in their hearts for me, but they will not stand up before my father. And my mother—the only person in the world who might have defended me before them all—is gone. On top of it all, I am a criminal, an arsonist. What I have done must be bad enough to make me a candidate for the slave galleys or even the Doge's prisons. The authorities are probably looking for me—a fire-starter, a traitor to my own family.

I consider my choices.

I have experienced enough to know that I cannot go on living like a phantom in my city, a pariah to society. It goes against every grain of my body, and I know that I don't have it in me to hide indefinitely. I also know that I cannot leave Our Most Serene Republic. I have no papers and nowhere to go. I know no one on the mainland. The only possibility to leave the city is to volunteer on one of the merchant galleys, a life that amounts to little more than slavery. No, I must stay in Venice. Besides, I cannot imagine leaving My Most Excellent City. I love it with all my heart and cannot imagine living in a place that isn't permeated with waterways. The city is part of me, and I part of it.

Is there a path for me back home? Is it possible that I might overcome my enormous failings—that I may find my family willing to forgive me, that I might rebuild the *squero* and resume my place?

Seemingly by instinct, I walk in the direction of my old neighborhood in Cannaregio, in the direction of the one person left in the world with the power—and perhaps the will—to answer these questions.

I RECOGNIZE THE oarmaker's studio from its second-floor balcony, which, though rickety, boasts an expansive vista over the Sacca della Misericordia, a view the *remero* brags is better than that of any palace on the Grand Canal. On the lower level, a ramp slopes into the canal, making easy access for boatmen to moor and have their oarlocks fitted, restored, repaired, and replaced. The building could almost pass for a *squero*.

I choose an isolated spot in an alley where I will not be noticed, and I squat so that I can watch the back door of the *remero*'s studio. I wait. At dusk, just as the sky begins to turn pink, I hear the familiar ringing of the church bells at Madonna dell'Orto, signaling the end of the working day. Moments later, I spot two of the *remero*'s assistants leaving for the day. The men exit the back of the studio, chatting as they stroll down the street near to the spot where I wait. Another five minutes pass, then I see Samuele, Master Fumagalli's new apprentice, dash out the door and down the alley.

It is time to make my move. I approach the *remero's* studio, rapping quietly on the back door.

After a moment, I hear footsteps. "Who's there?" Signor Fumagalli's voice calls from the other side of the door.

"It's me, *remer*. It's Luca Vianello."

"Mother of God!" I hear fumbling with the lock. The door swings open and Signor Fumagalli, with his sour apple face twisted in alarm, reaches around and snatches me by the collar with a firm grasp that takes me by surprise. He closes the door as quietly as possible and leads the way into the back storage room, which occasionally doubles as a bunk for assistants, firmly gripping my forearm. He pulls me down to sit on a straw-filled mattress, and immediately takes my face in his wrinkled hands.

"My Lord, son, I hardly recognize you." In the days since the fire in the *squero*, I have grown nearly a full beard. My hair is greasy and tousled. I peer down ashamedly at my filthy clothes. "The whole neighborhood is talking about the fire at the great *squero* of Master Vianello. The boatyard is burned nearly to the ground."

I stand up with a start. "And my family...?"

"No one was injured in the fire, son," the *remero* says. "By the grace of God alone, they were able to escape the flames in time. Your brother, your sister, the baby—they are all sound, at least physically. Even the house and those of the neighbors are standing. But the *squero* is a God-forsaken mess, every boat reduced to ashes. And your dear mother was buried on Murano yesterday. The Rosmarin brothers sent one of the finest gondolas from their *squero* to your father to bear her body away. It seems that the old rivalries can disappear in times of calamity."

I squeeze my eyes shut and cup my hands over my ears. "Please! I cannot..."

The oarmaker stops and grasps my forearms. "Boy! What the hell were you thinking?"

I slump on the edge of the bed, and the words begin to flow out of me. I recount to Master Fumagalli all the events that led to my careless act—my grief, the blame I placed on my father, my lashing out against him, the flames bursting and leaping out of control. The oarmaker watches my eyes as I speak, but does not say a word until I finish.

Finally the *remero* sighs and rubs his palms over his head. "Your brother has already come to me in tears, certain that I must know something of your whereabouts. I could not imagine where you had gone."

"I don't know what to do now, *remer*. How could I ever redeem myself after what I've done?"

The oarmaker remains silent for a time, contemplating the weight of his response. "My dear boy," he says finally, "we are human beings and, true to our nature, eventually our judgment fails. You are no different. But as for going home now, I fear that I cannot advise it in good conscience. Your father..." Master Fumagalli rubs his face with his hands, then looks at me with a pained expression that tells me more than any words he could have chosen.

My shoulders slump and I sink into the mattress.

"Stay here," he says, and pats my shoulder. "I will bring you something to eat. You must be starving. Don't make a sound, you hear? Until we figure things out I don't even want my cat to know you are here!" He rises and heads toward the door that leads to his studio. "Mother of God!" the oarmaker exclaims in a loud whisper, then disappears. I collapse onto the bed, and for the time that Master Fumagalli is out of the room, I drift in and out of sleep.

Finally I hear the lock turn, and I see the stooped frame of Signor Fumagalli in the doorway. He hands me a burlap bag without a word. Inside I find a piece of warm bread and some cured ham, along with an apple and a wedge of soft cheese. I silently devour it and thank the *remero* again for his kindness. For a time we sit together in silence.

"Perhaps for now I may find work as a day laborer in the Arsenale shipyard," I say finally.

"You? A *fachino*?" The oarmaker looks at me skeptically.

"Why not?" I say. "I am an able-bodied man. I could load and unload cargo on the merchant galleys. It would just be for as long as it takes for me to sort things out."

Signor Fumagalli rubs his shriveled jaw.

"What else am I to do," I ask, "join the inmates who row war galleys to Crete and the Barbary Coast?"

The oarmaker contemplates my face with concern. "Luca, look. I want to tell you something I've never told you before," he says. "Whatever success your father has won as a boat-builder has come to him through nothing more than sheer determination. *Casso*, maybe a little bit of arrogance, too. But you, my son, you are the one with God-given talents in your hands. I have seen it myself; in fact, I would have engaged you as my own apprentice from the time you were eleven years old, if you were not already the gondola maker's son. I would never tell your father this, of course. He has his pride. But you should know it. You are the one with the magic in your own hands. I have known many artisans in my time, men who inherit a workshop but not the passion, the natural ability for the trade. You, my boy, are different. Yes, of course it's your destiny to inherit your father's boatyard. But most of all, son, it's what you were meant to do. If you are able to open your eyes long enough to examine the depths of your soul, you will know that what I say is true."

"That means more than you know, *remer*. Thank you. But clearly I cannot return to my place as the heir to my father's *squero*. Not after everything that has happened."

Signor Fumagalli shakes his head. "Thinking of you working as a dockhand in the Arsenale... It's just that you are meant for much more than that in this life." The oarmaker manages a grin, and for a moment I glimpse the jovial character that I have always known. "You must stay here with me until we resolve all of this," he says.

"Thank you, *zio*. God bless you, Master Fumagalli, but for the sake of our families' friendship, our history together, for the peace of my mother's soul, I would not bring that on you. If my father finds out you are harboring me, he might murder us both with his bare hands. At a minimum, he will never do business with you again."

Shadows pass over the oarmaker's face and he turns grim. "For now, what is important is that you need some rest." He squeezes my leg with a firm grip. From his perch at the end of the bed, the *remero* watches me. The old man's face, heavy with worry, is the last thing I see before sagging into a deep and dreamless sleep.

At dawn, I awaken to a faint glow outside the window. The sun has not yet risen, but the sky is turning from black to pink and yellow. Soon the master will awaken, then his assistants will arrive, and the workshop will begin to stir with the day's work.

My mind is clearer than it has been in days. I must not bring more trouble to the oarmaker than I have already caused. I must move quickly now, disappearing before anyone catches sight of me. The damp morning air cools my face as I emerge from Master Fumagalli's house. Behind me, I ease the door closed, and I hear its iron bar scrape into the locked position.

THE STENCH EMANATING from the public latrines is enough to make passersby swoon. I have only been inside once, taking up two friends on a dare when I was twelve years old. Ever since, I have avoided these disgusting-smelling outlets at all costs. If I am away from my family boatyard and feel the call of nature, I do as most boys and men do: I relieve myself in the canal.

My current predicament in a crowded street gives me little opportunity to be selective. I breathe in a nose full of fresh, damp air, then hold my breath as I duck into the dark entryway of the below-ground latrine. I pause for a moment to let my eyes adjust to the dimness. After a moment, I make out a bench-like structure with four equally spaced holes. A small shaft of light appears from a hole where one wall and the ceiling meet, but otherwise the room is dark. The odor is overwhelming. Then I perceive movement from the corner of my eye, and I flinch as I see a figure coming toward me from the corner of the stench-filled room. It is a man, staggering toward me, and I immediately realize that he is drunk. "Excuse me," slurs the man, and as he moves toward the light of the door, I see his bulbous red nose, lined face, matted hair, and soiled cloak. I back up to the wall to let the man pass. When the man exits, I proceed to the back of the latrine and relieve myself as quickly as possible, then exit.

Climbing a short flight of stairs from the filthy space to the quayside, I suck in the damp, fog-laden air, drinking it in with all my might. Before me, a crowd is gathering at the façade of a church. It stands at the edge of the wide canal; only a narrow quay separates the boat mooring from a staircase leading to the church doors. Several gondolas stand docked at a quayside, and passengers are being discharged before the church. Decorative marble forms geometric patterns in the pavement in front of the church and up the stairway, appearing as an extravagant carpet leading people toward its portals.

People begin to form into a procession, one of the many religious pageants that fill the city each day it seems, to honor particular saints and other feast days. I pause for a moment, watching three Dominicans dressed in long cloaks instructing a group of boys who are slipping white robes over their street clothes in preparation for the procession. Two or three dozen men and women, elaborately dressed, cluster on the staircase.

Three girls emerge from one of the gently swaying gondolas docked at the quayside. Arm in arm, they chat as they process up the patterned marble stairs to the quay where the crowd is gathering. There is something familiar about the tallest of the three—the way she walks, the gentle movement of her skirts as she moves, the gesture of her hand as she talks to her sisters. The girls pause near the spot where I am standing, and the tall girl turns in my direction. She glances briefly at me, turns her head away, then turns it back sharply and fixes her gaze on me.

Her eyes widen in shock.

I freeze.

Annalisa.

Chapter 9

It isn't until that moment that I stop to consider what I must look like. Instinctively, I smooth my stringy hair away from my face and run my palms down the front of my waist-vest as if to smooth the wrinkles. I run my tongue over my front teeth. Now I am fully aware of my unkempt hair, my unshaven chin, my dirt-smudged vest, my mud-caked shoes. I wonder if I have carried any scent of the public latrines with me.

Annalisa snaps out of her state of shock at meeting her betrothed by chance on the street and starts toward me with a furrowed brow. "Luca, Luca, where have you been? Your brother is looking all over the city for you! My father says the *signori di notte* are probably looking for you, too! The *squero* is practically destroyed. Your mother... There was a mass for her at Madonna dell'Orto and everyone from the guild was there. They bore her body away on a gondola covered with flowers. Everyone was talking about you! They decided to bury her in her family's tomb on Murano. My mother and I paid our respects there yesterday. And the baby... They baptized him as Antonio; did you know that already? Your sister has taken him to a wet nurse in Dorsoduro..."

The crowd has now turned its attention on us. Annalisa pushes forward, gripping my forearms, and looking into my eyes. I can smell her skin, can see her straight teeth up close now, and her large brown eyes under a furrowed brow. "Please, please, you must come back home. Your brother and sister are... It's beyond words. And your father... Luca, you cannot run away. It's your fate! We are to be married."

She reads my expression, then loosens her grip and takes a step backward.

"Annalisa..." I consider my words for a moment, then start softly. "Annalisa, I am sorry. I cannot go back—ever. I have no choice."

Slowly, she drinks in my words, then covers her mouth with both hands.

As I speak, I am aware that my voice is beginning to crack. "Please understand. I cannot go back. It's impossible. I will not. The fire..." My shoulders fall. "My father disowned me. It is no longer my fate to follow, and I was never worthy of it to begin with." I approach her, now visibly agitated, my hands drawn tightly into fists at my side. Annalisa's sisters rush to her as I continue. "It was all his fault that she died, don't you see? All his fault!"

Annalisa is sobbing now. She continues to take slow steps backward, shaking her head slowly from side to side. The two younger girls bolster their sister upright. She is silent for a moment that seems like an eternity, her mind processing the events. I chew my bottom lip. The crowd of onlookers grows.

Annalisa's eyes seem to turn black, and a deep shadow of rage crosses her face. She explodes.

"Traitor!" she shrieks. "Traitor!" Her cries become louder, and churchgoers stop in their tracks. Their muttering fills the air. Annalisa's youngest sister wraps her arms around her, and Annalisa covers her face with her hands. Then she wipes her nose on her sleeve, takes a deep breath, and cries loudly, "You set the fire in the *squero*! How could you? How did you dare? You betrayed your own family!" She sobs even louder. "And now you've betrayed me, too! You are worse than a traitor! You are a criminal!"

"Annalisa, the fire was an accident!" I manage to say. "But don't you see... I can't turn back now. Things can never be the same again. I am not even my father's true heir! My brother is the one, not I. I am a fraud, a clumsy, left-handed impostor. They will carry on better without me. And..." my voice becomes very soft, "I cannot marry you."

Annalisa stands momentarily silent. Then she explodes a second time. She raises her fists and shakes them vigorously toward the heavens. She howls as loudly as she can, a shriek so horrible that it makes my scalp tingle. Her sisters force her away from me, and from the crowd that has formed to witness a public spectacle even more compelling than the procession they had come to see.

I turn on my heels, duck my chin, and walk away quickly, my heart rending as I hear Annalisa's shrieks and sobs grow muffled and distant. I feel the burning eyes of several dozen onlookers at my back, as if they could brand me with a searing glance. I walk faster.

It begins to rain. Cold, grape-sized pellets fall from the sky, making a haphazard cacophony of concentric rings in the canals. The crowd of curious onlookers who witnessed Annalisa's outburst disperses. Some raise their cloaks over their heads and run for cover in the church. Others scatter to arcaded walkways that line the edges of a nearby piazza.

I march away from the church with great conviction even though, in truth, I have nowhere to go. My shirt is soaked and clings to my skin, and my feet slosh loudly inside my worn shoes. Enormous raindrops splatter against my hair and splash onto my eyelashes. Through the great drips that streak my face, it is impossible to make out the tears.

As much as I may wish to turn around and recant everything I have just said to Annalisa, my feet march forward. Why would Annalisa have me now? She will do better to find a more worthy husband than I. I have set fire to my own family *squero*. I didn't mean to, of course, but it was malice in my heart, resentment of my own father, that drove me to do it. In committing this unwitting crime, I have sealed my own fate. I love my brother and sister, and I know I would love my baby brother, too, but the oarmaker is correct: Things can never return to the way they were before the fire.

My destiny may have once lain in my family boatyard, in Annalisa's bed, at the hearth of my own house, in the community of my fellow *squerarioli*, in the experience and the talent of my own hands. But I am no longer deserving of any of it. Perhaps I never was.

For the first time in my life, I am alone.

A PLACE FOR OUTCASTS, a place for those with nothing to eat and nowhere else to go. That is all I know of the almshouse attached to the Convent of Santa Marta. On Tuesdays at noon, the Augustinian sisters fulfill their mission to clothe the poor, nurse the sick, and feed the hungry. Until now, I have known it only by reputation, not by personal experience.

Arriving in the square in front of the convent, still dripping from the deluge, I find some three dozen forlorn-looking, rain-soaked souls waiting in line before two enormous wooden doors. I hang back near another doorway in the square and watch as the doors scrape open to allow the bedraggled crowd to file into the convent. I drop into the back of the line.

We move into a warm, dry, cavernous room. On one wall, a roaring fire occupies an open hearth, sending crackles and sparks into the chimney. A servant in a brown shift tends the fire, and another stirs a pot. Several long wooden tables are arranged in the center of the room. At one end, another long table, set perpendicular to the others, stands below an enormous wooden cross hanging on the wall.

From the iron pot, a laywoman, no doubt a member of the confraternity, is filling wooden bowls with a ladle. She passes each bowl to one of the sisters, who gives it to the next poor soul in line. "God bless you," nods the small woman with delicate skin who hands me a bowl of steaming rice with peas. Her blue eyes shine at me like crystals. I take my bowl to one of the wooden tables, and place it on the end. I hesitate for a moment, noting that everyone else in the room is still standing.

A tall, regal-looking sister enters the room and stations herself at the head table. Nodding her head to her motley guests, she addresses us with a prayer, thanking God for his mercy and for sustenance. We cross ourselves, then sit down to eat. I heave myself on the wooden bench, possessively reaching my arm around the bowl, and lower my face into the steam emanating from the pile of rice. In less than a minute, the bowl is empty.

Only now do I look up to survey my dinner partners. Two men sit at the other end of my table, pouring diluted beer from a blue ceramic pitcher placed in the center of each table. They are regulars, I think, from the commentary they run on tonight's choice of rice and peas. "Not as good as Sister Francesca's *risi e bisi*," one man with no teeth comments. His companion nods, but it doesn't stop either man from inhaling the steaming meal in front of them. "Hers is more mealy, and it has more spice," adds the critic. "This one's too bland, he continues," stuffing his cheeks with it. His friend nods in silent agreement.

From across the room, I spy a legless African whom I have seen performing impressive hand-walking feats in the Piazza San Marco. He wears ragged breeches that brush the stumps where his legs should be, along with a dirty shirt and a tight-fitting cap over his coarse hair. Alongside him, his scraggly-haired partner translates on his behalf in Venetian dialect for another pair of ragged-looking men seated across the table from them. At another table, a portly, street-wise looking man is regaling two others with a tale about a fight, describing in gory detail how one man had punched another one so hard that his teeth had exploded out of his mouth and rattled on the cobblestones. The other two men howl with laughter. The laywoman in the soup line casts them a cold, stern glance.

Soon a nun emerges from a small door with a stack of neatly folded woolen blankets. She moves from table to table, distributing them among the men. She seems to know everyone by name. She looks each one in the eye and inquires about his welfare—where he is sleeping, if he is working, what of his family, what of his health. A few of the men chat with her as if she were a close friend or sister. She listens intently to the woes and tales of each man and asks for God's mercy on behalf of each one individually.

Having talked with the sister and received their blankets, a few men rise from their tables and amble to the wall. They spread their blankets and sit. Out of view of the nuns, one man produces a deck of playing cards and begins to deal them to his friends. Another man rolls himself tightly in his blanket, lays his head on the cold bricks, and closes his eyes.

When she approaches my table, the sister scrutinizes me with a frown as if trying to recognize my face. She takes note of the spoon in my left hand and I see her recoil, though she quickly composes herself. "*Bonasera*," she says. "Have you been here before, *missier*?"

"No," I reply, lowering my eyes. "First time."

"And what misfortune, may I ask, brings a young man like yourself to a place like this?" she asks.

I hesitate. My mind goes blank.

Seeming to consider my appearance, after a moment, the sister asks, "Are you a tradesman?"

"I work—I worked—with boats." I cast my eyes to the floor.

"I see. Are you ill? Or in trouble with the authorities?" she asks.

"No," I reply too quickly. Again, I hesitate. "Just unlucky, you might say." Her eyes wander briefly to my left hand again.

"Hmm," says the sister, with an expression that I interpret as a combination of sympathy and doubt. I must admit that I look out of place amongst the other men in the room.

"What a shame," she replies. "It is our mission here to feed the hungry, aid the poor, help the sick. We serve meals here on Tuesdays and Saturdays, if you are in need."

I nod, continuing to inspect the floor.

"May God have mercy on you," says the sister, dropping a drab woolen blanket on the bench beside me and moving away from my table.

Behind the nun, a kitchen maid approaches, clearing the table and wiping it with a rag. She leans toward me but does not meet my eyes as if, like me, she is trying to remain invisible.

"Excuse me, *missier*," she whispers. "Please forgive me, but I overheard you say that you are a boatman," she says.

I do not answer.

"If it serves you, my brother is the station master at the ferry dock near San Biagio. On occasion he hires day laborers to help with the boats. Perhaps you would find work there. You must ask for Master Giorgio."

I try to meet her gaze, but the servant woman's braids and face are mostly hidden behind the folds of her bonnet.

"Thank you," I say.

She nods. "God help me if I have presumed too much, *missier*, but it seems to me that there would be no reason that a young man like yourself might not be apprenticed. I wish you well."

I watch her disappear into the convent kitchen.

Chapter 10

Chicken droppings streak the faded black hulls of three gondolas moored at the Traghetto San Biagio. A rancid odor fills the air around the old ferry station.

A strapping man with a silver beard is loading crates of live hens onto one of the boats. The man wears breeches and a gray shirt—both in need of washing—covering muscular, suntanned arms. Each time he plunks one crate on top of another with his stumpy hands, the chickens squawk and flutter their wings, then squat nervously as the boat rocks gently from side to side. Lost in his work, the man is suddenly aware that someone is standing on the quay alongside his boat. He steps back with a start but catches his balance on the rocking boat.

"*Dio Mio*, boy, you gave me a scare."

"Excuse me for startling you, sir." I remove my hat. "I'm looking for work."

The man wipes his lined brow on his grubby shirtsleeve, then looks me in the eye. "Is that so?" He brings his hands to his hips and frowns.

"Are you the *gastaldo* of this ferry station, sir?"

"Going on thirty years," he says. "Do you know how to row a gondola?"

"Yes, sir. My father was a gondolier, so I learned from him." I surprise myself with this lie, which seems to have materialized out of thin air. "I know the city like the back of my hand. My parents died when I was ten, and I've been apprenticed to a carpenter since then, but he died of a terrible affliction. Last week. I need to work."

The ferry station's master considers my story, eyeing me suspiciously as he balances his strapping frame on the gondola. "You have no other family?"

"None. I am alone in the world."

"Hmph." The *gastaldo* runs his hand over his head of lustrous silver curls. "It is not every day that a stranger appears wanting work. All of my dock boys come recommended by my cousins or my closest colleagues." He carefully inspects me.

I straighten my back and continue to look the stationmaster squarely in the eye. "Your sister from Santa Marta directed me here, sir."

He hesitates, then lets out a gruff chortle that causes the gondola to sway. Then he pulls his stout frame out of the gondola and heaves himself up the four stone stairs to the quay. He stands close to my face, and I note that he is slightly shorter than I am. He slowly looks me up and down from head to foot. I feel the skin on my arms and scalp tingle. "My sister... What is your full name, son?"

"Luca... Fabris." I swallow hard.

"And how old are you, Luca... Fabris?" The stationmaster mimics my hesitation with a hint of sarcasm.

"Twenty-two."

"Where were you born?"

I hesitate again. "In... In Dorsoduro, sir."

"Can you lift heavy loads?"

"Of course."

The stationmaster scratches his head and circles me slowly, sizing me up from behind. "Son, do you realize that I run one of the largest ferry stations in Our Most Serene City? More than eight dozen boats go in and out of here every day. All of our boatmen are part of the corporation: they are elected, they pay their membership, they own their own boats, they follow the rules. They entrust me with collecting dues, scheduling their shifts, maintaining this ferry station, and most importantly, screening any potential new members of our corporation." He raises his gruff voice and pokes his chest with a stubby thumb. "That means it's up to me to keep out any of the *salabràchi* that give our profession a bad name!"

I examine the ground.

"However," he says finally, completing his circle, "you find yourself in fortunate circumstances. I am buried under deliveries right now, and it just so happens that I lost a dock boy this week; stupid kid had *càca* for brains." The man projects a large wad of spittle onto the cobblestones. I blink hard. "I'm willing to take a chance with you for one day, provided that you play by my rules. So... you want to start right now?"

"Yes, sir, thank you, sir!" My shoulders fall in relief.

He holds up his hands, displaying large callouses on his palms. "Now I'm not promising anything. We'll give you a try, but just for today, understand? Then, tomorrow's a new day, and we'll see how you do. If things work out, I will provide you a place to sleep and I will pay you eight *soldi* per day, paid every Saturday, which you can spend on food and drink. You will do exactly as I say, go exactly where I tell you, keep your nose clean and your opinions to yourself. Stay out of trouble, and you and I will get along just fine. Got it?"

"Yes, sir," I manage.

"And," he adds, pulling his sour-smelling face even closer, "you make one mistake, you're out on your ass."

I nod.

"Marchese's my name." He shakes my hand. "You can start right away, then. Finish loading the chicken crates from the warehouse onto the three boats moored here. When you're finished with that, come to the station house, and I'll give you further instructions." Without another word, Master Marchese ambles to the station house, little more than a grimy, wooden, thatch-roofed shack along the quayside. At the door of the station house, he turns to size me up again from a distance.

I PAUSE AT THE THRESHOLD of the boathouse to let my eyes adjust to the darkness. The cavernous stone building lies low along the canal-side. Heavy wooden doors latch with an ominous-looking lock, a wonder of ironwork that must have taken a blacksmith weeks to fashion. At the center of the boathouse is a boat slip, accessible through the enormous sliding door. I judge that the boat slip is wide enough to accommodate four or five gondolas at once. Boats pull directly into the slip inside the building, making it easy to unload goods into the adjacent storage areas. A pedestrian door opens onto the quayside. On one side of the boathouse, oars the length of two men stand stacked in special holders. Beyond, I glimpse the station house, where Master Marchese is chatting animatedly with a gray-haired gondolier who has just docked his craft. From across the ferry station, I can only make out the men's deep-throated chuckles and a few choice swear-words.

On the other side of the boathouse stands the ferry station itself, little more than a dock where passengers wait to be ferried out to the Grand Canal and to stations elsewhere in the city. For a mere *bagattin*, a passenger can go as far as the quayside opposite the canal. For another five *ecus*, he can have the gondola and the gondolier all to himself and go wherever he pleases. For a little more, and if he is so skilled, he can rent his own boat, either a gondola or a canal raft, for an errand or a picnic on one of the lagoon islands.

The stench of sweat, poultry, and rancid water fills my nostrils. I shiver against the dampness and wish for my woolen waistcoat, which I imagine hanging on the hook beside my bed in my parents' house. My father's house, I correct myself.

On a simple wooden table in the corner of the boathouse, I find a pair of dirty leather gloves, and I slip them over my hands. The chicken crates are stacked high in one corner of the building, and one by one I bear them to the gondolas. I listen to the nervous bruck-brucking of the mottled hens and eventually grow accustomed to the putrid odor of their feces as I work. For the next two hours, I allow my mind to go blank, gratefully engrossed in the mindless task. I feel myself begin to breathe easy for the first time in days. Make money to eat—that's all I need to think about right now.

The stationmaster appears at the pedestrian door of the boathouse. Simultaneously, a gondolier glides his black craft into the boathouse slip. I recognize the boat. I know the emblem on the aft deck: three carved roses that are the signature of the Squero Rosmarin. Its proprietor is one of my father's rivals. For a moment I am lost in examining the boat's keel, its fittings, its prow, its oarlocks, but Giorgio's gruff voice snaps me out of my dream.

"What are you waiting for, son? Grab the towline and unload this gentleman's cargo!"

"Neither time nor money is wasted at the Traghetto di Giorgio Marchese!" jokes the gondolier, emerging from the boat and offering the stationmaster a vigorous handshake. "Especially not money!" he laughs.

The boat is loaded with a dozen wooden and wicker boxes. I cannot see what is inside; I only know that they are exceptionally heavy. Following Giorgio's direction, I stack them along the left side of the boathouse, next to a gathering of crates full of vegetables that reach the height of two men.

Gondoliers come and go in a steady rhythm throughout the afternoon. I dutifully load and unload their goods: containers of spice, sacks of flour, bolts of silk. Most of the boatmen are older, each with his own distinctive boat. One gondolier has skin the color of coal, and I suppose that he is a freed slave who has worked his way into the corporation. I continue my endless task of moving objects in and out of boats, from one side of the boathouse to the other, sometimes for no apparent reason. At first I use a cart whose wooden wheels get stuck between the cobblestones. Finally, I give up and rely on my arm strength. I am soon drenched in sweat.

I come to understand that Giorgio's *traghetto* has three boats of its own. They are squalid, coated in layers of indefinable grime. I wonder if they had ever been cleaned. Another boat is outfitted with a broad *felze* made of green fabric to keep off the rain and a simple upholstered seat for carrying passengers. It is only a little cleaner that the gondolas used for cargo. I would be ashamed to own a boat in such a state.

In the distance, Giorgio sits on a rickety chair outside the station house with a pair of rough-looking gondoliers. The men are playing cards, engrossed in their wagers, alternately swearing and laughing as the sun sinks lower in the sky. Noticing me watching him, Giorgio excuses himself from the game and heads down the stairs to the gondola mooring. For a moment the stationmaster pauses to observe me polishing the *fòrcola* of one of his boats with a rag.

Then he stops dead in his tracks. The boat I am working on is far from spotless, but it is cleaner than it was just a few hours ago. The white streaks of chicken feces have been scrubbed clean, and the black paint reflects the shifting dusk light from the canal waters.

"Hmph," grunts Giorgio. He seems to restrain himself from commenting. Finally, he clears his throat. "Tomorrow you'll work with Alvise, one of my most experienced *gondolieri*. You will go with him to make a delivery to the studio of Master Trevisan. This Trevisan is a prestigious painter, and he's one of my best customers." He wags a chubby finger at me. "Don't screw it up. *Capito?*"

He leads me to a low-slung stone building adjacent to the boathouse. Its wooden roof is riddled with holes that open to the dusk sky streaked with pink clouds. I follow Giorgio down a short flight of stairs and into a cave-like storage room filled with barrels, bails of straw, and crates. In the corner is a lumpy, straw-filled mattress lashed to a bed frame with ropes, a tattered blanket thrown over the foot of the bed. A rusty chamber pot peeks out from beneath the bed. The room reeks of rotten barley and urine.

Without another word, Giorgio hands me a brown cloth with its four corners tied together, then saunters back to the station house. Unraveling the package, I find a piece of stale bread and a pear. I devour the meal in seconds, then fall into an exhausted heap on the mattress.

That night, the canal outside my new home echoes with the sounds of the Castello quarter. Women giggle, the tinkling sounds of their voices lifting into the air. A screaming match between two lovers breaks out, their agony and passion echoing across the water. The fight abates only to be replaced by the shrieks of battling street cats. Toward the wee hours of the morning, someone vomits loudly into the waters of the canal. The clamor of this Venetian symphony only licks the edges of my mind. I surrender to sleep, the best I've had since that night, hardly a week ago, when, by my own hands, my life was reduced to ashes.

Chapter 11

"Pellegrini!" Master Giorgio shouts. "Take the new kid with you!"

"*Cavolo*, Master Giorgio has ensnared a new recruit, I see!" A chestnut-haired boatman flashes a smile at me from where he stands on the quayside next to an ancient-looking gondola docked there. "Give me a hand, will you?"

The boatman gestures to a large wicker container sitting on the stones. I lift one side and he lifts the other, and carefully we board the boat. We nestle the heavy box onto the floor of the gondola. I take a seat on the aft deck. The boatman unties from the metal mooring ring on the quayside, letting the gondola drift. He seats himself next to me and wraps one arm around my shoulder in an amicable embrace. "Greetings! What'd you say your name was?"

"Luca. Luca Fabris."

I squirm under his embrace as he offers me his free hand in a tight handshake. "Alvise Pellegrini. It's a pleasure. I guess we're colleagues, as of this moment, anyway." Two of his teeth are black with rot, yet Alvise manages to pull off a remarkably charismatic smile. He releases his grip on my shoulder, stands, and maneuvers the gondola out of the narrow passageway where the ferry station stands.

Alvise is older and shorter than I am, a muscular mule of a man with deep creases in his cheeks and lively eyes. His hands are cracked and scarred; dried blood appears across two knuckles on his right hand.

"Old Man Marchese has dispatched us to Master Trevisan's studio," Alvise informs me. "We make deliveries there often. He's some kind of famous painter, but it makes no difference to me; I just go where the old man sends me. Marchese... he's a lecherous old *strónso,* is he not?" I blink hard, unaccustomed to the foul language for which Venetian boatmen are famous. "But I must give him some credit," Alvise continues. "He knows how to make money and keep it. He'll work your ass off. Just watch your back, that's all I can say. So, where'd you come from, Luca Fabris?"

"Um..." I stammer, not knowing where to begin, and trying to ensure that my story lines up with the lie I have already constructed for Giorgio.

"A man of mystery," Alvise smirks. "That's alright, you don't have to reveal your dark secrets if you don't want to."

"No, it's alright," I say. "I needed work, that's all."

"Don't we all... So, did Old Man Marchese tell you why he hired you?" Alvise raises his eyebrows.

"No, but I don't care. I just needed to earn a few *soldi* to eat." I gaze into the canal as if I can see the bottom.

Alvise smirks. "Well, you might care about this: Your esteemed predecessor got knocked off in a brawl last week by one of the servants from the Ca' Servadei."

"Really?" My jaw falls as I check Alvise's face to see if he's joking.

"Really. The guy—Paolo was his name—was an imbecile. And constantly drunk, *macarón.* Paolo's job was delivering wood and wine from Rialto to the Servadei household. Paolo and the servant who accepted deliveries at the palace were constantly fighting—calling each other names, punching each other at the slightest provocation. Would have killed each other already if I hadn't stopped them on more than one occasion. It was all over a woman—*inbeçiíli* both of them." Alvise releases one hand from the oar to make a dismissive gesture.

"The other night Paolo was out with some men from the ferry docks. They spent the evening in a tavern down near Rialto," Alvise explains, gesturing vaguely with his thumb to an area over his right shoulder. "They see this man-servant, and he's with Paolo's lady friend. Paolo flew into a rage. Needless to say they got into a fist-fight, and the guy chased Paolo onto the bridge near the Ruga Vecchia. Well, that's one of those old-fashioned bridges with no rails, you know. Paolo was drunk, like I said. The guy punched him good in the face, and he went over. Never came up." Alvise nods his head and smiles as he finishes the sordid tale.

I am stunned for a moment. "So, what happened?"

Alvise shrugs and continues rowing. "What happened? Well, you showed up, that's what happened." He snickers and raps me on the shoulder with the back of his hand. "Who knows? Maybe we'll find Paolo floating in the canal on our rounds. Now, here we are."

Alvise slows the gondola as we approach an impressive-looking brick *palazzo* that dwarfs the buildings adjacent to it, a grand house with tall windows and several chimneys reaching their long columns toward the sky. A stone stairway leads from the waters of the canal to a landing beneath an arched wooden door. At eye level, the door is pierced with a small, sliding portal, which has bars so that the occupant can see who is at the door without opening it. Below the portal, a window box displays yellow and purple flowers. Alongside the impressive-looking door, a glazed window with diamond-shaped panes stands at the level of the canal.

While Alvise ties the boat to the artist's mooring, I stand and find my balance in the boat. From this vantage point, I am able to peer inside the large leaded window, and I pause to take in the scene.

The painter—who else could this man be—sits with his back to the window. He wears a silk shirt the color of a ripe peach, gathered at the shoulders with the sleeves rolled up to expose strong forearms. Velvet breeches the color of rubies cover his stout legs, and his hat sits askew on gray curly locks. Deep in concentration, he perches atop a stool with his knees wide apart, examining a canvas on the easel before him. In his right hand he holds a paintbrush; in his left, a stick to steady his hand. On a small wooden table sit a palette with several colorful smears and a dingy rag.

Sensing our presence, the artist wheels around to face the window. A surprised expression crosses his face, then he rises and moves quickly to the door. I hear heavy footsteps approaching, then the iron bar that locks the door scrapes against the wood.

"*Dio Mio*, how you startled me!" the artist cries as he pokes his head around the door. I see a shock of silver curls, a thick beard, and piercing gray eyes that examine me.

"Good day, Magnificence, and please excuse us for startling you," Alvise bows to the artist. My cheeks turn hot in embarrassment. Alvise and I work together to lift the box out of the boat, and we carry it up the stairs and through the doorway of the artist's studio.

"Come in, come in." The door swings wide and for the first time I take in the full presence of the artist.

Trevisan is a strapping, virile man with strong arms and long yet stout legs like the trunks of pine trees. He wears his aristocratic clothes with flair. His beard and mustache are closely cropped, but his curly gray hair remains tousled and unkempt. The artist stands with his back perfectly straight and looks down his nose at me, though somehow without haughtiness. His girth implies gluttonous habits but also lends him an air of authority. I manage to bow slightly, an awkward and unpracticed gesture. I avert my eyes.

"You will come into the studio and wait for me, please," the artist says, wiping his hands on a rag and throwing it across one shoulder. "I have another delivery that you may make on my behalf now that you are here."

It takes a moment for my eyes to adjust to the interior light. Dust-flecked sunbeams illuminate the studio, a space so richly appointed that I stand dumbfounded. Apart from the basilica of San Marco, I have never seen a place so splendid in my whole life. On one end of the room, a fire crackles in a tremendous stone hearth carved with winged feline creatures with human heads. Two rich carpets from the East blanket the floor with fantastic red and blue designs. From one wall hangs an enormous tapestry with a hunting scene, a nobleman sounding a trumpet and dogs leaping after a stag. Dark panels of wood make decorative patterns across the ceiling. They decorate the walls, too, but I can hardly see them, as paintings cover the walls from the floor all the way to up to the wooden beams that line the ceiling. I cannot begin to count the number of paintings that hang from the walls. There are portraits, saints, horses, mythological figures that I fail to interpret, and so much more that my eyes can hardly take it in. Candelabra taller than a man stand clustered around the artist's easel, lighting his work. I have only seen such massive candelabra inside my parish church. A crimson, velvet-upholstered divan sits before the easel, with purple silks draped across the back.

The artist leans over a large wooden desk, writing something on a parchment folio with a feather pen. Alvise stands before the desk waiting, hat in his hands. Light from the window filters into the room, illuminating the artist's workspace, as well as the painting on the easel.

And that's where my eye stops.

The painting shows a woman's face. Her skin is smooth, her lips full and moist. Fine wisps curl around her forehead and temples, then the image disintegrates into brushstrokes. One hand rises to her flushed cheek, but the artist has not yet fully painted it. In fact, the picture remains little more than a colored sketch, yet in my whole life I have never beheld something so beautiful. Without a doubt, this is the most captivating woman I have ever seen. I stand transfixed.

Worried that the artist might be observing me, I glance at Trevisan. He paces slowly across the studio, pulling on his beard as he reads the document in his hand, lost in concentration. Alvise waits silently. My eyes turn back to the picture on the artist's easel, and I move closer. It is remarkable; the woman seems to be looking straight at me. Brown hair frames her delicate face, and her greenish eyes have an alluring quality that I cannot begin to describe.

Never has a woman looked at me this way. My collar seems to tighten around my neck, and I need some air.

Wheeling around on his heel, Trevisan breaks his trance. "Very good, very good." He returns to the wooden desk near the hearth, pulls the feather pen from its inkwell, and signs the document with a flourish.

"I need for you to deliver this contract immediately to my client's palace in San Marco." He rolls the signed contract into a scroll.

"Magnificence," Alvise says. "With all due respect, this service falls outside the normal course of today's delivery." Alvise gestures to the box we have just placed on the studio floor. "Master Giorgio is expecting my colleague and me back at the *traghetto* to attend to our work. An additional delivery would require a premium on today's fees. Of course, my colleague and I would be delighted to provide this service at a lower rate if you will work directly with us."

The artist fixes his silent, piercing gaze on me, and pauses. Finally, he demands, "What is your name, son?"

I hesitate. "Luca, sir. Luca Fabris."

"My dear boatman Fabris and my dear boatman Pelligrini," continues Trevisan, "I have been waiting for this contract for three months. I'm not about to wait one more single minute. I fail to understand how people's minds work at times. How can they expect me to work without a contract? I've already begun the oil sketch," he says, blowing air and gesturing toward the picture that has so captivated me. "That's more than I do for most of my patrons. Without a contract, there will be no painting. I have other commitments, and I have no more time to wait."

I hope the artist cannot see my hands trembling.

Trevisan looks at me again. "I have instincts about people, and I have a good feeling about you, son. You seem like a trustworthy person, unlike many of the blaspheming gondoliers who extort their customers and give your profession a bad name. Hmph!" For a fleeting second, his gaze flickers toward Alvise. "Now, if you will kindly deliver this contract to the Councillor, I am prepared, of course, to pay the customary rate for this service, and I will pay it directly to Master Giorgio on my next visit to the *traghetto*." The artist fixes his eyes, the most remarkable shade of gray, on Alvise.

"Yes," says Alvise, and bows exaggeratedly. "As you wish, Magnificence."

"You know the Ca' Leoncino, on the Grand Canal just beyond San Marco?" the artist asks. "It's the palace with the pink and white stonework, the pointed windows like they used to make during the time of Doge Venier, and the painting of Venus and four *putti* on the façade."

I struggle to imagine what *putti* are. Alvise says, "Yes, Magnificence, I am familiar with the palace."

"*A presto*, then," says Trevisan, his head cocked to the side and his piercing eyes fixed on me for a moment. He swiftly rolls up the contract and ties it with a green ribbon. Then he hands it to me.

Chapter 12

Propelling the gondola down the Grand Canal, Alvise lets loose a outburst of cursing, most of it directed toward the artist Trevisan. "And who does he think he is, the Doge? He's nothing more than a painter," Alvise says.

But I am hardly listening. I sit on the aft deck holding Trevisan's contract in my hands. All I can think about is the painting in the artist's studio. That woman, My God, who is she? Is she real or just a figment of the artist's imagination? I take a deep breath. Pull yourself together, I tell myself.

We pass the Piazza San Marco, and Alvise slows the gondola before what must be the Ca' Leoncino. This is not just any house; it is a palace, its foundation of large, coursed stones and the upper parts of its façade decorated with pink, coral, and white stones laid in a zigzag pattern. Even the artist's studio pales in comparison. Just as Trevisan described, the tall windows of the main floor are dressed with pointed arches, now considered old-fashioned but still elegant.

From the canal comes the shrill whistle of a gondolier, followed by the scrape of a pair of iron gates that protect the palace's private boat slip from the vagaries of the canal. I can see that the slip houses no fewer than three elaborate boats, including a stunningly outfitted gondola with carved and gilded swans ornamenting the passenger compartment. Alongside the boat slip stretches a long private quay studded with metal rings for mooring boats, as well as two large mooring posts painted with red and white stripes.

There is already one gondola there, a masterpiece of a boat that I suppose was made by Samuele Malatesta, another of the city's master boat makers and one of my father's rivals. The gondola is spotless, its black sides gleaming and reflecting light off the waters. A great steel dolphin adorns the prow. I gauge that the dolphin itself weighs double that of the prows we fastened to the gondolas in our own boatyard. The *felze*, secured with thickly entwined red silk cords, covers a bench richly ornamented in red damask fabric with leather insets. The oarlock is a masterpiece, no doubt the work of my dear *remero*, Master Fumagalli. No one else in the city makes oarlocks like that.

I admire the boat for a moment as it rocks gently in the shimmering water. This gorgeous gondola makes the boat we are rowing look like a shabby heap of wood, its paint peeling, its finish dull even though I have spent hours polishing it. Alvise slows the boat near the quay, and I reach out my arm to grasp its cold, damp stones. I expertly tie a knot to one of the mooring posts, then climb out of the boat and up the stairs to the quay. I grip Trevisan's contract, guarding it with my life.

I am nearly to the canal-side doors, which I judge to be a delivery entrance, when I realize that Alvise remains in the boat. I turn and shrug my shoulders at him.

"I'm going to let you handle this delivery yourself," he tells me. I hesitate. "But..."

Alvise raises his palms in a sheepish gesture. "Let's just say I'm not in this household's good graces."

Two enormous rings, wrought from twisted iron, hang from the mouths of lions. Above hangs a door knocker in the shape of a dolphin. I reach up to the dolphin and knock four times, cringing a bit at its harsh metal sound. My heart races. I have never made a delivery alone to a patrician palace, not even knocked on the door.

I have only gazed at such magnificent buildings from the canals. I clear my throat and wait. In a moment, I hear footsteps approaching the door then stop.

The door does not open. Instead, a small wooden window slides open at eye level. A pair of wrinkled yet clear blue eyes peers at me through an iron grille. "*Sì?*" a woman's voice asks curtly.

"I have a delivery from Master Trevisan, the artist," I say as confidently as I can.

"And you are...?" the voice asks, again curtly.

"I... um, I am... from the Traghetto San Biagio. The painter Trevisan sent us to deliver a contract to His Most Excellent Councillor at this house." I shift my weight from one foot to the other. My finger twirls one of the loops of the green string that binds the contract.

The eyes narrow. "*Un momento,*" the voice says. The wooden window slides shut, and I hear footsteps retreating.

I look up and marvel at the hulking building, its pale pink and white stones towering over my head. A windowsill made from a single slab of marble projects outward one story above. A pigeon peers down at me from its perch; even the bird carries a haughty air.

Finally, I hear footsteps approaching the door again. This time the metal bar scrapes, and the door opens to reveal a man. The man is about my age, and from his clothing I surmise that he is a manservant. He gestures for me to enter the house. I step across the threshold into a room paved with giant stones. The space holds a single piece of furniture, a narrow, uncomfortable-looking bench against the canal-side wall. Before me stands a curved marble staircase that disappears into the second story, from which I perceive only darkness.

The manservant sizes me up, then looks me in the eye. "You have come from Master Trevisan's studio?" he asks."

"Yes, to deliver a signed contract for a painting," I say. By instinct I extend the contract to the manservant with my left hand, but he does not take it. I meet his gaze. The man grins slyly with tight lips. I switch to my right hand, and he pulls the contract toward him.

"Are you Master Trevisan's new *barcherolo*?" he eyes me suspiciously.

"I... no. Yes," I stammer. "I mean, well, I run important errands for him. Like this one."

IN A MATTER OF WEEKS, Alvise has become my master in the art of gondoliering, and I, his unwitting apprentice. I live vicariously through Alvise, not sure I could ever hope or want to be so brash.

I watch Alvise charge four *soldi* for a trip to San Marco to a Venetian citizen who puts up a fight; for the same route, he asks for triple that price from an English couple who pay the fare with a trusting smile. On another day, Alvise makes the rounds of his favorite tavern owners, lashing the gondola to a half-dozen docks to collect his commission for ferrying passengers to his list of personally recommended establishments. By the end of his rounds, I calculate that Alvise has pocketed at least half of a gondolier's daily salary on tavern kickbacks alone. All the while, Alvise regales me with stories of his days on the water, most of them so outrageous that I think they can only be true.

A steady stream of clients approaches the ferry dock in the mornings and afternoons, and the time passes quickly. Alvise and I transport a group of foreign visitors to the Lido for a picnic, where they play music for half the day on lutes and another stringed instrument that I do not recognize. We ferry middle-class passengers: shopkeepers, artisans, merchants, foreign visitors. We even sometimes carry patricians like Nardo Battistini, a wealthy banker who regularly contracts Giorgio's boatmen to ferry him around as needed for business errands. "Costs less than maintaining his own boat and hiring a private boatman," Alvise explains to me after dropping Signor Battistini off one afternoon at the exchange. "*Strónso,*" he adds with a frown.

Giorgio dispatches Alvise and me to deliver wood, wine, supplies, market provisions, documents, and messages to various fine houses around the city. Until now, I have rarely traveled outside my own quarter in Cannaregio, having spent my days cooped up, hard at work in my father's boatyard. I have never been inside the house of a patrician, and I am compelled by these passing glimpses into the lives of the city's upper classes. I come to recognize the distinctive canal-side façades of each residence, as well as their much plainer dockside doors that make for easy deliveries from our boats. I steal glances into cavernous kitchens, warm and dry from the fires in their giant hearths. Rarely do we encounter the upper-class inhabitants of these residences. Instead, Alvise introduces me to a host of servants: the cook with a large backside at the Ca' Venier, who always wears an apron tied around her girth; the manservant with a harelip at the Ca' Rossini, who regards Alvise with obvious disdain, though Alvise doesn't seem to notice.

I begin to absorb the unspoken language of Venetian boatman, a complex set of hand gestures this cadre of men has developed over generations to communicate silently to one another across the water. Some of the signals are easy to divine: twirling fingers for "Let's meet for a plate of pasta at the midday meal" or a left thumb over the right shoulder for "incoming tide." Soon I learn the most common needs for communication: "high tide," "low bridge," "I will wait to enter the canal until you pass," "I intend to tie up my boat there," and "back up so I can pass." Many other gestures I must ask Alvise to translate for me.

From Alvise, I also learn how to rent boats to those who prefer to row themselves around the city from our ferry dock. For just a few *soldi* an hour, a customer can take out a *puparin* or a *sandalo*, smaller versions of a gondola that even a novice can row. I fit people with

the right-sized oar, ensuring that the oarlock fits snugly in its socket
and that the oar is neither too tall nor too short for the rower. Of
course, I already know how to do this by instinct. Of all of our
tasks, fitting the oar to the rower is the one in which I take the
greatest pride, even if my skill remains my own secret.

When we do not have passengers, we spend our time working
in the boathouse or on the dock, loading and unloading goods
from the steady stream of gondolas affiliated with Giorgio's *traghetto*. I now recognize a surprising number of boatmen, though
I only know the Christian names of a few; everyone is called by a
nickname instead. One of the men is named Nedis, but everyone
calls him Lupo. His face is stuck in a permanent snarl, and I try
to keep my head down whenever Lupo approaches the dock, as he
seems only to bark commands and insults, nothing else. Another
regular is an enormous hulk of a man everyone calls Little John.
The other boatmen treat him with quiet respect, tiptoeing gingerly
until he rows out of sight. Alvise tells me that Little John has served
on the galleys and was even taken into slavery in Tunis but escaped
by murdering his captors with his bare hands.

When the traffic slows, Alvise gives me a formal tour of the
boathouse. I have toiled inside it nearly every day since my arrival,
but out of respect for my new teacher, I pretend to know nothing. With dramatic sweeping motions, Alvise describes each aspect
of the boathouse as if he were describing the interior of a grand
palace. He reviews a vast variety of ropes suspended along one wall,
describing the purpose of each one: tying down boats, towing rafts,
fashioning pulleys. I don't tell him that not only do I already know
all of these ropes, but I also know how tie them into several dozen
specific knots, each for a different function.

I rarely speak, which is a relief, as I do not wish to explain
myself. Alvise, on the other hand, talks constantly. He explains
how the *traghetto* guild has reelected Giorgio numerous times and
pays him to keep the station running.

"He's a callous old *strónso*," Alvise chuckles, "a man of few but choice words. He may be an employee of the guild, but you and I know that the old man earns his salary the way they all do—kickbacks, side jobs, gambling, selling off any goods that linger in the warehouse. He's on the inside with all sorts—bankers, costume renters, glassmakers, water-sellers, you name it. Now that I think about it, he's very skilled at pocketing extra money along the way." Alvise grins.

"Does he have a family?" I am curious.

"Not anymore. He used to have a wife, but she died. Poisoned... Nobody really knows what happened, but..." Alvise makes an incomprehensible gesture with his hand, and I struggle to understand what it means.

Alvise snickers. "The Old Man's the only one I know who's actually been put in the stocks for cursing. You and I both know they don't enforce the public cursing law, but I guess if you break it too many times, they have no choice. You ever notice that scar on his calf?"

I shake my head.

"The rumor is that Giorgio was tortured with fire for spitting in the face of one of the censors. Needless to say, it's no wonder we've reelected him so many times as our *traghetto* warden. He's a hero!" Alvise laughs again.

Alvise lowers his voice and moves close to me. "Okay, you're a quiet kid, so I'm going to let you in on a little secret that only I and a few others know. On the side, Old Master Giorgio singlehandedly supplies young boys for those in the city who, well, those who *want* them." He winks and clicks his tongue. "Know what I mean? That's where the real money is."

I suck in my breath, trying to absorb this information.

"That's one of the reasons that painter Trevisan uses Giorgio's services. He hires male prostitutes as models for some of his pictures." Alvise chuckles. "I'm sure the ones he hires must consider posing for a picture easy money compared to the alternative."

Alvise is already onto the next topic, but I am still grappling with the thought of the gruff, unkempt Giorgio as an underground broker for what I have only heard described from the pulpit of my parish church as the great Sin of Gomorrah. All I know is that homosexuals are supposed to burn at the stake, though I person-ally have never witnessed that particular punishment meted out between the columns of justice in the Piazzetta San Marco. I force myself to refocus on what Alvise is saying. I wonder why he has shared this detail with me, apart from being proud of himself for owning this choice bit of information about our master.

Giorgio has a name for each of his boats, Alvise is telling me now, and even treats them as if they were pets. One of the gondolas is called Vecchina since it is the oldest of the fleet. I admire the old carving of a sea nymph on the aft deck, which I know requires great skill to achieve; I know of no one who carves like that anymore. Nerina is Giorgio's favorite, Alvise tells me, and that's the one he normally takes when he is running his own personal errands. Alvise is moving on to tell me about the cargo rafts when Giorgio's gruff voice interrupts us.

"*Cucco!*" Giorgio calls out Alvise's nickname, then gestures with his thumb to the passenger dock, where a man is waiting. Alvise leaves me behind in the boathouse, and Giorgio remains framed in the doorway with his arms crossed, regarding me closely. Something in the man's gaze makes goosebumps appear on the back of my neck. He has been observing us from this position, for how long I do not know.

Chapter 13

Giorgio charges Alvise and me with picking up Nardo Battistini, the banker, and his wife to go to a private masked ball in Dorsoduro.

Alvise mans the oar, and I take a seat on the aft deck of one of the passenger gondolas. I slide my fingertips across the mahogany planks beneath me, a subconscious gesture I must have repeated thousands of times in my life. I polished them two days ago with a special mixture of olive oil tinged with muriatic acid that I improvised from neglected materials I discovered in the boathouse. The boards feel slick and clean beneath my left hand, and I feel pleased with my work. Alvise steers the boat westward toward Dorsoduro. Near the Rialto market, he turns left.

"I thought we were going to pick up the Signori Battistini," I say.

"We are, my friend. But first, we have a little personal business to take care of," Alvise grins. He maneuvers into the tight sliver of water lined with boats docked on both sides, then ducks to avoid hitting his head on the rickety wooden bridge that spans the canal. He scowls back at it. "Shoddy craftsmanship."

He brings the gondola to a stop and moors it to a post outside a private residence. The narrow house stands some four stories high with a crooked façade and tall, arched windows covered with iron grilles. Like many canal-side façades, this one is painted in bright hues, with trailing green tendrils around the arched doorway.

His face raised upward, Alvise cups his hands and emits a low, bird-like whistle. We wait in silence for a moment, then Alvise repeats the whistle. Finally, we hear footsteps approaching the canal-side door. The arched, wooden door creaks open, and a man's lined face appears, bearing the closely trimmed facial hair in the fashion of the day. "My guests are readying themselves for an unforgettable night. We won't keep you waiting long!" He smiles, and I notice that several teeth are missing.

Alvise bows exaggeratedly toward the man. "At your service."

"Signor da Ponte," Alvise whispers to me. "I don't know much except that he hosts visitors from the foreign embassies. It's my job to make sure that they enjoy, shall we say, a memorable night in Our Most Serene City." He grins, then adds quickly, "but you must not utter a word to Master Giorgio! This little piece of business is strictly mine, understood?"

I nod. "Your secret's safe with me."

Alvise shrugs in defense. "If I want to buy a few tankards or wager on cards, I can hardly afford to do it on the pittance that Old Marchese pays us. Besides, if I bring the ladies some good foreign customers, sometimes I can earn some extra perks myself, if you get what I mean."

The door of the crooked house creaks opens again, and Signor da Ponte steps out with two fair-haired gentlemen who are nothing if not out of place. The first, a bloated man whose pasty white skin is streaked with fine blood vessels, grips the mooring post to keep from keeling over into the canal. His distended belly seems ready to burst, and his tightly cinched belt appears to restrain his stomach rather than to keep up his breeches. His legs emerge below like wooden stilts. I hold out my hand to him for support as he steps into the gondola and toddles toward the passenger cabin with uneasy steps. I smell alcohol on his breath—a potent, stringent stench.

The man heaves himself onto the seat and grins tightly at me. The second man, equally fair-skinned but scrawny, has an easier time with the journey from the house into the boat. He seats himself next to his portly companion. From his coat pocket, he produces a pewter flask, which he raises in a toast to Alvise and myself. The two men exchange a few flat-sounding, nasal words, but I do not begin to interpret their meaning.

Finally, Signor da Ponte emerges from the house, smartly dressed in a navy tailcoat and a cap with a stylish white plume. His chest held high, he steps effortlessly into the boat and winks at Alvise. "Onward, my dear boatman! These fine gentlemen have but a few precious hours to sample the best of our renowned Venetian pleasures!"

"Right away, *missier*." Alvise pulls away from the mooring and maneuvers down the canal.

As no more room remains in the passenger cabin, Signor da Ponte seats himself on the aft deck next to me. "You're nurturing young talent, I see!"

I take my cue from Alvise. "It's my pleasure, *missier*."

Signor da Ponte pats my shoulder convivially. "Son, these two fine gentlemen have brought me some excellent whiskey all the way from the green shores of the Kingdom of Hibernia. He raises his own flask, then throws his head back and swills the foul-smelling liquid into his cheeks. "Care to sample it?"

I shake my head.

"Well, then," Signor da Ponte continues, taking another swig, "from one earthly pleasure to the next!" Alvise laughs.

Alvise's swift strokes bring us to a narrow house in the Rialto quarter whose stones project out over the canal. The canal-side door is festooned with a metal door knocker in the shape of a lady's hand. A cat leaps onto a stone windowsill and crouches to watch me as I lash the boat to a metal ring while Alvise taps on the door with the knocker. He turns toward the men in the boat and winks.

One story above, I hear shutters open, and I gaze up to see an extraordinarily beautiful woman lean out over the windowsill. Her dark hair sweeps away from her face and spills over her shoulder in waves. A ring of flowers frames her brow, highlighting cheeks en-hanced with color and perfect white teeth. The neck of her golden silk dress plunges low to reveal the gathered hem of a gossamer-thin chemise pulled tautly over plump breasts, and strings of pearls and colored jewels swing from her neck. Every one of her fingers, even each thumb, is adorned with a ring, each holding an enormous gemstone of a different color.

"My dear Alvise, we've been waiting for you. Barbara will open the door for your guests. See you in two hours, my love?"

Alvise bows dramatically, as if on stage, and the woman disap-pears from view.

The canal-side door opens, and an older woman I judge to be a servant gestures for the men to enter. The woman is plain, and creases mark her brow, but even she wears a pale pink silk gown with a plunging neckline and ribbons tied tightly beneath her small breasts. Tiny freckles dot her protruding collarbones, and a single green gemstone hangs from a chain around her neck. I have heard that the jewels Venetian women wear may cost as much as a house; but rarely does even a housemaid leave home without adorning herself with some bauble.

Signor da Ponte offers his hand to bring the two foreign visi-tors to a standing position, and Alvise and I help them climb from the boat onto the stoop of the whorehouse. The two men look bewildered and excited. Signor da Ponte fishes a small leather bag tied with a silk cord from an inside pocket of his tailcoat and pro-duces several coins for Alvise. In a low voice, he says, "Better that I pay your commission now, in case those whores decide to con us out of everything we have!" He winks at me, then says loudly to Alvise, "Always a pleasure doing business with you." Signor da Ponte alights effortlessly from the gondola and bows low before the servant woman. The door closes behind the men. Alvise drops the coins into his pocket and pushes away from the stoop with his foot.

At the corner of the Grand Canal, two elaborately dressed women loiter on the quayside. One of the women waves and calls out, "*Bonasera*, Signor Alvise! Who's your friend?"

"I'm not telling you! I want you all to myself!" Alvise retorts.

She giggles. "Then why don't you stop by later tonight, so I can repay my debt to you?"

"*Senz'altro*," Alvise replies, tipping his hat.

Alvise saunters to the rear of the boat, puts his feet up on the deck, and smiles. "And that is what I call an honest day's work. It looks like I'm even going to get more than one benefit out of this trip."

He hands the oar to me.

"And now, *figliolo*," he says, mocking Giorgio's new way of referring to me as Alvise's junior, "back to our official work."

Chapter 14

"Where is that no-good *slandrón*?" Master Giorgio emerges from his hut, his cheeks flushed and his eyes black with rage.

I look up from the quayside, where I am mucking grime from the keel of a boat in dry dock.

Alvise is nowhere to be found.

"It figures," Giorgio grumbles, talking to no one in particular. "On the day I have an errand for one of my most important clients, he deserts me. I treat that boy like my own son, and this is how he repays me!" He bangs his fist down on the wooden table outside the hut. "*Salabràco!*"

I flinch, returning my gaze to my vigorous scrubbing as the tirade continues. The quay alongside the boathouse accumulates with dirt quickly because of the foot and boat traffic. I watch the small clouds of dust, dirt, and bird feces lift into the air, then light on the surface of the dark canal waters. After a moment, the specks scatter with the ripples.

"*Figliolo!*" Giorgio booms, using the new nickname he's chosen for me. I cringe. "It's your lucky day!" Giorgio saunters down the stairs towards me. "Load the Nerina with those crates and row as quickly as your little arms will take you to the painter Trevisan's studio. I would never ask the likes of you to do it if you weren't the only one here. You mess this up, boy, and you're out on your scrawny ass without a *soldo*, understood?"

"Of course, Master Giorgio. Right away." I untie my apron and exchange my scrub brush for one of the oars mounted on the outside wall of the boathouse. I load the crates, then board the Nerina, moored at the dock. I push off from the quay and row swiftly through the waters, elated to have a chore outside the grimy ferry station.

As I row, I wonder just where Alvise could be. I form a picture in my mind of my new friend, snoring and sodden with drink. In my mind's eye, the brazen gondolier is sprawled at the end of the bed of the courtesan who had called to him from across the canal the night before. I don't know Alvise well, but I know enough to imagine that my guess is accurate. Or perhaps Alvise has met the fate of my predecessor, punched in the jaw by some woman's husband, falling to his death from a bridge into the stinking canal. In that case, I think, my training is over and I am truly on my own. I stifle a grin.

I effortlessly maneuver the ninety-degree turn into the canal that borders the house of the artist Trevisan. I slow the boat as I approach Trevisan's boat slip, a cavernous space that allows direct access from the underbelly of the great house into the canal. Nearly every house of any size possesses a boat slip where its owner locks up his watercraft, safe from the vagaries of the canal.

A pair of ornate wrought-iron gates, closed with an impressive lock, marks the opening to Trevisan's boat slip. The space is constructed with a barrel-vaulted ceiling. The sound of the murky water licking the sides of the boat slip reverberates and amplifies into great lapping slurps. Light enters the cavernous space from the wrought-iron grille of the access door as well as from a line of fan-shaped windows under arches across the back of the boat slip. A broad landing creates a U-shaped edge around the water, allowing boats to be charged and unloaded. Even in the gloom, I discern that there is a magnificent gondola moored inside with what appears to be a new green velvet *felze* and elaborate, gilded carving on the prow. Balancing my weight in Giorgio's gondola, I move close enough to grip the gate. I press my face to it in order to get a better look at the boat and whistle under my breath. I wonder who made this fine craft.

Peering further back into the shadows, I observe what appears to be years' worth of neglected belongings: furniture covered in drapes, shelves stacked high with discarded tools, household goods, and more. Within this jumble, my eyes begin to make out the shape of another gondola stored in dry dock, turned upside down on a pair of trestles. The boat is partially covered with a large swath of canvas, but from the portion of the craft that is visible, I see that it is very old and neglected. The paint is dull and scratched, and part of the wood is split on one side, probably the result of some long-ago crash.

My heart leaps as I notice the carved maple leaf emblem on the prow of the boat. Even through the darkness, I would recognize it anywhere: the old gondola was made in my father's boatyard.

Chapter 15

I grasp the wrought-iron gates with my hands and push my head between the bars to get a closer look at the old gondola made in my family *squero*, now stored upside down in the shadows of the artist Trevisan's boat slip. I cannot help myself. The old, dusty boat is from the Vianello workshop, of that I am certain. I would recognize it anywhere. The boat is at least seventy years old, I judge, probably turned out by my grandfather. An image of my father and brother working in the *squero* crosses my mind. I feel a pang in my gut and turn away.

I propel the Nerina by walking my hands along the wrought-iron gate, then bump against a mooring post nearest the canal-side door to the artist's studio. Stay focused, I tell myself. I do not want to make a bad move; I cannot afford to lose my position at the *traghetto*. I moor the Nerina, ascend the stairs from the canal with the first crate, and rap loudly on the studio door. One of Trevisan's assistants opens the door for me, and I bring in the crates from the boat.

Each time I enter the artist's studio, my eyes are drawn instinctively to Trevisan's easel in front of the window. I crane my neck to catch a glimpse of the picture of the woman that so captivated me. It is as if the image of her face has seared itself into my mind, and it will not disappear. I see the back of the frame; but the picture is turned toward the wall, and I can see nothing of the canvas.

The artist enters the studio from another part of the house. "Boatman Fabris," he greets me. I manage a bow toward him.

I turn to leave, then hesitate. "Magnificence," I say haltingly. "May I ask you a question?"

"Of course," replies the artist, surprised.

"The boat you have in dry dock in your boat slip..." I begin. "The old one. Is it yours?"

"Yes. Well, actually I inherited it from my father. It's damaged and probably should be converted to firewood, I'm afraid." He chuckles. "Too bad, for it's a beauty, a work of real craftsmanship. I've never had time to restore it. I use my newer boat instead. Why do you ask?"

"Well, if I may, Magnificence, it would not be too difficult to restore it. You would need the proper materials of course." I seem to forget that I am merely making a delivery to the artist's studio. "But, properly returned to service, it could be not only a means of transportation but also a work of great beauty."

Trevisan cocks his head and looks at me curiously. "My son, are you one of Master Giorgio's boatmen or are you independent?"

"I'm neither, sir. I'm just a dock boy at the *traghetto*. I'm taking the place of one of Master Giorgio's boatmen today."

"I see," says the artist. "I thought you looked too young to be a boatman. But you obviously know how to handle a boat."

"Yes, very well."

"How long have you been with Master Giorgio?"

"Just a short time."

"Are you a member of the guild?" asks the artist.

"No," I answer haltingly. "Not yet."

"Hmm." The artist presses five cool coins into my palm. "Signor Fabris, thank you for your service."

I AWAKE TO FIND THE *traghetto* coated in white. I emerge from the humble building where I sleep, pull my vest snugly around me to ward off the chill, and shuffle into the snow that has fallen silently to the ground during the night. Normally the prows of the black boats buck against the gentle wake that laps against the quayside, but they now stand motionless and silent under a white coating. The water appears like a giant mirror, and I marvel at the stillness of the air, the unusual reflective quality of the light, and the remarkable glassy surface of the canal. It is early, and the *traghetto* remains silent. Giorgio's hut is dark and quiet. A few stray flakes fall from an eerie gray sky tinged with pink. I loosen the tarps covering the gondolas and fluff them like bed sheets, sending showers of snow into the canal.

Then, she catches my eye—the Blessed Mother. Sculpted into the side of a building flanking the *traghetto* stands a stone tabernacle depicting the Virgin holding the Christ Child. Of course, it has been there since my arrival, and I have already taken note of the shrine, but in the purity of the snow, it is if I am seeing the image for the first time. I fetch a stepladder and a pair of gloves from the boathouse and prop the ladder against the building. I climb up so that I stand eye to eye with the image. It was sculpted long ago, I surmise, for the stone is already eroded in the spots where it is exposed to the elements. Below the image stands a stone container for flowers. The flowers that were last put there now amount to no more than wilted twigs. I remove them and toss them to the white ground below, making a note to collect some fresh ones to place in the box.

Snow collects in the crevices that were etched out years ago by some now-forgotten carver. With a gloved hand, I remove the fluff to expose the cold relief of the stone. Below the Mother and Child stands the familiar image of gondolas, and I understand that the *traghetto* probably commissioned this tabernacle long ago to protect this particular brotherhood of gondoliers. For a moment I look into the eyes of the Christ Child. His face holds an expression that could be read as serenity or boredom, but which, I am not certain. The Virgin, though, is exquisite, with even features and an expression of eternal peace. She is painfully beautiful, and the image of a mother and her baby touches me somewhere deep inside.

Suddenly something icy hits the back of my neck, sending freezing droplets down my back.

Alvise has returned.

I turn just in time to catch sight of my mentor winding up to launch another snowball at me from the quayside with his tongue between his lips. I scramble down off the ladder and prepare to retaliate by gathering snow into my palms, but the sight of Giorgio, who appears from around the corner, makes me think twice. Without a word, I move to the boathouse and begin my work.

Behind me comes a sudden stream of cursing. Giorgio shouts at the top of his lungs, a fearsome outburst about Alvise's unexplained absence that travels all the way to the boathouse. I cringe and smile simultaneously, visualizing Alvise's reaction: the shrugging shoulders and the sheepish yet confident dismissal of authority that only Alvise can pull off and still manage to keep his position. I do not dare to emerge from the boathouse to see for myself, for fear that I would make an easy target for Giorgio just by virtue of showing my face.

With my master's tirade as background noise, I busy myself with a boat in need of repair. One of the wooden seats that spans the center of the gondola they call Vecchina has split down the middle. I don't know what happened but imagine that someone put a load on it that was too heavy. I wish for some of the wood glue that my father and I used to mix in our shop just to repair such damage, but I improvise by mixing a concoction of gum arabic and turpentine from discarded supplies I find on a cluttered table in the shadows of the boathouse. I secure the mended piece with another slat recovered from a heap of scrap wood and nail it with two forged nails I retrieve from a pile of hardware collected in a glass jar nearby.

Finally, Giorgio's words begin to fade, and the tirade ceases. I look up from my work to see Alvise entering the boathouse with a strange expression on his face, a smirk and a look in his eye that I am not sure whether to read as embarrassment or amusement. When he catches sight of me, Alvise lifts his eyebrows sarcastically. "So, Fabris, I understand you can row a boat on your own after all."

"What makes you say that?" I feign ignorance. I pick up a broom and begin to stab at the stones.

"Because Old Marchese has an important errand, and he's dispatching you instead of me." Alvise flashes his incongruously rotted yet chivalrous smile. Giorgio enters the boathouse, and both Alvise and I cast our eyes to the floor.

"Wash up at the fountain, *figliolo*," Giorgio says. I shake out my broom over the canal waters, then prop it against the wall.

"Your man Trevisan's got another errand, and he asked specifically for you." He sizes me up once again, and I feel the skin on the back of my neck tingle. "Seems you made quite an impression on that painter."

Chapter 16

I recognize Signora Baldi's costume-rental shop from Master Giorgio's description. As I maneuver the Nerina into the narrow canal, I spy racks of colorful fabrics fluttering in the breeze along a long stretch of the quayside. The frocks are organized by color from light to dark, a rainbow palette of silks, satins, and velvets of every shade: indigo, saffron, crimson, emerald, and rose.

Before leaving the *traghetto*, Master Giorgio informed me that Signora Baldi operates the best costume-rental shop in the city, providing an ever-changing supply of fashionable costumes, party frocks, and masks to some of the finest families in Our Most Serene Republic. She single-handedly supplies costumes for the Doge's ball at carnival time.

Signora Baldi stands alongside stacks of wicker crates staged near a stone stairway that disappears under the level of the canal waters. She is a tall, elegant woman with an aristocratic countenance. Signora Baldi wears her hair in a fashionable coif with curls framing her face, the rest pulled into a tightly braided knot, studded with pearls, at the back of her head.

Signora Baldi seems to recognize the *traghetto* gondola as I approach the quayside. "Are you here for Master Trevisan's costumes?"

"Yes, Signora."

"Patrizia!" she calls. "Please show Master Trevisan's boatman where the crates are for the Carnival party." A girl around my age, a younger version of her mother, emerges from the shop. She catches my eye and smiles. Her mother looks on warily. I load two crates onto the gondola.

"Please tell the artist that I personally hand-selected these choices from my best stock," Signora Baldi says. "The ones in the top crate are for the artist—wide enough around the middle to accommodate his girth, yet tailored to suit his tall frame. I know he prefers the hats with the wider brims, not the newer, more tight-fitting ones. I've also included a new royal-blue waistcoat with the cords and buttons. The bottom crate has some choices for Master Trevisan's young journeyman."

Leaving the costume-rental shop behind, I row out into the Grand Canal, then into a narrow waterway that leads to Trevisan's studio. As I make the sharp turn into the canal alongside the art-ist's house, out of the corner of my eye, I catch sight of another gondola careening toward me. Alarmed at its speed, I instinctively grip the sides of the gondola and prepare for a crash. Surprisingly, the brawny gondolier masterfully oars his craft from a steady clip to an instantaneous halt, and I breathe a sigh of relief. Its boatman greets me curtly with a nod, then ties the gondola to the mooring before the artist's house. He jogs up the stairs to Trevisan's studio door and rings the brass bell. The boat is fantastic, I note, covered in carving, paint, and gilding from prow to aft deck. It's the kind of gondola I would expect two men to row, but I only see the one boatman at Trevisan's door.

The artist's studio door opens, and a woman with a gentle ex-pression appears. She wears a simple, elegant silk gown the color of sparkling white wine, trimmed with delicate embroidery around the neckline. A black cloak is draped across her shoulders. The gon-dolier reaches out his hand to her to help her climb into the boat, and she remains standing in the gondola, her hands clasped before her, as if waiting for something to happen.

Then, a second, younger woman emerges from Trevisan's studio. I hear the clomping sound of what I know to be platform clogs—

their heels as high as a pig's back—that are fashionable among patrician women. The woman is covered from head to toe in a black cloak with a hood trimmed in weasel fur. Delicate hands emerge from the fur-trimmed sleeves, and I spot at least five gold bands with large colored gems. In her arms she cradles a small brown dog, only his trembling head emerging from her voluminous sleeves.

The gondolier extends his hand to help this grand lady into the gondola. The woman waiting there—I judge her now to be the lady's maid—extends her hand to help her mistress toward her seat. As the woman climbs into the boat, she pushes her fur-trimmed hood back from her head, then turns her face toward me, as if startled by my presence in the gondola next to her. For a moment that passes ever so slowly, the woman fixes a pair of clear green eyes on me. A thin veil covers her hair, but a few brown curls emerge, twisting around her face and entwining the small drops of pearls at her earlobes. Her cheeks are flushed pink, her lips parted. She carries a slightly surprised expression on her face.

I watch as the two women seat themselves on the bench under the *felze*, whose curtains are tied to the side to allow air into the compartment. The gondolier leans his weight into the oarlock to power the craft away from Trevisan's house. I watch as the two women grow smaller and out of focus as they glide away from me. Finally, their gondola turns the corner into the adjacent canal, and they disappear from view.

A collage of images sears through my mind, and my thoughts race to make sense of images so foreign and yet strangely familiar: the green eyes, the gaze, the parted lips. Then, I feel as if someone has punched me in the stomach. A sudden ache spreads just below my ribs.

It's the girl in the painting.

Chapter 17

His Girls. They are his most prized—and most private—pictures.

The Councillor follows the narrow corridor that leads from his study into the small yet ornate chamber that holds these little treasures. He enters the dark room and pulls back the curtain. Sunlight illuminates the jewel box of a space, with its gilded-coffered ceiling and paintings that cover nearly every inch of its scarlet, fabric-colored walls.

Long ago the Councillor commissioned a plush chair upholstered in blue velvet just for this gallery, and now he positions himself in it so that he may enjoy an unobstructed view of His Girls. Each one looks out at him in return from their gilded frames—a private view for one pair of eyes only. From this position, he relishes the memory of each one.

Signorina Faustini was his first, and he begins by looking at her portrait. The artist did well to portray her startling gaze, her large brown eyes and thick eyebrows. The Councillor runs his eyes along the silhouette of her waist. Then there was Signorina Contato, whose hips were luscious though it turned out that she talked too much. There was another one whose name escapes him; he remembers only that her father insisted that the artist portray his daughter as the mythical Flora, with one pale nipple exposed and a flower in her hand. The Councillor chortled at this thinly veiled attempt to imagine the girl, who turned out to be surprisingly ardent, as a coy mythological goddess.

Hmm, groans the Councillor smugly to himself. He plucked each girl like an apple at the peak of ripeness, devouring her sweetness, then discarding her core. Thrilling every time.

In exchange for each virginal deflowering, the Councillor pays a substantial sum to the girl's father. Only rarely does the father refuse. Inevitably, a reasonable man sees the logic in getting compensated, in lieu of outlaying a sizeable dowry, for his daughter. After the fact, she is no longer marriageable anyway. Then her father can whisk her away to a convent along with a respectable endowment and plenty to spare for his own pocket. After all, the girl has the rest of her cloistered life to atone for her own sins, not to mention secure a place for her family in the life hereafter. It makes sense for the father, the family, and of course, the Councillor, who never tires of the chase.

In addition to paying off the father, there is of course a pretty penny to pay for the portrait of each girl. Over the years the Councillor has commissioned some of the city's best painters to craft each one of these little souvenirs.

This very moment, he thinks, his latest prospect may be sitting, shivering in the damp studio of Master Trevisan, whose contract is now signed. He thinks about the first time he noticed her at a party, his eyes drinking in the girl's flushed cheeks, the nape of her neck. He felt the usual twinge of attraction overtake him, then the obsession grew.

Even though this negotiation was far from normal, which troubles the Councillor somewhat, he is unable to turn back now. No, he must have this dark-haired beauty. At the same time that he anticipates the encounter, he thinks about how he will rearrange His Girls to make a space for a new picture.

Chapter 18

My work as Alvise's assistant in the *traghetto* has returned to normal, but in truth, things can never be the same, for I cannot rid myself of the image of the girl. I find myself distracted, engrossed in my work yet far away, turning over images in my mind of her face, her eyes, her hair, her teeth.

"This one is yours, *cucco*!" Giorgio's voice booms across the ferry station. A man carrying a satchel over his shoulder is waiting at the dock. "Take *figliolo* with you." The two of us board the boat.

"Good day, *missier*!" Alvise flashes a smile and tips his hat with an exaggerated gesture toward the passenger waiting on the dock. "Where may we escort you today?" The man—I take him to be a shop owner because of his costume and businesslike demeanor—steps confidently aboard and ducks into the seat under cover of the *felze*. "Drop me off at the new ferry station in San Polo," the man rattles off in a brusque voice.

"Of course. Right away, *missier*," replies Alvise. He places the oar into the lower notch of the oarlock and tilts the oar to the right. The boat responds immediately and pushes away from the quay. Once the craft is set into motion, Alvise moves the oar to the upper lock and plies his strength into it. The gondola gathers speed. The gondolier's body sways rhythmically as he rows, a natural movement that makes him seem as if he were part of his craft. Soon fanciful façades appear as nothing more than a blur of arches, pink and mauve stripes with wavering mirror images in the canal. Alvise begins to hum a popular tune under his breath, a satisfied look on his face. The humming grows louder, and then breaks into whistling. Alvise rows to the rhythm as he hums and whistles. The boat skims along silently with a gentle rock. For the first time since I left home, I savor the familiar sensation of riding in a gondola, with wind in my hair and the sun on my face. A wave of contentment washes over me. We pass under several bridges, gliding at such a clip that I have the feeling that the bridges are moving toward us rather than the other way around.

Alvise turns the boat into the Grand Canal. The great basin teems with boat traffic. I recognize the flat-bottomed water barges we call *burchi*, surprisingly strong, from which owners sell fresh water by the bucketful. During times of drought, when people's wells and cisterns go dry, these water vendors make a fortune transporting fresh, clean water from the Brenta and floating around Venetian canals shouting *"acqua fresca!"* then doling out eight buckets for a mere *soldo*. A hunting boat slides stealthily out toward the lagoon, carrying two patrician men with crossbows. Cargo barges carry firewood, produce, and other supplies. I recognize two public ferries, today unusually empty. Alvise waves to a friend rowing another gondola some twenty yards away and greets other acquaintances with a lift of his chin or a hand gesture I cannot interpret. His body sways rhythmically as he rows, a natural movement that makes him seem as if he is part of his craft. Alvise Pellegrini, rowing confidently across the Grand Canal, is in his element among these boatmen.

Somewhere along that stretch of Grand Canal, I notice that Alvise begins to slow his strokes. He places the oar in front of the oarlock and even swirls the oar in a seeming backward motion. The craft decelerates, and I am confused. Alvise's countenance remains the same. A grin on his face, he continues to hum his contented tune without skipping a beat. Catching my eye, he winks.

Alvise maneuvers the craft around a bend in the Grand Canal and into one of the *ghebi*, the network of small canals that feed into the lagoon. I recognize this particular *ghebo* as a cut-through from the Grand Canal to the northern basin. Alvise expertly slides the craft into the cramped space, and slips by another gondola moving in the opposite direction. I marvel that the two boats glide by one another so closely without touching, a mere inch or two apart. As the two boats pass, Alvise and the other gondolier extend their arms and wordlessly salute one other with a quick clasp of their hands, a fierce yet fleeting arm-wrestle.

We approach San Polo. Alvise slows the gondola and drifts toward the quay. The side of the boat skims the algae-covered stone wall near a short flight of stairs leading up to the street. The shopkeeper emerges from the *felze* and gathers his belongings.

"Here we are, *missier*! What a delightful ride, if I do say so myself! That'll be four *soldi, per favore*."

The man's bottom lip drops slightly, and he looks at Alvise with a confused expression. "*Quattro?*" the man clarifies. "But you only ferried me from Castello. That should cost no more than two."

"How right you are, sir," Alvise replies diplomatically. "But don't forget, sir, that today is the Feast of San Rocco, so the rates are higher, naturally. And, sir, I don't know if you remarked—if you're not a boatman you may not have noticed—but on the smaller canals in this section of town, the current runs east to west when the tide goes out. I was rowing against the tide, sir, and that always takes longer," Alvise counters. He continues to flash his crooked smile.

The man purses his lips, and his expression hardens. He drops his satchel on the floor of the gondola with an exasperated gesture, then raises his finger to Alvise's face. "You!" he begins. "You're trying to extort me! I'm not some stupid foreigner, you know! I'm a Venetian citizen, and I know how much it costs to go from your blasted ferry station to San Polo! It should cost no more than a *bagattin.* I'm giving you two and no more!" He continues to stare down Alvise.

"I'm sorry, sir, but I can accept no less than four. I must make my living, you know, with the cost of grain these days." Alvise crosses his arms and taps his fingers on his muscular forearm.

"You're nothing but a no-good thief! You boatmen are all the same! I ought to report you to the Great Council!" The man reaches into the pocket of his breeches, pulls out a coin, and flings it on the floor, then scrambles out of the gondola. Standing on the stairs, he turns to address Alvise again. "San Rocco, my ass!" He spits a large wad of saliva, which hits the inside rim of the gondola. I watch the wad of spit streak slowly down to the floor of the boat.

Alvise immediately breaks out of his diplomatic guise and raises his left hand to make an obscene gesture. "Well you can *kiss* San Rocco's ass as far as I'm concerned!" Alvise powers the gondola away from the quay, a self-righteous look on his face. He turns the craft into a narrow canal, then glances toward me and nearly collapses from laughter.

But I am hardly paying attention. My thoughts still lie in Master Trevisan's studio.

AT DUSK, THE ARTIST APPEARS at Master Giorgio's ferry station.

I am polishing Nerina's keel when I catch sight of Trevisan's hefty frame moving briskly toward the station hut from the shadows of the alley.

Startled, Giorgio looks up from his solo card game. "Master Trevisan!" he gasps, scrambling to his feet. "What a surprise... I usually expect to see one of your shop assistants! To what do I owe this honor?"

Trevisan motions with his hand for Giorgio to be seated, and the artist pulls up a chair to the other side of the rickety table outside the hut. "I have an acquaintance from the *scuola*—a certain Signor Brunelli of Dorsoduro. You know the type. Connected. Upstanding. Married. Very married—to a woman who is even more connected than he is. He needs a little diversion of the type that only you can provide." He looks at Giorgio and raises his eyebrows. "I was thinking of those twins you sent to Signor Fonta the last time? It requires the utmost discretion." Trevisan examines his own fingernails. "My acquaintance is prepared to pay you handsomely, of course."

"Are you... involved with this Brunelli?"

"Heavens no," replies the artist, waving his hand. "Strictly business."

Giorgio nods. "Consider it done, sir. As always, we'll take care of it. Anything else?"

"Yes, one more thing. Have your dock boy Fabris pack up his belongings and report to my studio first thing tomorrow morning." From the inside of his cloak, the artist produces a small velvet bag pulled tightly with a cord. He plunks it down on the table in front of Master Giorgio. It rings with the heft of a large mound of coins. Giorgio's eyes widen.

"If it please you, of course, Master Giorgio," begins the artist, using his most polite graces, then meeting the grubby station master eye to eye, "release your dock boy from your charge. I have a pressing need for a new boatman. Luca Fabris now works for me."

Chapter 19

"You're one lucky *fionàso*, did you know that?" Alvise guffaws at me from his seated position on the rear of the boat.

I grin and row the little *puparin*—a skiff that Master Giorgio affectionately calls Piccolino—into the canal. Reading my expression, Alvise continues, "Santo Stefano! Who has heard of a boy your age—not even part of a guild, for God's sake—hired as a private boatman?"

Before leaving the ferry station, I filled the flower box of the tabernacle with fresh flowers I purchased at a street market and bid a silent farewell to the stone faces of the Madonna and Child. From Giorgio, all I got was a gruff salute, but I expected little more.

We turn into the canal where Trevisan's house stands. The early morning light penetrates the shadows of Master Trevisan's cavernous boat slip. Through the streaks of sun, I can make out the artist's two gondolas—one fine, one dilapidated—hulking beasts penned behind the great wrought iron gates. As Alvise and I glide slowly by the boat slip in Giorgio's old skiff, Alvise regards the fine boat, shakes his head and whistles in quiet amazement. "What did I tell you? Lucky, lucky *fionàso*, you are."

"Thanks for the ride, *cucco*," I joke, handing him the oar. "And for everything else, too."

Alvise claps me on the shoulder. "Maybe you can talk your new boss into paying off Giorgio for me, too!" We laugh, then I heave myself out of the boat and walk up the stairs to knock on the artist's studio door. "Just remember to watch your back!" Alvise adds.

"You too!"

Alvise salutes me with two fingers, then shoves off with the oar, whistling to himself as he rows out of sight.

Trevisan greets me at the door of his studio with a strong, amicable grip of his hand and leads me inside. The artist's breeches alternate red and blue satin stripes, and his gold sleeves billow. His portly stomach threatens to burst the buttons off his blue waistcoat. He wears a two-toned cape and an elaborate hat with feathers on one side. His clogs clomp on the shiny tiled floor. On one side of the studio, a woman crouches on her hands and knees, wringing out a rag over a bucket of water.

"I have an important meeting with a patron this morning. You will take me there in my boat, and wait for me."

"Yes, of course, Magnificence."

"Luca, this is Signora Amalia, my housemaid. She can help you get settled and provide you with anything you may need." Signora Amalia is about the same age as my mother was, I judge. She is thin, with a lined face, and her ashen hair sweeps back from her face in a tight bun with waves around her brow. She greets me with a warm smile but does not rise from the floor, where she is using a wet rag and a stiff-bristled brush to scrub a paint stain from the wooden planks.

The artist opens a small door on one side of the workshop and gestures for me to follow. The door leads to a spacious kitchen, where dry heat emanates from an enormous hearth. Dozens of ceramic plates hang above a window along another wall, overlooking the narrow canal below. A wooden table occupies the center of the room, and on it lie three half-chopped onions and a carrot. On the right, a narrow, curved staircase leads upstairs. Through a slightly open set of double doors, I catch sight of a dining room with a round table that has an elaborate centerpiece and a chandelier above it, both made of blown glass from Murano. Even in the kitchen, there are oil paintings, at least two dozen hung floor to ceiling, just as in the artist's studio.

On the far side of the kitchen, Trevisan leads the way to an exterior door and opens it to reveal a narrow stone staircase. I catch a whiff of the cool, dank canal and understand that this door is the inside entrance to the boat slip. We descend into the shadows of the damp stairwell.

The artist unties one end of the canvas cover that protects his fine gondola moored in the slip, and I untie the other side. Trevisan lifts the cover with a dramatic gesture. This gondola, I note, was made in one of our rival boatyards, but it is a beauty all the same. The oarlock, the prow iron, and even the upholstery seem brand new, as if they have never seen the light of day. The rest of the boat is dusty and cluttered, but with minimal effort it could be a showpiece. What I admire most about the craft is that Trevisan has outfitted it so that it conforms to the Republic's laws about gondola ornamentation, yet at the same time it is more elegant than most fine boats on the city's canals.

Trevisan produces a key from his pocket and unlocks the tremendous padlock of the wrought-iron gate. It creaks as it opens outward. "You'll find an oar on the wall there," instructs the artist, climbing into his boat. In fact, there are a half-dozen oars hanging from a rack on the wall, some older than others. Instinctively, my eyes are drawn to one with a sharp, blade-like protrusion running from the handle to the paddle, the kind that my old friend the oarmaker always considered the most effective tool for rowing a standard gondola. I pull the oar from the wall and step into the back of the boat, using the oar to balance myself as I get into position to row.

"We're going to the Scuola Grande di San Teodoro, son. You'll want to approach it from the Grand Canal side."

Tentatively, I push off with the oar and emerge from Trevisan's boat slip into the sunlight. My heart flutters, and my chest swells with nervousness and pride. How did I manage to become a private boatman in a single day? It seems unfathomable, a pure stroke of luck. I row with purposeful strokes, not wanting to do a single thing to disappoint Master Trevisan. I hope that the artist cannot see how nervous I am. I try my best to look competent with the oar, but in truth I know that it will take some practice before rowing this particular grand craft becomes second nature. They say that rowing a gondola is like riding a horse; you may know how to do it, but each one is an individual. It takes time to develop confidence with each beast.

During the journey to the Scuola Grande, the artist does not utter a word. He remains inside the passenger compartment with the curtains tied open, either lost in thought or sketching with black coal on a piece of parchment. He sits confidently with one leg crossed over the other, as a gentle breeze tousles his silver curls. Even though his fingernails are perfectly filed and buffed, the artist's hands belie his true profession, marred with paint stains that must be impossible to remove. Otherwise, the man is impeccable and could be mistaken easily for a patrician.

When we arrive at our destination, I guide the gondola among the jungle of mooring posts that stand at odd angles at the entrance to the *scuola*. Trevisan instructs me to moor the gondola with a rope to an enormous metal ring driven into the stone quayside and to wait for him.

Trevisan is gone for most of the morning. During the long hours, I explore his boat in detail. In the light of day, I recognize that the gondola, though fine, is neglected. Dust has collected on the decks, probably as a result of the boat being grounded for so long after Trevisan's last boatman left. I make mental notes. The paint needs to be refreshed. Part of the hull should be waterproofed to prevent leaks. In the storage area under the aft deck, I discover a pile of dirty rags and tools thrown haphazardly into the space. I empty the storage compartments in the fore and aft decks and reorganize everything into neat piles. Then I set about shining the prow with a rag.

Throughout the morning, a steady flow of gondolas stops at the mooring to discharge passengers. Some are private gondolas with two rowers, which carry wealthy men and women. Others are plain black gondolas for hire like the ones from the ferry station. Each time a gondola stops, its gondolier greets me with an amicable "*come xea*" or one of many salutatory hand gestures that I have learned to interpret, thanks to my time on the canals alongside my mentor Alvise. It is as if I have joined a private alliance, an inner circle. I feel a double impostor now, for I do not consider myself a real boatman. With my hat pulled low over my brow, I return the greeting in a manner that becomes only slightly more confident as the hours pass.

As it nears time for the midday meal, Trevisan reappears. Another well-dressed gentleman walks alongside the artist, both engrossed in their conversation. The two men board the boat, and Trevisan instructs me to transport them back to his studio. Trevisan is so preoccupied with his conversation during our journey that the artist does not notice my efforts to beautify his boat. "Luca, you may wish to reorganize my boat slip as you see fit. After some time I'm sure to find it as organized and tidy as you made Master Giorgio's boathouse," says Trevisan as he and his guest exit the boat. I carefully steer the gondola into the artist's boat slip.

The silence of the cavernous space is broken only by the lapping of water against the stone walls. In the shadows, like a lurking behemoth, stands the now broken-down boat my grandfather made. I force myself to avert my eyes from it, wanting to take in the rest of the space first. The walls of the boat slip are covered in lichen, accounting for the dingy appearance and dank smell that fills it. Drips of water echo off the walls. Along with an impressive selection of oars, I note the three types of brooms hanging from the wall, and I put cleaning the boat slip on the top of my list.

In the far reaches of the covered area, I discover a lightweight *felze* of the kind used in the summer to protect passengers from the sun. Its wooden frame sits high to allow breezes in, and its sides are made of a lightweight silk fabric in light green. The silk is beginning to rot. I find another old one, covered in midnight velvet, that is used in winter, low and broad to keep off the rain but now ragged and rotted. I doubt that the fabrics can be salvaged, but I might be able to reuse the frames. I take stock of discarded supplies jumbled on shelves along one wall. Gels and varnishes, coated by years of dust, lie still in glass jars. I recognize turpentine and several types of oil, but I will need to open the jars and smell to be able to identify some of the others.

The dry dock extends far into the depths under the house, lit by lanterns along the wall. A narrow stream of light from a tall shaft illuminates the back of the dry dock. I follow the light and soon emerge into a small courtyard littered with belongings—discarded wrought-iron doors, a pile of scrap wood, sculpted stone capitals dating back what must be hundreds of years. In spite of the clutter, the space is usable, and I judge that I will be able to work here.

Finally, I return into the boat slip and approach the old gondola stored upside down on trestles. I take a deep breath to summon the nerve to push back the old canvas cover that conceals the boat. I close my eyes and run my hands along its hull, recognizing only by touch its familiar shape and curves, as if it were a long-lost lover. My fingertips divine its familiar surfaces, textures, its musty scent, its imperfections, its singular beauty. The sensation brings images, clear as day, flashing to the front of my mind. I see my grandfather varnishing a boat while I, just a small boy, run circles around the great black craft. My mind forms an image of my grandfather's lined and suntanned face, his subtle grin, his genteel voice, his old-fashioned Venetian words now rarely heard. He is telling me how the lumber must be stacked carefully in the *téza* and left to season for at least a year.

The pungent scent of varnish reminds me of our family *squero* in the spring, when people would bring their boats to us to be cleaned and revarnished. My mind races with images of our clients rowing their boats—a gondola, a *sandolo*, a *puparin*, a fishing boat they call a *scípion*—to the Vianello boatyard to have their keels cleaned. As if watching myself in a dream, I see my father and brother pulling the crafts out of the water up the ramp, then propping the boats on their sides. From this awkward position, we spent days scraping off canal grime, then coating the keels with *sottomarino*, a special kind of varnish that makes the boat watertight. I see the camaraderie among the men who bring their boats to be cleaned. I smile as I see my grandfather lightly tap these visitors on the shoulder with the back of his hand as he speaks to them, as if he is incapable of talking without touching.

I inhale the boat's scent, a musty mix of aged varnish, decay, and dank moss that transports me back to the reality of Trevisan's boat slip. Carefully, I tip the boat on its side so that I can view the inside of its hull. I recognize the planks of oak, walnut, and cherry that make the hull strong yet lightweight. The wood is in dire need of restoration, but I marvel that in spite of its damage, this old boat has stood the test of time.

At dusk, Trevisan appears at the door of the boat slip to find me mucking the lichen off the stones. He stands silently for a moment, watching me. He descends the stairs and clears his throat. "Luca, Signora Amalia has prepared some bean and barley stew. You may join her to dine in the kitchen. Afterward, she will explain to you how to find Signora Monti's boardinghouse, which is not far. I've already reserved a room for you there. I apologize for not being able to accommodate you here. I've had to pair up my four apprentices in my extra rooms in order to lodge them in my house. Unfortunately I have no space left. For the boardinghouse, I deducted the rent out of your first week's salary. Starting next week, you may pay the proprietor, Signora Monti, directly from the salary I pay you on Saturdays. Agreed? That is, unless you have some other accommodation for yourself."

"No," I respond quickly. "That is fine. Thank you, Master Trevisan, for your kindness." Glancing beyond the artist's shoulder, I see a narrow slice of the kitchen and the hem of Signora Amelia's skirt, then the aroma of the stew curls through the air. I replace the broom then climb the stairs to the kitchen, where Signora Amalia is ladling steaming broth into a bowl.

Trevisan continues, "I've also arranged for Signora Baldi to provide you with a selection of clothing from her stock, something suitable to a boatman in my charge. These will get you by for the short term. I do have a certain image to uphold, you know."

Chapter 20

The artist's house runs more like a manufactory than a residence.

On my third day with Trevisan, the artist finds the time to bring me into his studio and introduce his new boatman to his assistants. When I visited the artist's studio the first time, I was so overwhelmed by its rich appointments and by the painting of the mysterious girl that I lacked the time to appreciate the organization and operation of the workshop itself. Several stations manned by assistants occupy the corners of the enormous room. Trevisan's easel stands in an open space, placed so that the artist may sit with his back to the window to allow in light. Instinctively, my eyes travel to the painting on the master's easel, but just as before, it is covered with a drape and turned toward the wall. Under another window stands a rustic worktable and a shelf filled with glass jars and different-colored powders; it brings to mind an apothecary shop. In a shadowy corner of the room, a large board is placed on trestles. On the far wall, paintings in various stages of completion are propped against the wall, some turned outward, some turned toward the wall so I can see the wooden frames across which the canvas is stretched. A second easel is set up near the great hearth, where one of Trevisan's assistants applies paint from a smudged palette in delicate stabs.

I count three assistants in the room and wonder how many more the artist employs. Quickly I surmise that Trevisan's highest-ranking journeyman is a young man named Valentin, who looks near my own age. Valentin stands before a large easel, painting a tree in a landscape that forms the background of an incredible picture of a saint in agony as he is crucified upside down. The boy seems to work in slow motion, in intense concentration. I catch a whiff of the boy's perfume, a heady combination of flowers and musk strong enough to be detected even above the smell of paints. His wheat-colored hair is cropped neatly at his chin, and his jaw is clean-shaven and soft. Suddenly aware that he is being watched, Valentin looks my way with a faint smile. The boy's eyelids are heavy, almost as if he were sleepy. His shirt is unbuttoned to reveal a smooth chest, so smooth that it seems glossy. I can make out the boy's collarbones and the taut muscles of his breast. A silver chain hangs around the boy's neck, and on each hand, he wears gold rings with small gems on the thumb and index finger.

In addition to Valentin, a younger apprentice named Cesare, a boy about fifteen, stands quietly at a worktable wedged along the wall under one of the studio windows. With a mortar and pestle, he grinds an emerald-colored paint pigment, then wipes the extra powder from the side of several glass jars on an adjacent shelf. The boy appears older than his fifteen years, as he walks with a slight limp like an old man. Hobbling to the makeshift table constructed of a board on trestles, he wraps a large framed canvas in blue paper.

The youngest member of the studio is a slight boy with a cow-lick and widely set blue eyes, no older than ten. He is introduced to me as Biondino, little blonde boy, but I don't learn his given name. The boy's main job is to clean up after everyone else. He wears an apron and sweeps the studio floor as the other men work, occasion-ally stopping to wipe his nose on his sleeve or look out the window until one of the older assistants tousles his hair and reminds him to return to his chores. Biondino is also dispatched to answer the studio door when the bell rings at the canal-side that borders Trevisan's house. All day long, it seems that someone—usually a neatly dressed messenger or boatman—is clanging the little bronze bells suspended above the canal-side and land-side doors. The ringing is incessant, and Signora Amalia or, if she is occupied on the upper floors, Biondino, is constantly opening the doors, accepting invitations and messages scrawled in elaborate script addressed to the artist, delivered by private messengers.

In spite of the presence of Trevisan's many assistants, it is clear that Signora Amalia is the one who keeps things running in the house. She cleans and cooks all day long, scrubbing floors, stirring pots, fluffing bedding, chopping parsley with a *mezzaluna* blade, dusting windowsills, heating milk. Beneath this tough exterior, though, I sense a warm heart. I like her immediately, and finally, it occurs to me why. She reminds me of my own mother.

"THE PROBLEM WITH BOATMEN is that they become more interested in profiting from their side jobs than being paid for their primary one." Signora Amalia pauses from chopping onions at the massive table in Trevisan's kitchen and points her knife in my direction. "I have served Master Trevisan for nearly thirty years. During that time I have lost count of how many boatmen have come and gone; finding a reliable one has not been easy." She pushes the fruit bowl across the table to me, then resumes chopping the onions with great force. I select a ripe apple.

"Master Trevisan had one boatman who became so involved with a gambling scheme that he showed up less and less for the artist," she continues. "Finally he disappeared without a trace. Another one became so successful running a prostitution ring that involved some of our neighborhood wives that he no longer needed to work as a private boatman. Ha!" She shakes her head. "Later

Trevisan got word that the man ended up in prison." I taste the crisp sweetness of the apple. "And if they're not criminals they're just plain lazy," she complains.

"In that case I'd better get to work," I smile, tipping my hat to her as I exit the kitchen for the boathouse.

"Don't forget your vest, *caro*," Signora Amalia cries from the kitchen. Her voice echoes down the stairs and into the depths of the boat slip. "The clouds are collecting above the Giudecca, and that means we'll have rain today for certain."

I thank her as I push the artist's gondola out of the gates and moor it to Trevisan's canal-side dock so I have enough light to work. If there is to be rain later, I'd better make as much progress as I can in polishing the wood on the foredeck and the metal prow. By candlelight the night before, I mixed up an old familiar concoction that I feel sure will remove the grime and oxidation on the metal fittings. I get to work and soon find myself engrossed.

Every time a gondola makes a turn into the canal outside Trevisan's studio, my heart leaps, then falls when I realize that I do not recognize the gondola. In my heart, I know I am waiting for the girl to reappear.

Chapter 21

My room in the boardinghouse is little more than a monk's cell, four sparse stucco walls with a barred window framing a swath of coral clouds. The bed frame is fashioned of raw pine planks, on top of which sits a straw-filled mattress pressed hard from years of use. A table and chair stand against the far wall. My sole possessions in life—a straight razor and a comb I purchased after working for a few weeks in the *traghetto*—lie on the table. One leg stands shorter than the others, and the table wobbles when I place my implements on it.

The only thing my housemates have in common is poverty. Every last one of them is a poor wretch with no home and no hope. One man, Stefano, tells me that he is a tailor but has few clients, perhaps as a result of the sad expression seemingly frozen on his face. He is a droopy-eyed dog of a man, permanently cast into melancholy. Another fellow introduces himself as Bardo, and I am told he spends his days begging in the streets of Dorsoduro. Others have physical woes on top of their economic ones. Signor Paduca, a ham seller, suffers from severe stomach ulcers that keep him from regular work, and I have witnessed him vomit into the canal on two occasions. Another man, whose dialect I cannot place, suffers from an appalling itch, his skin raw and scaly. A particularly poor soul, Michele, is afflicted with a condition so painful that he defecates loudly on his chamber pot, alternately cursing and calling out the names of a litany of saints.

From the front door of the boardinghouse, we enter a shadowy common room with a few pieces of rickety furniture clustered around the hearth. Signora Monti, a sour-faced woman in a shapeless dress, presides over this space. From her post behind a bar in the back of the room she doles out watered-down beer and stale bread to a steady crowd of unfortunate souls who spend part of their day in this room. Whether I want to hear it or not, my new housemates regale me with their stories as I take my breakfast. Two of the men seem permanent fixtures at Signora Monti's bar, as immovable as the table in the center of the room. They play dice games and solve all the affairs of the Venetian state. I am thankful that my room stands on the third floor, which affords some fresh air and light from the small window.

As I lay on my mattress at night, I am aware of something crawling beneath me. Insects in the mattress are unavoidable of course, and apart from tolerating this minor inconvenience, I resolve to distance myself as much as possible from the boardinghouse. I return there late at night after closing up Trevisan's boat slip. By dawn, I am already walking through the fog to the artist's house as my housemates sleep, my breath visible in the damp air. I stop taking my breakfast in the common room, preferring to wait for the hearty lunch that Signora Amalia will have prepared for me at midday in Trevisan's kitchen. I will not let the fate of the men in the boardinghouse become my own. I throw myself into my new role, ferrying the artist to his many appointments, taking responsibility for caring for the boat slip and the gondola. I feel it is my duty, my calling.

My destiny.

"YOU WORKED UP QUITE an appetite cleaning that boat," says Signora Amalia. She stands at the chopping table in the center of the kitchen, hacking lamb feet into chunks with an impressive-looking blade. Blood streaks the front of her apron.

At a small wooden table in the corner of the kitchen, I devour a bowl of fish soup. I shovel mouthfuls of broth, cabbage, and fish meat into my mouth. My mind is elsewhere. In fact, the only place my mind has been for days is on the mysterious beauty from the painting, the one whom I saw emerge in person from my own master's house. She is real, flesh and blood, not just a figment of Master Trevisan's imagination. I have trouble focusing on the details of my daily life—working, eating, sleeping. My mind struggles to remember every detail of her face: her eyes, her nose, the curve of her lips.

"Thank you for the soup," I say, finally snapping out of my dream-state to pick a thin sliver of fish bone from the stew and place it on the table. "Fantastic, as usual." I smile gratefully at Trevisan's maid. Earlier, a client's boatman arrived to fetch Trevisan for a private party, so I am free for the evening. I enjoy a few moments to savor the meal and the warm fire in the hearth.

Signora Amalia wipes her hands on her apron, then removes it and hangs it on the back of a side door. "I'm off to my chores in the bed chambers. Rinse out your bowl and leave it on the table for me, *caro*." She gestures to the large basin where she pours the buckets of water she collects each morning from the communal well in the nearby square. She exits the kitchen through a narrow door on the opposite side of the room.

I run my hand over the knots and cracks of the tabletop. Suddenly, a noise catches my attention. I hear the door to Trevisan's studio close; his young apprentice, Biondino, is finishing work for the day. The house falls silent. I rise, inexplicably drawn toward the door that leads from the kitchen to the artist's studio. At the threshold, I pause and put my ear to the door. All is quiet except for Signora Amalia's humming on one of the upper floors. I crack open the door to the artist's studio and peer inside.

The soft light of dusk filters through the leaded diamonds of the canal-side windows. One of the window panels is cranked open, ventilating the strong smells of the studio and letting the sounds and dank odors of the canal enter Trevisan's workspace. I drink in the sights that so impressed me on my first visit to the artist's studio: the carpets, the mantelpiece, the paintings hanging floor to ceiling, the candelabra, the easels. Several large pictures are propped along the walls. Two of them are portraits, a man and a woman in left and right profiles; they look like they have been made to hang together. The paint is still moist and glistens in the light filtering into the giant room.

All the while that I take in the sights and sounds of the studio, I feel compelled to look at Trevisan's easel. If discovered, I will have little excuse for being in his studio. My heart begins to pound, but I cannot stop myself. Driven by an irresistible force, I tiptoe across the wide floor planks and approach the picture. Carefully, with a thumb and forefinger, I lift the corner of the velvet drape that covers the painting.

My heart leaps—the girl from the boat. There is the face again, the face that obsesses my mind and fills my body with tingling. I drink in the flush of her cheeks, the delicate shape of her chin. Trevisan has begun to sketch out the background now, and I can make out leaded windows in the back, as if she is seated in some kind of interior space similar to the artist's studio. I recognize that the artist has begun to replicate in paint the velvet-upholstered divan in the corner, with its fine, cloth-covered buttons and trim. He has even captured the way that the light streaming through the leaded glass panes makes soft shadows on the cushions. The rest of the painting remains vague. Only the face has been carefully con-ceived. I feel compelled to reach out and touch her cheek, but as I bring my hand to the canvas, I stop myself, not wanting to leave a trace of my visit.

The sound of a male voice makes me jump. "Come, let me show you the progress made so far on the portraits of you and your wife. I think you'll be very pleased, *missier*, with Master Trevisan's work." I recognize the voice of Trevisan's journeyman Valentin coming from down the hall. I let the drape fall back into place, then scamper out of Trevisan's studio and back into the safety of the kitchen as quickly and quietly as possible. My heart is thundering in my chest.

I hear Valentin and another man enter the studio from a hall-way that leads to the studio from the land-side entry of Trevisan's house. The two men seem unaware of the soft latching of the kitch-en door as it closes.

IN MY NEW POSITION as Trevisan's *gondolier de xasada*, no two days are the same. The artist's home is a beehive of activity. From dawn until dusk, a stream of personal messengers delivers invita-tions to parties, balls, galas, and festivals. The incessantly ringing bells and loud rapping at the canal-side and land-side doors are enough to drive Signora Amalia into a state of exasperation. Private boatmen drop off contracts, supplies, and their own masters, who have commissioned the artist to paint them. I begin to recognize the subjects of Trevisan's portraits among the patricians and dignitaries who alight from their expensive boats. I make the acquaintance of their boatmen, who wait at Trevisan's studio-side dock while their masters sit for the esteemed artist to capture their likeness in paint.

While Trevisan is working in his studio, usually in the morn-ings, the artist charges me to ferry Signora Amalia to the market for her daily shopping. I wait for her at the quayside, enjoying the bustle of the market, the artfully arranged pyramids of pears, oranges, and figs. I come to recognize the faces of individuals in the neighborhood: an attractive housewife, a rotund fruit and veg-etable seller, a vendor of fuzzy-headed chickens in crates, a beggar, a man with a stump instead of an arm. Some days, Signora Amalia delegates the entire task of marketing to me, dispatching me with a stack of empty baskets for bread, carrots, and turnips for her stew, or for a sack full of rice. I relish the chance to climb out of the gondola and take in the sights, sounds, and smells of the market, which make me nostalgic for my sister's cooking.

After a short time, I have become so adept at launching and docking Trevisan's gondola that opening and closing the great iron gates of the boat slip is second nature. Some days, the errands and appointments are so closely spaced that it isn't worth storing the boat in the slip at all, and I dock the boat in the sunlight before Trevisan's studio door. While waiting for my master, I take advantage of the light to brush a coat of varnish on the boat's decks, to polish the *fòrcola* with oil, and to beat the seats with a rag, sending puffs of dust rising into the air. At dusk, if the artist is not attending a party, concert, or other gala, I take time to dismantle all the trappings on the gondola and carefully store them in wooden chests lining the boathouse wall, a process my grandfather used to call "putting the boat to sleep."

Trevisan pays my salary every Saturday. The sum would be considered a pittance compared to what some boatmen earn, but in truth, I have not yet found any reason to spend anything beyond my boardinghouse rent. The artist is more than generous with meals, prompting Signora Amalia to prepare enough food for me as well as his own workshop assistants. With a roof over my head, my stomach full, and my days filled with work, I want for nothing. My little salary, paid in heavy coins, collects in a burlap bag that I store in the rear of a shelf in the boathouse.

The artist's time is filled with a host of professional and social obligations that take us across the city. Within the first three weeks, I judge that I have ferried the artist to several dozen of the city's most elegant residences, either for an afternoon appointment with a patron or an evening celebration. Each time I moor Trevisan's gondola at one of the canal-side entrances of one of the city's great palaces, servants appear as if out of thin air to greet the artist, catering to his every need. A flutter of domestic servants rush to help him alight from the boat, take his cape, and offer him food and drink as if he were the Doge himself. Trevisan views all of his appointments as opportunities to gain new patrons and cultivate existing ones. The artist makes no distinction between his business and social engagements. The man and his work are one in the same.

Trevisan never emerges from his home without being dressed in the most luxurious fabrics and colors—burgundy velvet breeches, a waistcoat with puffy sleeves lined in golden silk, matching stockings and meticulously polished shoes. I have never seen him wear the same thing twice, and I come to realize that Signora Baldi, the proprietor of the costume-rental shop, regularly refreshes Trevisan's wardrobe. At first glance, it is hard to believe that Trevisan is not officially part of the patrician ranks. He engages in what is, after all, manual labor, little different from how any Venetian glassblower, ironsmith, carver, or other artisan spends his day. The time and effort Trevisan spends on his appearance helps raise his social status to the point where the artist is considered an equal among his elite Venetian clientele.

I wait for hours for Master Trevisan outside the Scuola Grande. Because of the boatmen who like to chat while we wait for our masters, I have learned that Trevisan is a devoted patron of the institution's charitable activities. The artist has contributed toward founding a hospital for the poor, to dowering painters' daughters, and to supporting boardinghouses for the homeless, including, I discover, the one where I myself am lodged amongst a crowd of poor souls. Some years ago, I learn, the *scuola* engaged Trevisan to paint a series of wall paintings for its chapter room. I have not been invited inside the building, so I have no idea what it entails, but I imagine that it must be an impressive project based on the number of supplies I ferry to the site and on how much time the artist's assistants spend there. Often I ferry Valentin, Trevisan's highest-ranking journeyman, to the *scuola*, and when I pick him up hours later, his hands and smock are covered in plaster dust and splatters of paint. At the end of each day that Valentin spends there, I ferry Trevisan himself to the *scuola* to inspect the work.

As I ferry the artist and his assistants around the city, my eyes scan the landscape. Subconsciously, I am hoping to catch a glimpse of the girl from the painting. She is clearly a patrician, and if I linger at the city's great homes with the artist long enough, I am bound to see her again. I want to know her name, where she lives, what she eats for breakfast, what the back of her neck smells like, how her hair would feel against my cheek.

Most of the time, my mind flickers with these fantasies of the dark-haired girl, but during my periods of idle time at Trevisan's house, I begin to formulate another dream: restoring the old boat—most likely crafted by the hands of my own grandfather—that now lies neglected in Trevisan's boathouse. Restlessness rises inside me, an inner urgency that will not be quelled.

Chapter 22

I struggle to build up the nerve to broach the subject of the old gondola with Master Trevisan. The artist is busy, wrapped up in his commissions, in his social engagements, and in managing his workshop. Clearly he does not care enough about that old boat or he would have already taken it himself to any one of the city's four dozen *squeri* and paid a *squerariolo* to have it repaired. But when I regard the dilapidated gondola, my mind's eye sees what it could be: a boat worthy of any craft on any canal today, a fine antique, a beauty. As I carry out my chores around the artist's boat slip and dock, I keep the old Vianello gondola ever in the corner of my eye. I imagine myself removing the cover, flipping it over, and repairing the ribs. In my mind, I reform the prow, sand the decks, refine its decorations, scrape and varnish the hull—tasks I carried out every day of my life up until the calamitous day of the fire in my father's boatyard. I utter a deep sigh.

Finally, one moment as I wring out a rag in the canal waters, I feel myself inexorably drawn to the gondola, as if it were calling to me. I approach its familiar curvilinear form outlined by the drape of its canvas cover. Carefully, I push back the dusty cloth, just for a look. I run my palms along the hull, feeling a rush of warmth, the same feeling one gets when caressing a dog or embracing a friend.

The canvas cover slips off the boat hull, falling into a heap on the cold stones.

Flipping a gondola over on trestles normally necessitates the strength of at least two men. The boat stretches the length of some five men laid head to toe and can weigh equally as much. But on this day, to my surprise, the energy coursing through my body gives me the force to complete this task on my own. I corral my strength into propping the boat into a tilt, then awkwardly I flip it right-side-up on top of the wooden trestles. It is the first time that I have had the chance to examine the interior of the old boat. The seat upholstery, which once comfortably seated two passengers, is ripped, its stuffing rotted, no more than a rat's nest. The boards of the aft deck are split open; the boat has been involved in a significant crash. A gaping hole mars the hull, its boards splintered up into the boat itself. I open the aft deck to find a few stiff rags and an empty green-glass wine bottle. Two large spiders scuttle out, and I recoil.

The *ferro* that adorns the gondola's prow is measurably smaller than the ones being made now. I think of the hulking iron forks that Annalisa's father turns out, as much a measure of the man's bravado as of current taste in gondola ornamentation. This old one is still heavy, though, its short prongs decorated with delicate swirls and swags incised into the metal. Although this old boat was made before the era when the Doge began handing down decrees against ostentatious decoration on gondolas, I judge that this understated prow could pass muster against any sumptuary law currently in force. I admire the serpentine shape of the iron fork as I run my fingers over its cool, pitted surface.

This boat can be restored; I am certain. I have restored countless gondolas—granted, usually in much better condition than this one—alongside my father and brother. Thoughtfully brought back to its original state, this gondola could be fine, a masterpiece. I am lost in my memories, in my intimate exploration of the boat, when a voice emanating from the stairwell breaks my trance.

"Son, what are you doing with that old boat?"

I CAN HARDLY BELIEVE my good fortune.

My master is not angry with me for disturbing and working on the dilapidated old boat. In fact, he seems pleased. A strange smirk crossed Trevisan's face when I hurriedly explained my vision for the gondola, how it could be restored to its original glory, working even better than it did when it was first launched into the canal, long before I or even Trevisan himself was born. The artist seemed amused when I listed the advantages of having two boats in working order. Trevisan did not even seem to be concerned that the restoration project would take time away from my other duties.

I slip out of the boardinghouse before dawn. The common room stands empty except for Giuseppe, the unemployed tailor, a permanent fixture at the bar. He sits slumped over in a chair, snoring. I quietly unlatch the lock and move into the alley. I stop at a rusty spout that projects from a nearby wall. I place my head under it and fill my cheeks with cool water. A thick mist rises from the canal waters as I walk to Trevisan's house, and the damp air chills my skin. I stuff my hands inside the pockets of my waistcoat. Trevisan plans to work in his studio for the morning, which will afford me the time I need to work in the boat slip. I am eager to get started.

I rap softly at the land-side door, and Signora Amalia lets me in; I do not have a key to Trevisan's house and probably never will, given most people's distrust of their own boatmen. I pass through the kitchen, where Trevisan's simple breakfast of fruit and cheese has been prepared on a tray. I grab an apricot from the fruit bowl for later and stash it in my pocket, then descend the stairs to the boat slip.

Dawn's light has not yet penetrated the dark, dank space, and I shiver and rub my palms together, watching vapors of my breath puff into the dimness. I push the canvas cover gently off the boat and stand back to take in the whole thing in one glance. I hardly see the splintered wood, the crusted, flaking varnish, the rotted upholstery. In my mind's eye, I only envision the finished gondola. Still, I fully understand the work that must be done to get it to that point. To properly restore the boat, I must sand off every last bit of canal grub that has crystallized on the boat hull over the years. That will take some serious work, but once I have the gondola sanded back down to bare wood, I can bring it to sea-worthiness once again.

But first things first. On the side of the boathouse opposite Trevisan's working gondola, I set up a space where I can work. I shift the clutter to the back of the boathouse, then sweep the dust and grime off the great stones and into the black water that laps against the walls. I pull the trestles out from against the wall, dragging them carefully across the stones so that I can access the gondola from all sides.

In the far reaches of the boat slip, a set of shelves is cluttered with old, forgotten supplies. I take stock of what might be of use in the gondola restoration. The turpentine is probably worth salvaging, as it hardly ever goes bad. The varnish, on the other hand, will have to be thrown out—a pity, for it will be expensive to replace. As I work, I compile a list in my mind of the supplies I wish I had: sandpaper, a saw, a mallet, some planks of elm, a bag of wooden nails, some paintbrushes. I will have to make do with what I have or locate what I need as I go.

The morning passes in what seems like mere seconds. At midday, Trevisan appears at the door. For a moment he seems disoriented as he glances around the new state of his boat slip. He seems to notice that the shelves have been wiped clean, the storage containers neatly organized. The cobwebs have been knocked down, and the corners swept. Even the moss has been scrubbed off the stones so that only a faint trace of the fetid odor remains. Trevisan clears his throat but makes no comment other than to ask me to ferry him to the *scuola* to inspect the progress of his frescoes.

By the time I lay down my broom and pick up an oar, I have already transformed the back half of the artist's boathouse into a makeshift *squero*.

"THAT'S QUITE a project."

A man—I perceive him to be a private boatman—peers around the doorway to the boat slip. I am wiping down the prow of the old gondola with a wet rag. Decades of dust have collected on the boat, and my first order of business is to remove it so that I can fathom where to begin this project. It has taken me some fifty hours of work to remove the dirt caked in every crack and crevice of the boat. I feel gratified that someone has taken notice. I smile.

"Yes. Well, it's not much to look at now, but it will be a beauty once it's finished. That is, after many hours of work."

"Indeed. You must be Trevisan's new boatman." The man enters the boathouse. He wears close-fitting pants in the fashion of the day, one leg white and the other black. His shirt is also close-fitting, with a white collar and a red and black diamond design across the breast. He wears a sleek cap and black leather shoes polished to a gleam. In my mind, I make a rough estimation of the cost of the man's clothes, even if they are rented. My own new clothes, though an improvement for me, pale in comparison to this boatman's finery. Something about the man is familiar. I search my mind to think where I have seen him before. I step forward to greet him. "*Come xea, vecio?*" I offer, and the man greets me back with the camaraderie that I am beginning to grow accustomed to since my entry into the world of private gondoliering.

Outside the boat-slip door, I notice the prow of the man's boat rocking gently in the canal. At once, I recognize it, as well as the boatman steering it. The girl. I suck in my breath.

Mistaking my expression for a reaction to his boat, the man smiles. "A beauty, is it not? And it's a dream to row, too," he says, inflating his chest. "Usually there are two of us, but the prow man was sent on another errand at the markets today." I nod. Only the wealthiest in Our Most Serene Republic can afford to employ two boatmen, one for the fore and one for the aft. The front man sometimes doubles as a butler or house servant, which would explain why his partner has been dispatched to the market.

"Giacomo da Molin," he extends his hand. "But you can call me Beppe. Everyone does." I am hardly paying attention. My heart is pounding. "You mean old Trevisan managed to find a boatman who restores boats as well as rows them?"

"I suppose," I hesitate. "I have to keep myself busy during the quieter hours. I'm sure you understand."

"Of course. But I don't know of any of my colleagues who spend their spare time like this! You're an industrious soul," Beppe bursts out laughing. "I guess you heard what happened to Trevisan's last boatman?"

I hesitate again. "Actually, no."

"How could you have missed it? At the guild hall it was the topic of conversation for a good month." I can see that that won't stop Beppe from relishing the tale again. "The man stripped Trevisan's gondola clean. Stole the *felso*, the oarlocks, even the upholstery." He shakes his head. That would explain why all the trappings of the boat Trevisan uses every day are brand new, even though the boat itself is dusty and neglected.

"No one's seen the man since, as far as I know. Probably left the city already," he says.

I am eager to turn the conversation toward the girl. "You work for the lady in the boat?" I wince immediately, regretting how stupid the question sounds.

He smirks. "No. I work—worked—for her father. It's most accurate to say that I work for the whole family. The upper class wouldn't dream of letting their daughters go around in a boat with just anybody, or subjecting them to the vagaries of street traffic. So, here I am." He sweeps his hand dramatically from head to foot then laughs again, a deep-throated chortle.

"Of course," I open my palm but imagine that my gesture must appear unconvincing. "Who is she?"

"Giuliana Zanchi. Yes, that Zanchi—the banking family. She's having some kind of picture painted here," says Beppe, waving his hand in the general direction of Trevisan's studio.

"Is the picture for her husband... or, um, fiancé?" I utter the question, then hold my breath.

The boatman smirks. "Signorina Zanchi? Married? Hardly... Though any man in Our Most Serene Republic would sell his soul to Satan in exchange for ten minutes alone with her."

"The Zanchi family... Is that the Ca'Leoncino?"

The other boatman smirks again. "Goodness, no. You must be kidding! No, it's the big pink brick palace further down the Grand Canal, the one you can see from the Church of San Silvestro. Care to have a look at the gondola?" Beppe asks, and I follow him from the boat slip onto the sunlit dock. My gaze goes straight to the leaded glass window of Trevisan's studio that overlooks the canal. The curtain has been drawn, and I can see nothing except the dull side of the green velvet.

Beppe begins a detailed tour of the Zanchi gondola, and I feign fascination. Even without the dolphin emblem carved near the prow, I have already recognized the boat as a product of the Squero Delfin, a rival *squero* that produces beautiful boats. The *ferro* decorating the prow is enormous, a hulking iron fork engraved with flowers and grape vines; it is a wonder of metalworking. I gasp in genuine surprise when Beppe demonstrates how the top half of the *ferro* can be ingeniously folded in half, to avoid bumping low-lying bridges. The stern *ferro* is hardly less ostentatious. The oars are painted with the family coat of arms. The oarlocks, too, are nothing short of masterpieces.

The *felze* is one of the newer enclosed kinds that allow passengers to travel in utter privacy. The frame of the cabin is constructed of wood, but you would hardly know it. Every single inch is carved, painted, and gilded. Whereas by law, all *felze* with certain exceptions are supposed to be black, its cloth cover, at least the one for this season, is made of bright royal-blue velvet with fringe and tassels. Beppe gestures for me to have a look inside. Wooden, louvered doors open to an interior space that I can only describe as a jewel box. One wall is covered in mirrors, which reflect the gilded damask fabric that upholsters the remaining walls and ceiling. The two seats are upholstered in royal blue velvet, and behind the seat stands a mahogany panel richly carved with scrolls and shells.

"And there are two more fine boats in the Zanchi boathouse," Beppe tells me. "Over the years Signor Zanchi has paid enough *zecchini* in fines for breaking the sumptuary laws to buy ten new gondolas. A small price to pay in his view, I suppose." I gasp.

On any other day, I would have been thrilled to explore every single inch of this fine craft, but I am distracted. Throughout Beppe's tour, my mind is focused on the door to Trevisan's studio, straining to hear or see something—anything—from inside. I hear the clang of the bells of San Biagio. A solid hour or more has passed since the boatman poked his head around the corner of the boat slip. Beppe chats about the new guild regulations on boatmen's salaries, and I pretend to listen.

Finally, I hear the lock scrape against the wooden door that leads to the artist's studio. Beppe continues to talk—something about guild elections this time—but I am no longer listening. The gondolier's voice recedes into the background, and the pounding in my chest takes over. My eyes are fixed on the canal-side door to the artist's studio.

As the door opens, her face is illuminated in the light. She is laughing at something Trevisan is saying to her as he escorts her down the stairs to her boat, her hand looped through the crook of the artist's arm. Her maid is following the pair, carrying her mistress's brown dog. Trevisan leads Giuliana Zanchi to the quayside, where her boatman is now waiting with a gallant gesture to help his lady board the gondola. As they pass, she turns and looks at me. My heart in my throat, somehow I manage to nod to her in greeting.

Trevisan pauses for a moment, then says, "Signorina Zanchi, may I introduce my new boatman, Luca Fabris?" To my surprise, she meets my gaze with her bright green eyes. "Signorina," I greet her, unlocking my rigid pose. I bow in her direction, which feels awkward and unpracticed—I can't recall ever having done this before for a lady.

"Signorina Zanchi," interrupts Trevisan, turning his attention back to her, "Will I have the pleasure of seeing you again on Saturday at the Councillor's party?"

"I wouldn't miss it," she replies.

Beppe extends his hand to help the lady into the boat, and she accepts it, stepping gingerly from the steps into the rocking gondola. Her cloak covers her entire body, but I drink in every detail of her face, her hand, and her foot as she boards the boat. Seemingly aware that I am watching her, she looks directly at me with a curious expression. Behind her, the girl's maid follows her mistress into the boat. She regards me with a disapproving glance. Trevisan's assistant now appears at the door, paintbrushes in one hand, and bows slightly to the ladies in the boat. I stand transfixed for a moment, not believing that I have finally encountered this woman, the one who has filled my mind for weeks.

The two women disappear into the passenger compartment of the gondola. Beppe salutes me with two fingers to his forehead, then pushes away from the mooring, expertly backing the boat and turning out of sight around a narrow corner of the canal.

I return to my work in the boat slip, my entire body on fire.

Chapter 23

I uncork a bottle of varnish, draw it under my nose, then make a disgusted face. It is rotten, and I can only imagine how long the bottle has been sitting there, collecting dust in Trevisan's boathouse. Too bad. I will have to figure out how to procure the ingredients I need to mix a new batch. I am intent on stripping the split wood from the gondola's hull. Several of the oak planks are water-damaged and warped, a result of sitting partially sunk beneath the surface of the water for so long. I inhale the pungent, moldy scent of the wood, a strangely comforting smell that transports me to the past.

I locate a pair of stiff leather gloves from the back of the boathouse and figure they will suffice to protect my hands from splinters. With the help of a hammer and saw I locate in the jumble, I wrench the pieces of splintered wood out of the bottom of the boat and toss them into a pile on the cobblestones. Those, I think, may be recut and fashioned into wooden nails of the kind I have made ever since I was a little boy.

After a solid three hours of work, I have managed to clean out the splintered wood from the hole. Thankfully, most of the *corbe*, the structural ribs that I know all too well, are not damaged except for two small V-shaped members near the prow, which can be easily replaced. One of the *masse*, the long elm boards that normally run the length of the boat on either side to protect the craft from scraping alongside docks, has been stripped off. It will need to be replaced as soon as possible to ensure the structural integrity of the boat.

What remains of the original upholstery, as ragged and rotten as it is, proves surprisingly difficult to strip. I prop myself on my knees in the bottom of the boat and tug on the faded velvet with all my might. None of it is salvageable, and I move it to another heap.

I test the soundness of the prow by pushing my weight into it. It does not budge, and I smile, satisfied that even on a damaged boat, the techniques of my own family's *squero* have withstood the test of time. I run my hand up and down the prow as I imagine my grandfather forming this shape on the dirt floor of the Vianello workshop. My fingers bump over the slight notches in the wood, and I am certain that I have held the ax that made these marks in my own hands.

I WEAVE THROUGH boats docked along the narrow canal to Signora Baldi's costume rental shop. Trevisan's gondola is laden with two large crates, filled to the brim with costumes that the artist has worn. I recognize the wicker containers as the same ones I picked up some weeks ago, in what I now realize was a test that Trevisan had organized to see if I would prove a trustworthy boatman.

I arrive at the canal-side entrance of the costume-rental shop just as Signora Baldi is helping another client. She references a list scrawled on a large parchment, stretched across a piece of wood, as a gondolier calls out the contents of a box to her. Signora Baldi acknowledges my arrival with a businesslike smile and a nod, and the other gondolier greets me with a silent hand gesture. Behind him, another gondola awaits.

Signora Baldi stifles an exasperated sigh, then finally instructs me, "I'm sorry. Tonight's party at the Ca' Leoncino has made me fall behind. Go inside the shop. My daughter Patrizia will help you. We have the crates ready for the artist." I moor Trevisan's gondola and climb out, staggering slightly as I ascend the stone stairs to the costume shop, bearing the weight of one of the crates with the costumes inside.

Inside, Patrizia sits mending a shirt with a needle and thread. She looks up from her sewing to face me. She looks startled, then composes herself and smiles. "You're Trevisan's man, right? I thought I recognized you from the last time." She sets down her sewing and, in a self-conscious gesture, smoothes the front of her dress. "Come... I'll show you where my mother has put aside the new cartons for the artist."

I follow the girl into the storehouse behind the shop front. As she walks, she reaches up and pulls a pin from her hair. I inhale a floral scent as she lets her hair cascade down her back. She turns her large brown eyes on me and twirls a lock of loose hair with her finger. She gestures for me to follow.

"Isn't it time we exchanged that waistcoat?" I look down sheepishly at my coat. She smiles. "I think we can do better than that." Patrizia files through a rack of men's costumes, fingering a rainbow of velvets, silks, and taffetas. From this bundle of fine fabrics she produces a stylish-looking coat. "Here it is. Try this one."

Reluctantly, I remove my waistcoat and toss it onto a chair, then thread my arms through the coat that Patrizia holds out for me. She squeezes my arm and leads me to an enormous mirror propped on the storehouse floor. I look at my reflection while Patrizia runs her hands slowly over my shoulders and back, tidying the coat. In the mirror, she peers out from behind my back. "Just as I thought: this jacket is perfect for you, with your eyes—almost like fire! You can borrow it if you like, as long as you think of me when you wear it," she giggles. "Just return it to me when you come back with Trevisan's costumes."

I emerge from the storehouse with the large crate full of next month's supply of Trevisan's costumes, and load it onto the gondola. "I've also packed a separate box with several possibilities for tonight's gala," Signora Baldi gestures to another container on the quayside. She watches her daughter follow me out of the shop and stares in disapproval, seeming to take note that she has let down her hair. She frowns, then turns her attention back to me as I load the second crate onto Trevisan's gondola. "Please have Master Trevisan make his selectionss and return the remaining choices to me by next Thursday since I'll need to have whatever he does not select available for other clients. The other costumes he may keep until next month, as usual." She waves as I unlatch the boat from the shop's mooring. "I'm glad to see that the artist has finally found a trustworthy person to carry out his errands. He has had his fair share of tribulations with boatmen."

I have begun to row back to Trevisan's house when a thought occurs to me. I pull out of the Grand Canal and into a small side rivulet where there are no boats or people in sight. I moor the gondola to a giant iron ring on the side of a building. Looking around to make sure no one is watching, I lift the lid off one of the wicker crates. Inside, Signora Baldi has carefully folded a dozen or so garments from which Trevisan may choose, each fully accessorized with stockings and hats to match. A red and black ensemble catches my eye. Swiftly, I roll up the costume and sweep it into the storage compartment under the aft deck. I look around again, then swipe the matching hat, a broad-brimmed affair embellished with a single, long gray goose feather.

I make sure that the rest of the costumes in the crate appear undisturbed, then close the lid and row toward Trevisan's house.

"THERE IS TOO MUCH boat traffic for me to wait for you here, Master Trevisan. I must moor the gondola away from the palace." With one hand, I grasp a mooring post outside the Ca' Leoncino.

"Of course," says the artist. Valentin, Trevisan's journeyman, climbs out of the gondola first. Next, Trevisan exits the boat with his usual spryness, which surprises me given the man's age and portliness. A younger man dressed in an elaborate blue cape and an onion-shaped hat greets the artist with a smile as he climbs out of his own boat. Within seconds, Trevisan is surrounded by a crowd of fawning friends, patrons, and acquaintances. The group moves from the docks up to the palace's canal-side entrance. Another crowd of talkative partygoers makes its way up the side alley to enter the palace from the land-side.

Pushing off from the docks, I glide away from the Ca' Leoncino and the many boats clustered around it. I round the corner and search the canal for an ideal spot. Not far away, I find a lone mooring pole next to a dark, silent canal faced with narrow houses, all of which have their shutters closed. I approach the pole and lash one of the boat's ropes to it. I open the aft deck and snatch the costume I have stored there. I duck into the passenger compartment and draw the curtains closed.

In truth, I don't really know what I am doing, so I follow my instincts. With some awkwardness, I ply myself into the red and black costume. The silk breeches feel slippery across the skin of my thighs, an unfamiliar sensation. The pants, silk shirt, and vest are of course sized for Trevisan and are much too baggy for my lean frame. Improvising, I roll the excess fabric of the waistband, and then fold the extra material of the shirt into neat pleats at my waist. With some care, I place the hat on my head at an angle, appreciating that it is the most extravagant thing I have worn in my life. I have no choice but to wear my old shoes, which look ridiculous with this elaborate outfit. I hope no one will notice.

I exit the gondola and duck down the alley nearest the mooring post. The alley opens to a broader path, and from there, I can
hear the sounds of the party—music, laughter, conversation. The
great doors that mark the land-side entrance to the Ca' Leoncino
are closed, but warm candlelight emanates from the upper-floor
windows. I position myself in the entryway to a grand building
nearby, and wait for an opportunity. After a few minutes, a group
of a dozen party guests approaches the building, talking amongst
themselves. One man pulls the cord outside the door, ringing a bell.
I emerge from the doorway and fold myself into the back of the
group. When the doors open, I slip into the palace behind them.

While the exterior of the land-side entrance is relatively plain,
the interior of the building takes my breath away. Beneath my
dusty shoes, the floor is composed of rose and white marble slabs
formed into the shape of a giant star. Several people sit under al-
coves around the edges of the entryway, on benches festooned with
jewel-toned velvet cushions. Mythological scenes are painted on
the walls. I look up to a coffered ceiling some twenty feet above
my head, punctuated with gilded flowers. Silks embroidered with
coats of arms line an enormous staircase, its marble steps gleaming
like mirrors.

I tuck myself toward the back of the crowd with whom I entered the house. Ascending the stairs, we reach the main floor with
an arched *portego* overlooking the moonlight reflecting on the
canal waters. The party is underway. Several men gather around
an enormous hearth that is the keystone of the room, a hulking
fireplace carved with gilded mythological figures that stretch from
floor to ceiling. At a nearby table, guests sip from wide-rimmed
glass goblets so transparent they are nearly invisible. At another
table, a black man with a turban-like headdress pours wine from a
blown glass pitcher in the shape of a ship.

In the center of the room an enormous table overflows with
food beneath ornate glass chandeliers. I have never seen such abun-

dance: a vast bounty of fish and fowl, grapes, pomegranates, eggs, eels, and braided breads, all displayed on red fabric with silver and glass candelabra illuminating the feast. I have eaten meat only on a few occasions over the last year, and I have never tasted the game birds that I have seen patrician men hunting with bows and arrows in the lagoons. Now, here before me splay artfully arranged carcasses of peacocks, pheasants, mallard ducks, quail, guinea hens, and partridges, with the feathers of these birds making up part of the table decoration.

My mouth waters as I load my plate with a precariously balanced bounty of delicacies. I duck to the periphery of the room, where I find a gilded, tapestry-covered stool. The sights, sounds, and smells of the party grow dim and out of focus as I savor the unfamiliar flavors that slide over my tongue. With a two-pronged silver fork, I remove what must be a spleen or a kidney from a tiny bird on my plate. I separate a flap of bumpy skin from the sliver of dark meat. The cook has done his utmost to make the bird look appetizing, dressing it with soft sage leaves and a sliver of citrus. The sight of the creature's innards exposed, its limbs akimbo, the bumps where its feathers have been plucked, makes me squeamish, but it tastes surprisingly delicious. Finally, two crayfish legs and a pile of empty cockleshells are all that remain on my plate.

Satiated, I scan the room. I catch sight of Trevisan's assistant, the sleepy-looking Valentin. He stands at the balcony of an open window, his elbow resting lazily on the railing. His unbuttoned silk shirt reveals his smooth, shiny chest and a large gem hanging on a chain. An older man has engaged Valentin in conversation, so I don't worry that he might recognize me. Still, I pull the brim of my hat down lower on my face. I scan the room for Trevisan, but I don't see the artist.

The party spills into the next room, and I file into another enormous chamber with coffered ceilings and luxurious fabrics draped over the windows. The chairs have been pushed back against the wall. In one corner of the room, a trio of musicians plays stringed instruments while several guests dance in a circle, holding one another's hands high in the air. Others stand in clusters, chatting, drinking, and observing the dancers.

At one end of the room stands another enormous *portego*. Its lace-like arches frame a view of the Grand Canal. I pause to take in the vista. A full moon hangs in the sky, making shimmering, metallic patterns in the water. A large gathering of boats—mostly the boatmen of the people at this party, waiting for their masters—clusters in the canal. It appears that the boatmen are enjoying a party of their own. Several boats have been lashed together, their boatmen chatting loudly to one another and laughing. Each boat has a lantern suspended from the frame of its *felze*, and from this vantage point, they appear like hundreds of fireflies bobbing on the water.

The music stops and everyone claps. I turn my head, then freeze. There she is.

I only see her from the back, but there is no doubt in my mind that it is Giuliana Zanchi. She is taking in the same view that I am, standing at the *portego* alongside two men and an older woman. I approach slowly, moving so that I can see her from the side. Her hair is pulled back from her face in fine braids studded with tiny pearls and sparkling gems. A string of beads hangs at her neck, and a pair of platform clogs peek out from the hem of her emerald-green velvet gown. I can make out their white leather uppers pierced with a fine mesh of flowers and leaves, their tree-trunk-like heels making her nearly as tall as I am. My heartbeat reverberates loudly inside my head.

One of the men, a gallant-looking patrician, is doing his best to engross the women in conversation. He moves close to Giuliana and leans down to talk near her ear. My heart fills with uncontrollable jealousy for this stranger of whom I know almost nothing. I inch closer to her along the balustrade, to a spot where I can observe her while at the same time appearing to observe the twinkling lantern lights in the canal. I do my best to seem inconspicuous, as if I have found something fascinating in the canal to watch.

From the corner of my eye, I notice that one of the house servants is watching Giuliana as closely as I am. The slight man, whom I judge to be a North African, nearly disappears into the richly ornamented fabric on the wall, where he stands with his hands behind his back. I may not have noticed him if not for his seemingly abiding watch over Giuliana Zanchi. He is also watching the man talking to Giuliana, as if waiting for the man to make a false move.

I am now close enough to hear the man recounting a story about his exploits in the Dolomite Mountains. From the corner of my eye, I see the other lady in the group stifle a yawn. I listen vaguely to the man's monologue, but all my senses are directed toward the girl in the green dress. After a few moments, I muster the nerve to turn directly toward her. From this vantage point, I can see the delicate skin behind Giuliana's ear and wisps of brown hair loose at the nape of her neck. I inhale, trying to catch her scent, but only the rotten, damp vapors of the canal fill my nose.

Giuliana seems suddenly aware of a presence behind her. She turns her head slowly. My heart leaps, and I look away, pretending to gaze again at the twinkling gas lamps swinging in the boats in the canal. Giuliana fixes her eyes on me with a blank stare for a moment. Then she smiles.

"I know you!" she exclaims. "Master Trevisan's boatman!"

Chapter 24

"That's a pretty good disguise! Well, except for the baggy pants." She utters a deep-throated laugh. "And the shoes." I look down at my sagging breeches and my embarrassingly scuffed shoes, which I now realize look even more ridiculous than I originally thought. She leans toward me, and I can smell her perfume. I instinctively flare my nostrils, catching a mixture of daffodils and rose water.

"It's fine," she whispers. "Your secret's safe with me." She stifles a giggle with her hand. "What are you doing here, dressed like that?"

I gather my wits. I clear my throat and inflate my chest. "Well, I happen to be here on a secret errand for someone. I'm afraid I am not able to reveal more than that, Signorina Zanchi." I try my best to sound confident and serious, corralling all my force to conceal my sheer panic. I am not at all sure that I have convinced her.

"I see," Giuliana says, her expression now serious too, mirroring my own. I glance to see if the two men and the woman have turned to listen, too. To my utter relief, the tall man continues to drone on about the Dolomites, and the other two continue to listen to him politely. I turn my gaze back to Giuliana.

"I thought I recognized you," she continues. "I don't usually forget a face, though I often forget a name. What is it again?"

"Luca. Luca Fabris."

"Yes," she says. "Now I remember. Trevisan told me that he hired a new boatman. Poor man. He has had terrible luck with boatmen in the past. I'm glad to see that he seems to have found someone reliable. And how are you finding your work with the artist?"

I try to look confident. "Very well. You know, the artist has many important social engagements and business appointments, so I am very busy, too." As soon as the words come out of my mouth, I second-guess myself. "But of course, like every *gondolier de xasada*, I have a lot of time, too, for..." I hesitate, "my own tasks."

"Of course," Giuliana says slowly, as if her mind is processing the information, and she seems suddenly and deeply engrossed in her own thoughts.

At that moment, Trevisan enters the room.

I recognize the artist's portly, confident frame as it fills the doorway. A small entourage surrounds the artist, and the group heads toward the balustrade near the spot where I am standing.

This is my cue to flee.

"Excuse me," I say to Giuliana, then I duck my chin and make my way purposefully across the room, sticking close to the wall. I navigate through the crowd in the room with the banquet table, then jog down the great marble staircase into the main entryway of the Ca' Leoncino. A short-statured servant mans the front door. As I approach, the man opens it, bows, and wishes me a curt "*Bona serata, Signore,*" with a thick accent. I tip my hat briefly, then hurry out the door before I can be recognized by anyone else.

As I sprint down the alley to the gondola mooring, I hear the clanging of church bells. Blast! I have lost track of time. I reach the mooring and leap into Trevisan's gondola. Inside the *felze,* I rip off my silly costume in desperation, my fingers fumbling with what seem like thousands of minuscule silk-covered buttons. I stuff the outfit and hat under the aft deck, unlatch the mooring rope, then row with all my force to the alley adjacent to the palace.

The boat glides to a stop before the canal-side entrance of the palace just as Trevisan and Valentin emerge from the door. "There you are, Luca! Excellent timing!" exclaims Trevisan, still in the mode of gallant socialite.

"*Bonasera*, Master Trevisan," I respond breathlessly. The important-looking men I saw walking with Trevisan inside the palace are still with him. Each grasps Trevisan's hands and kisses his bearded cheeks warmly, then bids the artist farewell as he steps into the gondola.

I row the artist and his assistant home, struggling to calm my wildly beating heart.

I SMELL THE TANNERIES, the famous *scorzeri*, long before I bring the gondola to rest along a stone quayside on the island of Giudecca. The stench is overwhelming, a nauseating combination of animal carcasses and rancid water. An acrid odor—some kind of alchemical concoction—fills the air. It has been years since I have had any reason to row to Giudecca. Now I understand why the tanneries lie at a distance from the city center.

If Valentin notices the stench, he doesn't show any sign of it. The boy sits on the foredeck of Trevisan's gondola, the wind blowing his hair as I row. The sun shines brightly and there is a tinge of warmth in the air, a harbinger of spring. Valentin is a puzzle to me, a quiet and withdrawn young man who seems completely self-absorbed. From my vantage point rowing the gondola, I observe his profile. His skin is soft and delicate. There is something dreamy about him, as if his mind were far, far away, except when I find the boy narcissistically gazing at himself in the mirror of the master's studio. Although we are around the same age, it seems we have little to speak about. Trevisan has dispatched me to accompany Valentin to pick up supplies from a pigments seller in the Giudecca, and I think that it might provide an opportunity to learn more about what is happening inside the boy's head—and inside Trevisan's studio.

"Picking up supplies today?"

"Yes," replies Valentin, not turning his head.

"So, why the Giudecca?"

Valentin continues to look to the horizon but turns his body to face me. "One of the pigments sellers there carries some special materials that Master is using as an experiment. We've started grinding colored and colorless glass particles in with the pigments. When we apply them in thin layers on the new twill canvasses, they make the surface of the picture appear more... translucent." He makes an odd gesture with his hand, as if to try to replicate the effect of the paint.

"Hmm." I nod as if I understand perfectly. "What project are you working on?"

Valentin turns his face to me, and his expression softens. "Master and I are working on several commissions right now. There's the *scuola*, of course—that project seems never-ending. And as of yesterday we have a new commission from the Greek ambassador for a painting of Leda and the Swan. And we have our usual stream of portraits—everyone in this city wants to flatter themselves, it seems. We need to stock supplies since over the next month there will be a lot of work in the studio."

I nod. "Does that include the picture of the girl... what's her name again? Signorina Zanchi?" I feign ignorance.

"I don't know," replies Valentin. "I'm not working on that one. Trevisan's doing that picture by himself. It's small." Valentin puffs up his chest. "I usually work on the bigger paintings—mythological scenes or religious pictures like the new triptych we're doing for the church of San Giacomo dell'Orio."

I nod. I have no idea what a triptych is.

We fall into an awkward silence, and I turn my gaze back to the other side of the Giudecca canal, where I glimpse a line of *squeri* along the banks that lay between the Punta della Dogana and the Zattere. From my standing position on the aft deck of the gondola, I have an unobstructed view of the ramps where the boat makers launch their new boats. I know each one of the families—Pisani, Sanuto, da Riva—all colleagues of my father, not one a rival.

"Would you please drop me at the quayside next to the tanneries?" Valentin asks. "That's closest to the shop where I need to buy the supplies." Then he falls silent again, idly chewing his fingernails and gazing off into the distance.

While I wait for the boy to return, I watch a man scraping a large animal hide tied to a wooden frame next to the banks of the canal. It is backbreaking work, barely a step up from slavery. The stench—created during the process of curing the hides—is nearly unbearable. On the north side of the tanneries, animal carcasses are piled high, a hellish sight. The hoofs of the slaughtered beasts reach stiffly skyward with rigor mortis. I wonder how the tanners endure these miserable conditions and figure that they must grow accustomed to the ghastly sights and repulsive smells.

A young man, no older than fourteen, carries two wooden buckets with rope handles down to the water. He is shirtless, his muscles too developed for a boy his age. He is drenched with sweat. As he bends over to fill the buckets, I perceive the strip-like welted marks across his back. He staggers back up to the tannery with the buckets full of water, and I see the long lashing-scars across his back again. I shudder.

I don't want to see any more. I leave the boat at the quayside and, hands in my pockets, stroll down the wet alley. I pass a cobbler's shop, a tailor, and a few residences. The shops are little more than grubby hovels with dirt floors, their doors open to the street to allow light onto their workbenches. Yesterday's rain gathers in a trough in the middle of the cobblestone street, which forms a sieve that drains back into the canal. I step to the side here and there to avoid stepping into little piles of dog feces.

Ahead, a meat and cheese market stands cobbled together in a muddy piazza. Laundry flaps haphazardly like ragged flags on crisscrossed clotheslines overhead. I plunk a few coins on the table at one of the butcher's stalls, and a heavy-set man with blue eyes and a

bloody apron slices off a few wafer-thin pieces from a hock of prosciutto. I sit on the stone threshold of a door overlooking the piazza
and chew the fleshy meat, which tastes grainy, salty, and delicious.

I wander toward the street where Valentin indicated he was
going for the supplies. The street is lined with modest residences
and grimier, hole-in-the-wall shops. It is just as Valentin described,
a place where there are numerous specialists involved in the business of mixing things—alchemists in the service of painters, tanners, and other artisans. One shop catches my eye, mainly because
it is large, clean, and filled with light from the storefront. Behind
a counter stands a spry man, mixing several ingredients with a
mortar and pestle. He has a shock of gray hair, an intelligent face,
and a piercing gaze that makes me think of my dear oarmaker. I
remove my hat and cross the threshold of the shop. The shopkeeper
looks up from his work and greets me with a polite "*Bondì.*"

"*Bondì, signore.* I wonder if you have any muriatic acid?" I ask.

"I can make some for you," replied the man. "Do you want
cornstarch, too?"

"Perfect," I say. "Thank you."

While the man mixes the ingredients, I look curiously around
the room at the shelves stacked high with glass bottles and ceramic
jars. The shop resembles a fantastic apothecary, neat and organized,
with labeled jars stacked from floor to ceiling.

The man sees me observing his shop and smiles. "I can make
anything you want. I mostly work with the tanneries but I supply
quite a few of the boatyards, too."

"Really?" I ask.

"Well, mostly those along the Zattere. The boat builders in
Cannaregio and Dorsoduro have their own sources. Say, I hear that
the Squero Vianello is being rebuilt," he says.

My heart pounds.

"What a disaster of a fire; what a shame for everyone involved. It's
a wonder no one was killed. Do you know how the family is doing?"

I am speechless, my heart in my throat.

"No," I stammer, caught unprepared.

"Surely you are a *squerariol*?" asks the proprietor, sizing me up with a piercing gaze.

"Um, no," I say. "I am just helping out with restoring an old boat."

"Is that so?" asks the man, with a hint of distrust in his voice. "I would have guessed you were a *squeriariol*, without a doubt. And I'm usually right. There's something about you... Plus, only a *squeriariol* would know about the magic of muriatic acid. Whose boat are you restoring?"

I am anxious to leave. "I'm sorry. I just remembered that I am late to meet my friend in the square. How much do I owe you?" I count the coins that I remembered to put in my pocket that morning, pulled from the burlap bag in the boathouse where I collect my weekly salary.

I emerge just in time to see Valentin walking purposefully down the alley, a panicked look in his eye. Then I notice that a bear of a man—black curly hair covering his head, chest and arms—is pursuing the boy. The man is staggering down the muddy alley after Valentin, visibly drunk, his eyes wild and tongue wagging.

"Come, *caro*! Just fifteen minutes! How much do you want?" The man's voice booms, echoing through the alley.

I act instinctively. "Leave him alone!" I yell at the man.

"Why? Who are you, his lover?" the man booms, then howls with laughter, leaning over to slap his knees, which makes him take three sidelong steps before regaining his balance.

Valentin looks relieved to see me. We walk quickly, side by side, toward the quay where the gondola is moored. Behind us, the drunk man makes loud kissing noises, puckering his lips exaggeratedly and then cackling and hooting so loudly that a stern-looking woman slams the shutters of her house closed as we pass.

"Thank you," says Valentin. "I'm sorry to say that it happens to me all the time. For some reason they think I am a prostitute."

I pull the last slice of ham from my knapsack and share it with Valentin. The two of us board the boat, and once again, Valentin stations himself on the fore deck. As we move into the boat traffic in the Grand Canal, Valentin faces me, the wind at his back.

"You asked me before about Signorina Zanchi. Are you interested in her?" The boy chews the grainy piece of prosciutto and studies my face.

"No," I reply a little too quickly. "Just curious. Why?"

"No reason. But just in case you were, she'll be at the studio tomorrow morning."

A grin crosses Valentin's face, and once again, he falls annoyingly silent.

Chapter 25

Morning sunbeams streak down the canal, imparting radiance to even the dingiest façades, and I feel I can smell the arrival of spring. I approach Trevisan's house after fetching eggs from the market for Signora Amalia when I see the Zanchi gondola moored at Trevisan's dock.

I recognize the luxurious boat from a distance. I smooth my hair and shake my head at the abysmal state of my only pair of shoes, as well as my hands, covered as they are in sawdust and varnish. Beppe, Giuliana's boatman, greets me with a salute and a nod, then leaps out of his boat to help me moor Trevisan's gondola. He glances at the sack of eggs in my hand and smiles. "Fine day for a little side work."

"I try to help in whatever way I can," I reply, trying to sound casual and confident. Automatically, my gaze travels to the window of the artist's studio, but just as the last time that Giuliana came to call, the green curtain is drawn closed over the diamond-shaped leaded glass of the studio window. I appear to busy myself in Trevisan's docked gondola, wanting to stay outside the boathouse so that I may have another chance to encounter the girl. I try my best to keep up the idle chat with Beppe, who is more than happy to oblige.

Finally I hear the door of the studio open. Valentin escorts Giuliana and her maid down the stairs. My stomach leaps at the sight of her, and I attempt to look occupied with the boat. The smoky smell of the hearth fire inside the studio emanates into the cool air.

Today her hair looks different, I note, pulled back in the front with long cascades in the back. Her cloak falls open to reveal a blue gown and a large gemstone hanging from a chain around her neck. In her hands, she clasps her tiny brown dog and a small purse made of the same velvet as her dress. Her grim-faced maid follows, pulling her own cloak tightly to her throat to ward off the chill. Suddenly, Giuliana seems to take a few purposeful steps in my direction. Taken aback, I look up from my work to search her face. She looks steadily at me with large green eyes, walking toward me. Holding my gaze, she pulls her right earlobe and addresses her maid: "Carolina, I seem to be missing an earring. Would you be so kind as to go inside and fetch it for me?" Her maid returns to the studio.

Next, she hands her dog to Beppe, who caresses its head. While Beppe settles the dog gently in the boat, Giuliana fishes something out of her purse, then, slowly, she turns her back to me. She entwines her hands behind her back. Almost imperceptibly, she flutters her fingers.

I notice now that Giuliana pinches something between the second and third fingers of her right hand. It is a piece of parchment, a small yellowish scrap folded neatly into quarters. Without drawing attention to herself, Giuliana takes a few steps back to the edge of the dock, and without a sound, drops it into Trevisan's gondola. I watch the folded piece of parchment flutter like a leaf, then land in the floor of the gondola. Now Giuliana turns her head, cuts her eyes toward the bottom of the boat, then glances at me briefly to see if I am watching. My throat tightens.

At that moment, her maid returns, dangling a gilded, lace-like filigree earring in her hand. Beppe extends his hand to Giuliana, and the women board the boat. The boatman salutes me, and I watch the elaborate gondola disappear.

As soon as the lady's boat rounds the corner, I clamber into Trevisan's gondola and snatch up the folded piece of paper. I sit on the aft deck and unfold it, my heart pounding. A short message is scrawled in a long, elegant script:

Would you be willing to do a side job for me? If so, meet me on the street that runs alongside the vineyard at San Francesco when darkness falls tonight — GZ

Chapter 26

I double-check the security of the boathouse's lock as the sun sinks and lavender shadows extend across the alley that borders Trevisan's house. I jog all the way to the boardinghouse. In my room, I wash my face in a bowl of water and shave my cheeks with my straight razor. With a small pair of scissors I purchased at the market, I carefully trim my cropped beard and clip two stray hairs sticking out of my nose. Holding a broken piece of mirror that the last tenant left in the room, I examine my reflection. I run the comb through my hair and vigorously rub my teeth with a cloth.

Above all, I want to ensure that I don't look like an ass again, but my clothing choices are limited. I slide the flesh-colored silk shirt over my back, then pull on a pair of breeches and black stockings. I take the fancy waistcoat that Signora Baldi's daughter lent me and push my arms into it. I shine my scuffed shoes with a rag I've taken from the boat slip. I have even borrowed a small container of black gondola varnish, which I coat on the uppers of my shoes. Not bad, I think, as a sheen begins to appear across the toes.

In the square outside the boardinghouse, I rinse my mouth with water from a fountain, gargle it deeply in the back of my throat, then spit on the cobblestones. I smooth my hair again with wet hands, then replace my cap. I make my way toward the northern lagoon long before the *marangona* is likely to clang, hailing the arrival of dusk. Tonight there will be no moon. As darkness falls, the sky and the canal waters seem to meld together to form an ominous void. The only light comes from quivering candles in the glass lamps hung from an occasional corner shrine. I step carefully down the narrow paths toward the Church of San Francesco della Vigna.

I make my way alongside a long brick wall that marks the enclosure to the monastery where Franciscan brothers cultivate rows of manicured grape vines. I reach the alley where Giuliana has instructed me to wait. It is important to seem relaxed, I tell myself. I take a few deep breaths, shake out my hands, then roll my shoulders and try to look nonchalant, but I can't keep my feet from pacing back and forth on the cobblestones. My eyes scan the street. It is deserted, lit only with the dim flame of a lantern at the corner. The rest of the street is cast into complete darkness. I wait. The minutes elapse.

Just about the time the black fingers of despair begin to touch my heart, I detect footsteps in the distance. They grow louder, clomping on the stones. Finally, in the darkness, my eyes make out the silhouette of a hooded figure with a full-length cloak. The person is carrying a small hand-lantern that flickers as the figure moves forward. I hope with all my might that it is she. I move from the shadows into the middle of the street.

"Boatman? Is that you?" she calls out in a loud whisper.

"Yes, Signorina."

She quickens her footsteps. She holds up her lantern, and I make out the trace of her lips and chin under her cloak. With her other hand, she pushes back its hood. In the candlelight, I see her hair fall across her shoulders, and I make myself believe that I can smell its musky scent. She presses a package—something wrapped in dark fabric—under the crook of her elbow.

"Thank you for meeting me here," she whispers. "I'm sorry about the location, but there is an important task that I cannot be seen completing myself. I am prepared to pay you handsomely in exchange for complete secrecy. No one can know about it. I had a feeling that you might be the right man for the job. Can I trust you?" She searches my face.

"My lady, I give you my word."

"Good," she says, but continues to scan my face for confirmation. "I need for you to go to the Ca' Leoncino on the Grand Canal on Thursday evening at nightfall. There will be another private party. You need to make yourself invisible, disguised, just as you were when I last saw you there. You must appear as a member of the same class, as much a part of the crowd as anyone else in attendance. No one should think otherwise. Understood?"

I nod.

"You will need to locate a man—Jacobino Catarin. You will not miss him, for he will be the only Jew in attendance."

My mind is racing. "Of course. Signorina Zanchi, with all due respect, I do not think I can take Trevisan's boat. My master... if he finds it missing..."

"Not to worry," she replies, raising her palm. "You will need to go by foot and enter from the land-side. I've already taken care of your costume." She hands me the package from under her arm. From its softness, I can tell that it is a bundle of clothing, tied together with a narrow cord. Under the cord, she has secured a parchment envelope thickly stuffed with some kind of document.

"Your job is to ensure that this envelope passes into the hands of Catarin the Jew. You must make absolutely sure that you do not attract notice."

I nod again.

"You must give him time to read it and respond to you. When we meet again you will report to me every single detail. Understand?"

"Yes, but I am curious about one thing, Signorina. Why all the secrecy for a young woman like yourself?"

Nearby, footsteps echo on the cobblestones. Giuliana flips the hood of her cloak back up on her head. "Not now," she whispers. Beneath her hood, only her lips are visible. "We cannot meet here again. This is not a good location," the lips say.

I perceive a shadow, fleeting but a certain presence, around the corner. Someone is there, invisible in the darkness. The sound of the footsteps slows.

Giuliana turns her head toward the direction of the sound, then whispers quickly to me, "On Saturday evening, meet me inside the Church of San Giovanni Battista in Brágora. My family has a private chapel on the south flank of the church. Meet me there when the *marangona* clangs. And I will give you further instructions." She lifts her hood slightly and I watch her eyes search my face. "Understood?"

I bow toward her. "Of course."

"Then it's all settled." With a purposeful exhale, she extinguishes the flame in her lantern and hurries off down the alley. I watch her cloak flap and then vanish into the shadows.

THIS TIME, MY COSTUME fits. Without a doubt, this is the finest ensemble I have ever worn. The breeches and vest are made of a fine burgundy satin, and the cream-colored silk sleeves billow from where they are stitched to the shoulder with ribbon. I like the hat best of all, for it is ornamented with a small spray of reddish-brown bird feathers. She has even included a mask in the package, an unadorned black face-plate with the eyes cut out, which surely will help conceal my identity.

I pry open the parchment envelope that Giuliana put in my hands. Although I learned to read some Latin and Venetian as a child, I am unskilled and unpracticed. I run my finger slowly down the piece of the parchment and struggle to make out the words:

Twelve pewter platters with matching goblets
Four silver saltcellars, very finely wrought
An unusual set of silver, two-pronged forks (possibly from Turkey?)
A worn-out but serviceable bedside table made of elm and poplar

A large, finely made majolica platter from Umbria
25 miscellaneous pieces of kitchen crockery
A fine mirror from Murano with a small crack at the bottom
An exceptional marble-top table decorated with intarsia and decorative scrolls
A painting of the Madonna and the Christ Child, of artistic interest, to be valued separately from its frame (see next entry)
A very fine frame crafted of mahogany with gilded decoration
A pair of antique door knockers in the form of griffons
A box full of old keys, a few of them well-wrought
A very fine ball gown of dark blue taffeta with gold sleeves
20 assorted ball gowns, no longer in fashion but serviceable
A set of gold goblets with the family coat of arms
A gold crucifix attached to a rosary with enameled and glass beads
A set of two dozen kitchen towels
Two andirons, crafted of brass, in the form of snarling lions
Four X-shaped folding chairs of walnut, of Spanish origin

The list continues, the cramped ink covering the four folios front and back. Alongside each entry, someone—Giuliana, probably—has noted an approximate corresponding value. The total must amount to an astounding number. I compare the handwriting to the note Giuliana dropped into Trevisan's gondola. Although the text of the inventory has been purposefully condensed to maximize space on the expensive parchment sheet, the looping, elegant script is a match.

Guilt washes over me for reviewing this litany of luxuries. Surely it is intended to be private, but how can I help myself?

In the broken mirror that sits on my dressing table, I catch sight of my ridiculous appearance: a fine nobleman perched on the edge of a grubby boardinghouse bed, desperately peering into the private life of a woman of whom he knows nothing.

Chapter 27

I suck salty oil off my fingertips, careful not to drip any on my costume.

The banquet table is laden with Our Most Serene City's coveted delicacies—salted eels; black olives marinated in oregano; cured ham; fresh, jiggling oysters; hard-boiled quails' eggs veined with purple, just the perfect size for popping into your mouth. I watch a party guest engrossed in pulling the spine-like legs off a crayfish one by one, then pinching off the tails and the heads with their rotating eyes on stems, between his thumb and forefinger. Finally, he macerates their flesh between his teeth. I try to fathom how one host could afford to feed so many with such extravagance of fine tableware, cloth, food, and drink.

A pile of sardines marinated in onions fills my plate, a modest but no less delicious feast. One by one, I pick up each tiny fish by the tail, and pop it in my mouth. I crunch the fine bones, savoring the sweet yet salty taste. I survey the hundreds of party guests, looking for the man who must be Jacobino Catarin the Jew. I position myself so that I can observe the comings and goings of the partygoers from a spot that affords a view to the top of the grand staircase, the food buffet, and the vast ballroom where most of the finely dressed guests have already assembled. I watch as a servant with a wrinkled brow and beady eyes clears serving platters and returns to the kitchen to refill them.

I pop another tiny fish into my mouth. So far, I have not caught sight of the man Giuliana described. I scan the room for someone wearing the kind of red hat that Jews are required by law to wear in order to identify themselves, but I do not see one. I wonder why there is a Jew out at this hour at all and can only guess that his status must be special enough to allow him dispensation from the curfew that requires Jews to be in their homes inside the ghetto after nightfall. I imagine their dark eyes peering out from behind iron gates in their neighborhood in Cannaregio, not far from where I was born.

A handsome couple arrives at the top of the stairs to greet guests, and I take them for the party hosts. The lady is remarkably elegant, her graying hair swept away from her face and studded with gems. Her gown falls to the floor in layers of beige and cream satin. She encircles her arm through the crook of her husband's elbow. There is something familiar about the man: his sumptuous robe, his aquiline nose, the protruding abdomen—all signs of a successful, perhaps insatiable man. In spite of his cynical expression, the man emanates the kind of charm that can only be achieved by years of practice in high social circles.

The couple leaves the staircase to weave their way through the crowd. Party guests turn to greet them; many stop their conversations to nod or bow slightly. After a while, the woman moves off by herself, continuing conversations with her guests as she moves toward the banquet table. As she moves closer to where I stand, I see that beyond her superficial beauty the woman's face looks hardened—jaded, you might say—with a lined brow and deep-set eyes. Her husband feigns intense interest in a conversation with four or five other important-looking men. I notice that the man's eyes wander to the stairway, and though he continues his conversation with the men before him, his attention clearly is caught by something else. I follow the man's gaze to the stair. A fair-haired girl ascends to the top of the landing, a young beauty with dimpled cheeks, wide eyes, and a freckled décolleté.

The man excuses himself and, with a smoldering look in his eye, makes his way to the stair where he catches the eye of the girl. She gives him a knowing smile, and moves to allow him into her circle. The others in the group bow curtly to the man and turn their attention to him. The party guests continue to circulate, but the man does not let the blonde girl wander too far out of his range. He tracks her with a piercing gaze, and I think of a hawk ready to sink its talons into its prey.

It is only then that I see Jacobino's red hat. The man—the only Jew at the party, as Giuliana said—is standing just beyond the party hosts at a window overlooking the canal. I move toward him, glancing around to make sure no one is watching me. As I approach, I make eye contact with him, holding Giuliana's parchment envelope in front of my chest. I see the man's thick eyebrows lift for a fleeting second, almost imperceptibly. Then he too seems to scan the room to make sure no one is looking. I pass by him slowly and put the envelope in his hands, then stroll back toward the buffet table. I refill my plate, then find a quiet window ledge overlooking the canal. I savor a wedge of grainy, hard cheese so delicious I feel I might faint.

I wait. My eyes scan the ceiling, which has been painted to resemble a pastel sky dotted with billowing clouds. Baby angels peer down at me from the heavens, their mischievous grins flickering in the candlelight from a dozen blown-glass chandeliers. The walls, too, are covered from floor to ceiling with tapestries, crackled mirrors, and paintings, more densely adorned than even Trevisan's own painting studio. I spot the host standing before a massive painting of a nude man who has shot a stag with a bow and arrow. A dozen partygoers crowd around him, hanging on every word as he describes the meaning of some of the details in the picture.

Out of the corner of my eye, I see the Jew slip Giuliana's envelope inside his waistcoat and make his way to the buffet table. I approach the table as the hostess tells two female guests, "My husband says that boatmen represent the single greatest threat to peace and order in Our Great Republic. He tells me that every day the Council receives news of an infraction. Just today they reviewed a case involving gondoliers who were paid off to smuggle flour from the Republic's grain storage onto merchant ships in the lagoon—imagine!" Her guests shake their heads, and a stout lady clucks her tongue in disapproval.

The Jew and I make brief eye contact. We both begin to fill our plates as we move around the table, inching closer to one another. Finally we stand side by side, and I watch the man maneuver a set of silver tongs to place langoustines on his plate. At the same time, he leans so close that our shoulders are touching. I feel his breath at my ear: "Tell your lady that it will be my pleasure to consider her proposal. I will convey further instructions to her home by private messenger."

MASTER TREVISAN IS GOING away for several days. The artist tells me that he's going to visit one of the farms he inherited on the mainland, not far from the city of Padova. It's an annual trip, he says, to meet with his cousin and complete an accounting of the year's crop yields.

"You should take advantage of the situation," the artist tells me, "and take a few days for yourself. I don't often take time away from my studio, but it is long overdue. Besides, one of my clients has asked me to hunt ducks in the lagoon, and it's been years since I've shot a crossbow. With all the commissions I have right now, Heaven knows when it will happen again."

"If it please you, Master Trevisan, I would spend the time working on the old gondola," I tell him. "I want to procure the supplies
to restore the foredeck, as it's rotted in several places. As soon as
that part is complete, then I can begin sanding the rest of the boat
down to bare wood."

Trevisan considers my face, then smirks and shakes his head.
"In that case, let me give you some money to buy what you need,"
he says. "I admire your determination." He deposits several coins
in my hand.

"You might find what you're looking for at the brush and broom
market in Dorsoduro," Trevisan tells me. "That's where my father's
squeriariol used to go. There are excellent brush vendors there."

I already know where to go, of course. I just have to make sure
I choose a merchant who doesn't already know me. I find a grubby
burlap sack lying in a heap in the corner of the boathouse, which I
judge fit for carrying the supplies I need. Then, I clear off a simple
wooden table, which I began to set up as a makeshift workbench.
There, I judge, I may organize my materials, work on small-scale
wooden parts, and mix varnish.

Truthfully, all I want to do is work with my hands. I am filled
with nervous energy. I am to meet Giuliana in the evening and
report to her the events of the party at the Ca' Leoncino. I must
keep myself occupied, or the hours will pass too idly. I spend the
morning sanding the hull of the boat. While I work, my heart flutters every now and then, thinking of my meeting with Giuliana.
What is she doing? Why did she give the Jew that inventory? I don't
know, but I will get a chance to see her, to stand close to her. That's
all that matters.

My workspace is organized and I have salvaged what materials
I can. I have stripped the upholstery and the splintered wood. I
have stacked the wood by species: birch, oak, walnut, maple. I have
begun scraping the hull of the old gondola with a metal chisel,
plying away years of canal grime that has formed a crystalized black

crust on the wood. In small patches, the grain of the original wood is beginning to reveal itself, but it is going to take many days of scraping until the boat is clear of its old varnish.

As the layers of grime fall from the boat, I can finally examine the structural membranes. The ribs of the hull are in fine shape, but I feel I should reinforce them anyway. I have spent many hours fashioning *cugni*, small pieces of wood sawed into brackets, wedged under the oak planks that run along the topsides of the boat. My father introduced this simple yet ingenious solution into the Vianello boatyard, and these small wedges will afford the old boat greater structural integrity. My grandfather would have approved of such an improvement, I am certain of it.

The top deck of the prow is probably constructed of lime-wood, I think, though I won't know for sure until I finish stripping the varnish. They used it during my grandfather's day because it was easy to carve and work. However, it is less water-resistant than the larch panels my own father prefers. The lime-wood deck has not stood the test of time; it is soft in some spots and rotten in others. It will need to be replaced. It must be strong because it helps support the metal fork on the prow. For as long as I can remember, in our Vianello workshop my father divided up the work between two apprentices. One was the "prow man," the other the "aft man," and each was fully responsible for the work on his own end of the boat. This time, I am on my own. I judge that I have enough oak to shore up the areas where the *fórcole* are to be placed. It is important for these areas of the hull to be stabilized, as they need to be able to withstand the force of constant rowing. I will need to figure out how to get other pieces of wood I will need.

In the back of my mind, images of Giuliana drift in and out of focus, and I can't help but dream of what lies ahead in the evening. The hours pass, and I absorb myself in working on the Vianello boat. I am lost so completely in sanding it that I have nearly lost all track of time, so much so that I am startled by a voice at the entrance to the boathouse.

"Eh, *figliolo*, what do we have here?"

I turn to see a man standing at the pedestrian entrance to the boathouse. Immediately, I recognize the charismatic smile.

Alvise.

I DROP MY SANDPAPER and dust my hands on my breeches so that I can give my old friend from Giorgio's *traghetto* a proper handshake and a slap on the back.

"Looks like you're practically part of the paint here!" Alvise whistles and runs his hand down the hull of the old boat. "What a beauty."

I give Alvise a tour of the gondola, explaining my plans for the restoration piece by piece. While Alvise shares a few choice stories of Giorgio and the boatmen at the ferry station, I clean up my mess and brush sawdust into the canal with a long-handled broom. He colors his stories with his own exploits, mostly those involving women.

"And you?" asks Alvise. "You got a lady yet?"

"Not me," I reply too quickly and sweep the stones with great intensity. Alvise shakes his head in disapproval.

"You're working too hard, that's why, *casso*!" he chides, wiping a playful slap across my head. "A fine young man like yourself needs to be out on the town, not holed up here in a stinking boathouse! Come on, your master's away anyhow. Put down that damn broom and come with me. I'll take you to one of my favorite *osterie* for a meal. I guarantee you'll forget that boat of yours."

I grin. "Now that you mention it, I am hungry."

"Then what are we waiting for?"

The boathouse gate closes with a clang, and we wend our way down the residential alleys surrounding Trevisan's house. All the way to Rialto, Alvise regales me with stories of his exploits, and I realize that I haven't laughed like this in a long time. Alvise maneuvers through a tangle of dark alleys, seeming to know where to go by instinct.

In the tavern, the barmaid, orange-colored makeup smeared on her cheeks and her breasts pushed high with complicated corseting, listens to our order while she flits her eyelashes at Alvise. I ask for a plate of polenta with sausage of pork gut and a tankard of watery brew. The beer arrives, and I savor the warm, foamy liquid. While we wait for our food, Alvise continues his tales from the ferry station.

"And of course you haven't heard the best: one of the guys caught Giorgio in the passenger compartment of one of the gondolas with a manservant from the household of Signor Battistini the banker."

I spit my brew in a loud spray, wipe my mouth with my sleeve, and look at Alvise with my eyes wide.

Alvise cackles, slapping his knee and dabbing the table with a cloth napkin. "Don't worry, *figliolo*, he got out of it. You know that boatmen are sworn to secrecy about what happens behind the curtains of the *felso*. It was Giorgio's word against that of the gondolier who caught them, and no one produced any proof. You better believe that Giorgio and the servant lied their way from here to The World to Come." The barmaid brings our dinner. Alvise sits before a bowl piled high with steaming tripe and begins voraciously chewing the honeycomb-like wall of the cow's stomach.

Alvise recognizes a couple of other patrons in the tavern, boatmen from other *traghetti*, he tells me. There are also several women in the tavern, and they all seem to know Alvise. Alvise points out several girls to me and shares bits of information about each one. "If you're looking for a good prospect for later this evening, try the girl sitting with the man at that table," Alvise gestures by flicking his eyeballs to the right. "I think you could persuade her to leave her friend behind," he snickers. "And don't even think of wasting your time with the daughter of the tavern owner. It's not worth it, believe me." Alvise waves his hand. He grasps my sleeve and leans toward me. "Someone got a disease from her," he whispers behind a raised hand, pointing to a young woman with a nice face walking across the tavern. "I would stay away from that one." She looks perfectly harmless to me, but Alvise's face registers disgust.

About the time we finish our meal, a group of musicians enters the tavern and sets up in the back. "The party's finally getting started," says Alvise, saluting a man carrying a small lute. Alvise signals the barmaid for another round of beer. The room is already beginning to waver, but I drain my tankard anyway and wait for my refill. The warmth of the brew flows through my veins, and I feel more relaxed than I have in months. The music begins.

Alvise rises from the table and crosses the room to where the barmaid is standing, stacking glasses on a tray. He encircles his arm about her waist, and she lets out a squeal. Then he whisks her to the floor and spins her around. She feigns a protest, then throws her head back and laughs as he dips her low then runs his nose down her neck, inhaling deeply. The two dance as a group of patrons makes a circle around them and claps. Alvise and the barmaid entwine their hands high in the air, dancing together as if they've done it many times before. Alvise is in his element; I watch them from the table, enjoying the show and my watery beer.

The song ends, and the sound of the strings fades. Then, blended with the dying melody, I register the sound of bells. It takes me a moment to recognize the ringing somewhere in the distance. My heart stops momentarily, and my eyes widen.

Giuliana.

How could I have lost track of time? How could the hours have slipped by so quickly?

I leap from my seat, nearly overturning the table.

"I have to go," I report breathlessly to Alvise.

I dash out the door of the tavern before Alvise can protest.

Chapter 28

I sprint as fast as my legs will carry me.

I curse myself for not allowing the time to stop by the boardinghouse first, at least to change my clothes. I am still dressed in the same clothes I've worn while working on the boat all day, for God's sake, covered in sawdust and dirt. I glance down at my hands. They are a mess, dirt caked under the nails and smudged across my palms. I am sure that I stink of beer, too. In fact, my head feels fuzzy. What was I thinking? I let Alvise distract me into a night of taverning rather than paying attention to the task ahead. I curse myself again. It's not Alvise's fault. I allowed myself to be distracted with the idea of approaching one of the girls in the tavern. I have no one to blame but myself.

I feel an intense urge to urinate, but I can't afford to stop. By the time I arrive in the piazza before the Church of San Giovanni Battista in Brágora, I am sweaty, breathless, and I'm sure I must reek of beer. I stop for a moment to catch my breath, but still walk at a steady clip toward the portal of the church where am supposed to meet Giuliana. I picture her waiting in a church pew by herself. Will she be furious with me? Will she be there at all? It is dangerous for a woman to be out walking alone in the city in the dark, and I think that the information she wants from me must be important for her to take such a risk.

In the dark stillness of the piazza, I make out the church façade, an ominous silhouette against the night sky. I push the heavy door open with my palms. As my eyes adjust to the darkness, I spot a flickering flame in a side chapel. I tiptoe, yet each step echoes off the cold stones. As I approach the chapel, I make out a cloaked figure seated in the second pew. She turns as my footsteps approach.

"Signorina Zanchi?" I whisper.

"*Si*," she replies, and pushes the hood of her cloak away from her face. I feel my heart leap.

"Please, signorina, forgive me. I had an errand for Master Trevisan that ran late," I lie. "I am sorry for the delay." I sit on the narrow bench beside her.

"I was beginning to wonder if I was wrong to trust you." She raises her chin, but she is almost smiling, as if taunting me. "But that's no matter. Please, tell me, were you able to accomplish your task?"

I recount to Giuliana exactly what I did at the party, how I located the Jew and handed off her envelope. She listens intently and at certain points in my story, she stops me to ask for more detail. When I describe the man with the silk robes and the blonde girl, Giuliana poises herself on the edge of the pew, her skirts rustling as they spread across her lap. Her dog hops out of her lap onto the pew next to me, and pushes his tiny nose into my hand. I feel warm puffs of air in my palm as the dog inhales the scent of beer and stew on my hand. I stroke a soft ear, and he gazes up at my face with eyes like tiny, black glass beads. Giuliana leans over, resting her elbows on her knees, then wearily rubs her forehead with the heels of her hands. It strikes me as out of character for this noble lady, but at the same time a strangely authentic view, far from her usual façade of complete self-control.

"Signorina Giuliana, are you alright?" I reach out to touch her arm, and the tiny dog dances back across the pew to his mistress.

She lifts her chest and takes a deep breath, re-gathering her wits. The façade is back. "Of course," she says and meets my gaze with a self-confident stare.

"Signorina, who is this Jewish man? Why the secrecy?"

"He's a well-respected broker of second-hand goods, mostly those that come from patrician households," she says. "But that's none of your concern. You have told me what I needed to know, and you have delivered my envelope as instructed. Thank you for your service," she continues.

She fishes in her velvet purse and produces a handful of coins. She drops them into my hand one by one.

"Now," she says, "if you are willing, I have another job for you."

"Of course, signorina." My heart pounds.

"Do you know the jewelry vendors near the Pescheria?" she asks.

"Yes—well, no, not personally." I reply. "But I'm familiar with the neighborhood."

"Good. I would like to see how much you can get for this," she says dryly. From her purse, she pulls a long gold link chain with a red garnet stone that reflects the candlelight as it swings before my eyes. "You must try to get the maximum price for it that you can, paid in cash. I will give you ten percent of the price you are able to negotiate. However, you must not—under any circumstances—reveal who owns this necklace or how it came to pass through your hands. Of course I cannot afford to appear in a pawn-broker's shop myself."

I hesitate. "Of course."

"You might start with the jeweler called Balbi; he buys pieces like this. Just remember: he cannot know where you got it." She reaches to hand over the necklace. "I don't care what kind of story you have to invent—you don't know me. Let's plan to meet here again one week from tonight at the same time."

I act impulsively. As Giuliana lets the chain pool down into my palm, I seize her hand with my own. Surprised, she searches my face. I pull her hand toward me.

"Signorina Zanchi, have you ever seen the beach at the Lido?" I whisper.

"Well, yes, of course," she laughs nervously. "Who hasn't?"

"But have you ever seen the inlet on the south shore where the sea glass, the discarded pieces from Murano, collect in the sand when the tide falls?"

Giuliana looks puzzled. "Well, no..." she trails off.

"Then go with me there—tomorrow? I want to show you something you won't forget." The beer has emboldened me.

Giuliana's eyes widen, but she maintains her composure. For a few moments, she is silent, as if thinking of her reply. I imagine that I can feel her pulse in my hand.

"Not tomorrow," she says finally, matter-of-factly, pulling her hand away from me. "But I'll consider it for another time," she says, "if you are able to arrange a profitable sale of this necklace for me." She raises her chin again and gives me a slight smile.

"At your service, madam." I bow my head in an exaggerated fashion, thinking that Alvise has exerted a bad influence on me. "Consider it done."

She lifts her little dog under his chest and settles him carefully in her bag. His crooked ears tremble slightly, and he peers out at me with his glass-bead eyes. She rises and walks toward the church portal.

From the pew, I address her a little too loudly. "Sigorina Giuliana?" She stops and turns. "Has your father already betrothed you to someone?"

Although she doesn't slow her pace, as Giuliana turns her head I perceive a smirk—whether pleased, amused, annoyed, I cannot tell.

Her loud whisper echoes through the church. "My father is dead."

Then she disappears into the night.

Chapter 29

Valentin perches on the foredeck with his knees wide apart to help stabilize the painting propped in the gently rocking boat. The picture reaches from one side of the gondola to the other, an enormous rectangle packaged in blue wrapping paper that had required both Valentin and myself to transfer carefully out of the artist's studio. Trevisan has returned from his excursion to the mainland, and I have resumed my primary role as the painter's *gondolier de xasada*.

"It's not my favorite subject; nonetheless I am satisfied with the way the pigments helped render the drapery," Trevisan tells Valentin.

"One of your better works, Master," says Valentin. "I have no doubt that Father Dante will be more than satisfied with the result."

Trevisan nods, tight-lipped. "I trust that you are right, as he has offered a bonus for the completion of the picture by the feast of Sant'Agata so that it may be installed in the confraternity chapel in time for the feast day liturgies. With the number of preparatory pen drawings he required, I had my doubts that we would finish in time, but here we are."

I steer the boat out of the choppy wake in the Grand Canal caused by the passing of a cargo barge. As I weave the gondola into a narrow waterway with my master and his journeyman, I marvel at my good fortune. Somehow over the last months, I have managed to forge a new life for myself. Sometimes I must pinch myself to make sure I am not dreaming. I have a roof over my head—

nothing fancy, of course, but it's better than sleeping on the street. I have secure employment as a private gondolier, a position that few men of my limited age and credentials could manage. I have the opportunity to work with my hands, which, I have come to realize, is as vital to me as eating or breathing air. And working on the old Vianello boat has become cathartic. With each scrape of sandpaper, I transform myself into my own man, with a purpose and a plan, a new and better version of my old self. Most of all, I have the attention of Giuliana Zanchi. I need to ensure that it stays that way.

In the months I have spent at the ferry station and in Master Trevisan's studio, it's as if I have forgotten my former life as a gondola maker. It feels as if it happened to someone else a long time ago. My mother's death, the fire in the *squero*—it all seems like a nightmare, as if it never really happened but is only a horrible dream that I conjured in the dark corners of my mind. With each passing day, a little piece of myself transforms into Luca Fabris, and I grow into the role—more self-assured, less of a fraud. With each passing day, Luca Vianello burns down to smoldering embers, a dim flicker in my memory and imagination.

Alongside other private boatmen, I wait for my master at the docksides of palaces, markets, churches, and civic buildings. Against a backdrop of the great façade of some elegant palace, we boatmen tie our gondolas together, and I listen to their stories. Their tales range from the outlandish to the banal: complaints about their masters, exaggerations of sexual exploits, boasts about their moonlighting jobs. Of course, I am not naive enough to believe that these men do not take advantage of their masters, but I am astonished at the audacity of some of them, both in what they steal and in that they openly brag about it with their colleagues. One man proudly opened the aft deck of his boat to show me some expensive-looking jewelry he had taken from his master's house. Another reported that he had stolen a stack of silk garments from his master's chests and exchanged it with a black-market merchant at Rialto. I wonder how anyone could get away with such an offense. The answer is that they cannot, not for very long, as the faces on the boats change and change again. The turnover of private boatmen seems as high as the temptations that lure them to cheat their masters.

Most of the interchanges among us stick to ordinary topics. From one man, I learn how to recognize cloud formations that are sure predictions of fog. From another, I learn how to discern exactly how much time will pass before rain spills from a thunderhead, a tip that I find especially useful in judging how much time I have to get back to Trevisan's boat slip before the raindrops fall. From another gondolier, I hear about the fluctuating prices of flour. From still another, I hear more than I want to know about the anatomy of a particular shoemaker's wife in Dorsoduro.

Day by day I become more adept at using the sign language that allows our silent communication from boat to boat. It is even more complex than I had realized when I worked at Giorgio's *traghetto*. Now, using only my hands, I can indicate that I am taking a shortcut to the Grand Canal; that I will only be docked for a minute; that I am passing on the port side instead of the starboard; that I can accept or decline an invitation to the tavern for a midday meal; that I can thank another boatman who has signaled to me that my rowing technique looks especially impressive. I am astonished that these boatmen consider me one of them. I have entered a private world without even asking. No one questions me. I move freely among the pageantry of Our Most Serene City, weaving in and out like a thread in the great fabric of Venetian life.

Following the relentless rhythm of the artist's engagements, I wait for my master at the docksides of the city's most elegant palaces. These noble citizens occupy a different world far from the one we boatmen inhabit, from their embroidered sleeves to their roasted pheasants, their particular manner of speaking, their hours of leisure time, their preoccupation with ostentatious displays. Tucked away as I was in my father's boatyard my entire life, I had only viewed this world of Venetian nobility from the fringes. Now, I am immersed.

Giuliana is one of them, of course. She travels our city in the finest clothes, transported in a finely wrought gondola powered by two men. She has never had to labor to live, never had to power a boat in the rain, varnish wood, or use her hands to fashion nails. She and I could not be further apart in life if we occupied different continents and spoke different languages. And yet, there is something between us. At least I think so. Does she feel it, too—a magnetic pull, a spark of light, a leap of the heart?

At night, I stretch across my narrow, flea-infested mattress stuffed with matted hay and stare at a long crack in the stucco ceiling. My imagination transports me from this stark, monkish cell to a fine gondola overlooking a rose garden with a view of the sea. I close my eyes, and in my mind's eye I imagine holding her face in my hands, smelling the musk of her hair, running my fingertips over the fine hairs at the back of her neck.

In the light of dawn, I face the stark reality that she is simply paying me to do a job. It is only natural. People like her must pay boatmen to take care of undesirable tasks all the time. I hardly care about the money, which in any case will go toward defraying the cost of restoring the old boat.

All that matters is finding an excuse to be with her.

VALENTIN SEEMS IN AN uncharacteristically cheerful mood. He greets me with a silent smile as he boards the gondola, and the two of us head toward the brush market, to which Trevisan has dispatched his journeyman to pick up supplies.

"What are we going to the market for today, Signor Valentin?" I ask, not expecting much of a reply. I begin rowing swiftly. The sun creates long streaks across the sky.

With a dramatic gesture, Valentin produces the artist's supply list from his breast pocket. Scanning the list, he begins to hum a tune. I recognize the melody from a popular song that is performed in the city squares every year at Easter. It is a happy, lilting strain, and I am surprised to hear that Valentin has a knack for carrying a tune. I smile and adjust my rowing to match the beat of the melody.

Valentin begins singing Trevisan's list to the tune of the song: "My master wants purified linseed oil, four mink brushes, a large container of lead white and a smaller one of black ink." He begins slapping his knees to the beat, hums an interlude, then continues: "My master will have nothing less than a bag of nails, walnut oil, four rolls of canvas, the beautiful and coveted lapis lazuli, and powdered cinnabar!" At "powdered cinnabar," Valentin spreads his arms wide and belts it like a professional singer, then collapses onto the seat, giggling. I crook the oar under my arm and applaud.

Since I rescued the boy from the drunk who pursued him at the Giudecca, Valentin has opened up to me, or at least shows some level of trust.

"Powdered cinnabar? What's that for?" I inquire.

Valentin has finished his tune and now moves to sit cross-legged on the aft deck next to me. "Master has begun mixing it with *cristallo*—but don't tell anyone; it's a secret."

"What for?" I ask.

"It creates a shade of vermillion that is so lifelike and rich for replicating costume and drapery that our clients are stunned when they see the results. Word has already begun to spread about the 'red' from Master Trevisan's studio. Master has decided to rework the Leda and the Swan he's doing for the Greek ambassador to incorporate the color into the drapery."

Trevisan has already informed me that we are to stop by a grimy neighborhood near the Pescheria on our way back to the studio to pick up a woman who is to be a model for the new picture. "Trevisan is paying the woman what she must consider a small fortune to sit nude for him," Valentin tells me. "He persuaded her after tracking her in the market. Master Trevisan judges that she has just the right combination of innocence and maturity: wide hips and a pink flush in her cheeks. Any other minor defects, like scarring from childbirth, will be easily perfected with paint." It is more information than I have ever plied from Trevisan's journeyman, perhaps more than I care to know.

Valentin is still thinking about grinding paint pigments. "Trevisan has me busy experimenting with grinding other combinations of pigments with quartzite from Ticino and shards of Murano glass," he tells me.

"Lucky that Master Trevisan found you, then, especially since he has no sons of his own."

"Yes," Valentin ponders my analysis, his index finger pressed to his chin. "It's rare for a painter to achieve the level of success that Trevisan has without a handful of sons. It's not that he wouldn't like to have children," he says. "It's just that I don't think he wants a wife. See you in a bit." Valentin exits the boat at the edge of the market. He salutes me before darting into a thick crowd, narrowly missing a careening man staggering under the weight of a cart laden with cabbages.

I moor the boat to a lilting post near the docks. I recognize the market as the place where two of the city's best pigments-sellers operate their shops, providing painters, glass painters and enamellers with colors and supplies. I have heard that a number of pawnbrokers and jewelers cluster in the streets nearby. I exit the boat, then wend my way through a maze of narrow streets, looking back to make sure Valentin is nowhere in sight.

For the hundredth time during the day, I pat the outside of my jacket pocket just to make sure Giuliana's necklace is still there. So far, I think, my first official side job as a gondolier has not gone well. Two days before, I entered a jeweler's shop near the Pescheria, my heart pounding, and sheepishly asked the goldsmith if he would be willing to purchase the gold and garnet necklace I produced from my pocket.

"I know your kind," the slight man growled. "You domestic servants go around ripping off your masters, thinking you can make easy money by hawking some family heirloom. Well, I won't sully the quality of my stock with a stolen necklace."

Today, I find, is no different. Even though I gain confidence and refine my story each time I pull the necklace from my pocket, I am met with much the same reaction from the next jeweler's shop, and the next—and the next. Even if they are not as forthright as the first jeweler I encountered, I quickly read suspicion in their faces, in their body language. I find no luck even with the pawnbroker. No one is willing to take the risk of taking stolen goods into their inventory. It isn't worth their while.

Finally, I realize that I need to get back to the gondola before Valentin does, and I make my way to the docks. If I am going to sell Giuliana Zanchi's necklace, I think to myself, I am going to need the help of the one person who knows how to pull off a side job better than any other gondolier in Venice. I sigh, realizing that a certain level of teasing is going to be the price I must pay to get the necklace sold. I am going to have to put the necklace in Alvise's hands.

Chapter 30

The sharp, familiar smell of varnish remover stings my nostrils.

The vapors are beginning to make me feel nauseated, so I cork the glass bottle and walk to the canal-side door of the boathouse, where I can catch a breath of fresh air as well as a good view of the progress on the boat.

Now, with the bare planks beginning to reveal themselves from under layers of varnish, I admire the different types of wood my grandfather used to construct this gondola. The fore and aft decks are fashioned of mahogany and cedar, beautifully grained woods that also give off distinctive scents. I recognize cherry and walnut used for the *trasti*, the crosswise pieces of wood that stabilize the prow and stern as well as the wide span across the middle.

Originally, I realize, this boat was designed for a heavy-set rower. The stern has been raised higher than usual, a technique that my father and grandfather used to counterbalance a boat for a stouter gondolier. I am lean and not too tall; I will have to re-warp the boards that hug the prow so that the bow will rise off the water more prominently. That will take some time and a significant amount of labor with water and fire.

I consider the narrow planks of the aft deck, where the gondolier stands while rowing. In my grandfather's day, boat makers left this part of the boat relatively unelaborated. Now, I consider adding *soralai*, the two wedge-like footrests that can be adjusted to give the rower more leverage as he presses his heels into them, and which have become more common over the course of my father's and my generations. I will need to experiment with the pitch of the wedge to find what angle will give me the most efficiency in rowing. Idly, I polish the brass decoration on the prow with a paste mixed from corn flour and muriatic acid. Salt water has caused the brass to corrode to a not-unpleasant green color. I whistle a tune as I remove the corrosion, remembering how my father had ordered me countless times to make up this paste in the boatyard.

The sun begins to sink, and I tidy up the boathouse. Humming, I go through the now-rote motions of locking down Trevisan's working gondola for the evening. The *felze* is already stored, as I had asked Valentin to help me lift it from the boat when we returned from an errand earlier in the day. The contraption is not too heavy, just awkward, and Valentin took several sidelong steps trying to manage it. The two of us rested the *felze* on a pair of trestles in the boathouse. The winter *felze* is heavier than the summer one, though, its velvet curtains lined with damask. I press my weight into the oarlock—the most expensive accessory on Trevisan's boat—lift it out of its socket, and lock it up for safekeeping in a special compartment in the wall of the boathouse made especially for this purpose. I dust the inside of the gondola now, beating the upholstered seats with a clean rag.

As the sun sets, I lift the two lanterns sitting on the stone floor of the boathouse and extinguish their flames. As I lock the gates of the boathouse behind me, I realize why I am in such a happy state.

I am going to see Giuliana.

I ATTEMPT TO LOOK self-assured as I lean against the rough stone edge of a wellhead, but I cannot help myself; my foot taps nervously on the cobblestones. The ancient stone basin stands in the center of a small, deserted square near the larger one in front of San Giovanni Battista in Brágora. I feel the coolness emanating from the water and inhale the dank odor of the moss-covered stone. I imagine that countless women over the years have dipped their buckets into the fresh underground water, which flows from the source beneath. From this vantage point, I can make out a sliver of the brick church façade, just enough to keep an eye on its doors. I take in the trefoil silhouette of the church, its hulking yet elegant presence dominating the square. This time, I am early.

The streets are quiet, all except for a loudly chirping cricket, its shrill call echoing across the stones. While I wait, I review my plan. No matter what, I will convince Giuliana to come with me to the beach at the Lido. I don't know how I will take her there, though. I contemplate taking Trevisan's boat. No, I think to myself. It is too risky. If the artist finds his boat and his gondolier missing, I will be out on the street. The old Vianello boat is not yet seaworthy. For now, the only viable option I can contemplate is asking Alvise to lend me a boat from Giorgio's *traghetto*. I sigh, thinking that Giorgio's fleet must have returned to its squalid condition already since I was the only one who kept the boats clean and in good repair. I wonder if I can trust my friend Alvise with the revelation that I am interested in a girl, then shake my head thinking of the jeering and teasing that would prompt. No. There must be some other way.

At the sound of bells, I enter the church. It is cavernous, dark, cool, and overwhelmingly silent. Rows of candles cast flickering shadows. I walk as quietly as I can toward the south side of the church, but the shuffling sound of my feet echoes across the vast interior space. I locate the private chapel where we met the last time. Inside, a row of candles stands lit below a giant, time-darkened painting of a saint I do not recognize. I seat myself on a bench before the altar and wait.

After a few moments I hear the sound of a creaking door. All I can see is a cloaked figure, but I recognize her immediately for

I have memorized her walk, her frame. My stomach turns as she approaches the chapel. Saluting me with a faint wave, she tiptoes toward me, looking back twice to make sure no one is following. She pulls her full-length cloak tightly around her, her hood drawn over her head. I stand up straight.

"*Bonasera,* Signorina Giuliana," I say softly, trying to look casual and self-confident.

"*Bonasera,*" she replies, pushing her hood off of her head. My heart skips a beat. We squeeze into a narrow pew.

When Giuliana sits, her cloak falls open to reveal a satin gown the color of emeralds that rustles as she settles. Her little dog shudders out of the folds of her sleeve onto the wooden bench, shaking his body vigorously. He approaches me with his tail tucked, sniffs my fingers, then rolls onto his back and raises his tiny paws in the air. His beady black eyes search my face. I place my palm on his little chest and jiggle him gently. His lips flap back, and his tiny fangs appear in an amusing canine smile. Giuliana laughs. "He likes you! I can't believe it. He doesn't let anybody do that."

I smile. The dog quickly tires of me and leaps back into the satin pleats of his mistress's skirts. He flattens his ears and yawns.

"I was able to sell your necklace, signorina." I produce a handful of coins from my coat pocket with my left hand, and place them in her palm.

A surprised expression crosses her face. "Very good!" she says, counting the money. She consciously replaces her cool exterior. "Thank you for your service. Let me pay you your ten percent, as agreed." She counts out the coins and plunks them back into my hand. I feel the heft of the metal and slip my fee into my pocket.

I know that my commission for selling Giuliana's necklace will not stay in my hands for long, for I will need to pay Alvise for the service of hawking the necklace on my behalf. In turn, Alvise will pay a share to the prostitute whose skills far surpassed my own in convincing a certain jewelry dealer to buy the necklace. It makes sense, of course, for the jewelry brokers are already accustomed to buying baubles from prostitutes, who regularly receive gifts of jewelry from their customers and exchange them for cash. In the end, I was only able to shake my head in amazement at the amount of money Alvise's lady-friend was able to fetch. By the time I pay off my helpers, though, I will earn almost nothing from this transaction. I do not share any of this information with Giuliana. The money is the least of my concern.

"Was there something else you wanted me to do for you, Signorina?" I ask.

Without a word, Giuliana holds up her hand, and as the sleeve of her cloak falls back, I notice a shimmering bracelet studded with blue gems encircling her wrist. Giuliana fumbles to unfasten the latch of the bracelet with her free hand. After a few unsuccessful attempts, she says, "Could you help me please?"

Normally, I would never have the nerve to offer to help with such an operation. I reach for her wrist with one hand and work the latch clumsily with the other. In the darkness, she turns her palm upward, very close to my face so that I can see in the dimness. My heart begins to pound as I inhale her flowery scent. Finally, the bracelet comes loose, and she cups it in her hand, then hands it to me. I slip the bracelet into my pocket alongside my payment for the necklace. "I would like to sell this one too. I'm sure you'll be able to take care of it for me, won't you?"

"Of course," I say.

I summon my nerve. "Signorina, I'm very sorry if I offended you the last time we met. I did not know that you lost your father."

Giuliana continues to raise her chin in an aloof expression, no doubt practiced over years, but I notice that her bottom lip trembles slightly. "Thank you. It's all right; you didn't know. It happened only last month; it was very unexpected."

"How did it happen?"

She takes a deep breath. "We were sitting at the dinner table as usual—my mother, my brother and I. My father was laughing at something that my brother had said. Then, all of a sudden, he clutched at his chest and fell face-first into a plate of steaming rice. In a single instant—imagine—he passed from this world to the World to Come."

We sit in silence for a few moments. I contemplate this information. "And your brother..."

"Pietro."

"Is he taking over your father's position?"

"No, not exactly. Sadly, my father left no position for Pietro to take. After he died, we received the news that my father's bank had failed. It was a great shock, especially for my mother. She is still having trouble accepting it," she says. "I was very close with my father, so I had a feeling that something was wrong; but we had no idea of the magnitude of his debt. Once my mother learned of our situation, she was quick to agree for Pietro to be apprenticed to a silk importer in San Marco. He is twelve, just the right age. He is leaving for Flanders in a week's time."

"Hmm." I nod. "How will your mother be cared for?"

Giuliana sighs. "I feel pity for her." She shakes her head. "In one instant she went from being the wife of one of the city's richest bankers to having to sell her palace and all of its contents, just to repay her husband's debts. At first she couldn't imagine not living in our home. Now she is beginning to realize that if she doesn't sell it, there will be little left over for us to live. We must let go of our servants, all of our earthly belongings. Everything in our house will be put up for sale—even two of our gondolas."

She stares into the flickering light of the candles burning at the altar. Now I understand the reason for the inventory she had me place in the hands of the Jewish second-hand dealer. "Ah. The party..." I say.

"Yes," she says. "My mother would never agree to negotiate with a Jew, but I know that Signor Catarin will bring us a higher price than our family's notary will be able to realize. Besides, it has been painful enough for my mother to endure the public spectacle of my father's bank failure, his sudden death, and the loss of our family fortune. The last thing she needs is to endure a sale in the public square, with an auctioneer hawking some precious family heirloom from a pedestal. She has already been humiliated enough."

I nod, imagining people in the crowd shoving their way forward to consume such finery with their eyes if not their purses. "Catarin the Jew will arrange for the sale instead."

"Yes," she says. "We will visit our cousins in Vicenza while the Jews empty our house; it will protect my mother's emotions. They will take the goods to their warehouse in Cannaregio for safekeeping until the sale is complete. They will make personal visits to antiques dealers and the costume rental houses to broker the most valuable pieces. What's left—the bed linens, out-of-style frocks, and kitchen utensils—will be hawked from the back of an oxcart in the village squares of terra firma." She waves her hand in the direction of the mainland.

"Where will you and your mother live?" I ask.

She continues to stare into the candlelight. "For my mother, I suppose matters are simple. She will take her vows and enter the Convent of Santa Maria della Celestia. She has supported the sisters and has been a member of their lay confraternity for years. Surely my father had known about all this for some time, only he didn't tell us. He probably was working on a plan to get us out of debt. I'm sure he did not want to worry my mother."

She falls silent.

"He was very dear to you, wasn't he?" I prod.

She meets my gaze. "My father was everything to me."

"I know what you mean. I lost my mother recently, too. It is a great void."

She ponders my face. "I'm sorry," she whispers.

"Signorina Giuliana, what about you?" I say. I perch myself on the edge of the pew and lean toward her. Beneath the tie of her cloak at her throat, I watch her chest move up and down. I look directly into her eyes, and she meets my gaze. I corral all my inner strength.

Suddenly, we are interrupted by a loud "Psssttt!" Startled, we both look up to see Giuliana's maid peeking her head through the door of the church. I had no idea that she was waiting outside, and I now realize that she was stationed there to keep watch for Giuliana.

"Mistress!" the maid whispers loudly. "Please, my lady, someone is coming. Quickly!" She makes a frantic summoning gesture with her hand.

"*Santo Cielo*," Giuliana whispers.

She gives me a quick, wide-eyed look, then cradles her dog in her arm and jumps up from her perch on the pew. She scampers back to the door on tiptoe, her cloak flapping. Quickly, she flips her hood over her head.

It is only then that I realize I do not know when or how I will see her again. I cannot ask now. I can only watch her go.

Chapter 31

For several days, something has been nagging me. As I go about my daily chores, it is there, bothering me, filling my conscience. Finally, I realize what it is. I have no idea how I will come up with the money to finish restoring the gondola. In particular, I don't know how I will find the funds to purchase the new *felze* and the oarlocks that would be necessary to finish the boat.

If anyone knows the costs of these items, it is I. How many times have I heard my father—and my father's patrons, too—complain about the high cost of the fittings of these boats? They are among the most expensive parts of a gondola, which is why the truly rich spare no expense in their ostentatious displays. I count my meager boatman's salary, stashed away in the back of the boathouse. Even though I spend nothing, even though I've saved every *soldo* I have earned, at this rate it would take me years, maybe even decades, to earn enough to fit the boat with the proper *felze*, oarlocks, and other fittings. And I'm not even making anything on my side job since I turn over everything Giuliana pays me to Alvise.

I cannot bring myself to ask Trevisan for the money. It seems too much to ask of the man, who has already been overly generous with me, providing a roof over my head, food to eat, and the opportunity to get close to Giuliana Zanchi.

I run one hand along the back of the dusty *felze* that I removed from the old boat. It sits on trestles in the shadows of the boathouse. I allow myself to dream for a moment. If money were no object, I know exactly what I would do. My father worked with a *felze* maker in Dorsoduro, a man who still took the time to double-stuff the cushions and line the upholstery with silk. In reality, there is no reason to have a brand new wooden frame for the *felze* made, I think, when the old one could be salvaged. I have succeeded in stripping down the old frame to bare wood now, and I run my hands over the walnut, sanded smooth. Hands on my hips, I circle the contraption, which I have laid on the floor of the boathouse to consider. I admire the curve of the seat, which looks old-fashioned now after so many years. It is still beautiful. This *felze* frame will not be painted, gilded, or even carved. It will be stained simply, to reveal the beauty of the wood.

Although I would have liked to find a more sumptuous fabric, I decide that even something more modest could still provide privacy and protect the rider from getting soaked in the rain or burned by the sun. I make a note to ask the costume-renter's daughter for a suggestion.

Now there is the matter of the oarlocks. The front oarlock is simple yet serviceable; it will have to do. The rear oarlock, however, is missing and will need to be replaced. The problem is that I know every *remero* in the city, and more importantly, they know me. Somehow, I must commission one of these pieces without the *remero* knowing that it is the son of Domenico Vianello—now masquerading as a *gondolier de xasada* for the artist Trevisan—who is doing the commissioning. I sigh and shake my head, realizing how complicated my circle of lies has become.

Suddenly, out of the blue, the answer hits me. Even though I have never done such a thing, there is a first time for everything.

I will make the oarlock myself.

ONE OF TREVISAN'S APPRENTICES—the young boy every-
one calls Biondino—is leaving the artist's studio for good. The artist
seems visibly shaken by it, though I cannot divine the exact circumstances of his departure. The boy's parents come for him in a modest
water-seller's boat, which they dock outside the artist's studio. From
the boathouse, I catch snippets of their impassioned argument—
something about money, pre-arrangements, family promises.
Whatever the circumstances of Biondino's dismissal, it is a lucky
turn of events for me, as it opens a room inside the artist's house.

"It's not much too look at," Trevisan apologizes, "but it's clean
and dry, and you won't be out of pocket like you are now at the
boardinghouse." I thank my master vigorously, genuinely grateful for the man's generosity. Signora Amalia shows me to a small
garret tucked under the roof of the artist's tall house. No matter
how modest the space, I am thrilled with it. I happily gather my
few worldly belongings into a satchel and leave Signora Bondini's
boardinghouse for good.

The room forms little more than a compartment tucked under
one side of the sloping roof, accessed by a steep, narrow stairway
that climbs three stories from the kitchen. Each step is worn and
sagging in the middle, the result of decades of use. I must duck my
head to avoid hitting the top of the doorframe. A single window
allows light into the room, with a view to a tall, funnel-shaped
chimney from another house across a constricted canal, and the sky
above. A narrow iron bed is wedged under the sloping roof, and I
find the mattress to be softer than the one at the boardinghouse,
with a layer of goose feathers tucked over the straw. There is also
a small writing desk with a simple wooden chair and an elaborate
pewter candlestick holder. A small drawer holds a fresh supply of
butter-colored candles. A threadbare but once-fine woolen rug,
the kind I have seen the Eastern merchants selling in the markets,
covers the floor. One of the walls is made of brick, and I judge that

it is the flue of the kitchen hearth since it warms the room with a comfortable, dry heat.

Shelves line one wall, filled floor to ceiling with books. I have never owned a book. I approach the collection with trepidation and respect, running my fingers across the old-fashioned, faded handwritten script scrawled across their spines. Ghost-like goatskin bindings show the pores of the animals sacrificed for these massive books. At night, seated at the small desk in the candlelight, I turn each page in fascination. Most of them appear to be religious books—breviaries, prayer books, enormous monastic manuscripts with marbleized end papers and gilded-stamped words on their leather bindings. I examine the minutely gilded scrolls and swags that decorate the initial letters, as well as the richly colored pictures of noble people with their blue, green, gold, and red robes, crowns, and turbans. I make out many Latin words, but some of the books are written in Eastern languages that I cannot begin to interpret—perhaps Greek or Arabic, but I do not know. I run my fingers along the strange letters, imagining what they might impart if only I could unlock their meaning.

Like the rest of Trevisan's house, the remaining walls of my new room are covered from floor to ceiling with paintings. The ones in this room hardly compare to the giant, epic stories in the paintings on the main level of the house, but I find them fascinating anyway. There are several old portraits of patrician men and women, their somber expressions gazing out of their frames. From a tiny jewel-like Byzantine icon, Our Lady stares out at me with an impenetrable gaze. One painting of horses seems so old, so dark, that I can only make out the subject by standing very close and tracing the equine forms with my finger. I examine the paintings by candlelight, watching the colors emerge and the varnish shimmer as I raise my small flame.

One painting continues to draw my attention. It shows a nude woman reclining on a bed piled high with crimson-colored bedding and lace-trimmed cloth. She seems nearly asleep or perhaps drunk, her head lolling on her arm, her eyes half-closed. I move the writing desk with the candle so that it sits beneath this small rectangular frame. Now I can lie on my soft mattress and trace the voluptuous S-curve of her waist and hips with my eyes, spotlighted with a flame in a room otherwise cast into darkness.

The room has one window, and I open it and push my body through it. I discover that I can climb out to a cramped space on the rooftop of Trevisan's house, wedged between the windows, the tall stovepipes, and the metal gutters that dump rain into the canal below. I shove my hands inside the pockets of my woolen coat to ward off the cold air. With my left hand, I finger the slip of parchment that Giuliana dropped into my boat weeks ago. The paper has remained in my pocket ever since she gave it to me. Sometimes I pull it out and examine her handwriting, running my fingers over the words scrawled in a fussy, feminine script.

I hoist myself higher up on the roof tiles so that I can see over the peak of the roof. I suck in my breath at the awe-inspiring vista over the rooftops to the Grand Canal. I feel as if I could take in the entirety of my native city in a single vision, almost as if seeing all of its bridges, domes, bell towers, and squares from the perspective of a bird soaring high above it. The city spreads out like a vast panorama, shimmering on the surface of the water like a mirage. In the distance, I can make out the tower of Madonna dell'Orto in my old neighborhood. In my mind's eye, I see my sister stoking the fire in our kitchen hearth, my baby brother in the cradle. I imagine my father and my brother Daniele rebuilding the *squero* over the months since the fire. I wonder if they are making new boats, if they speak of me, if they think of me at all.

Chapter 32

I emerge from the narrow staircase into Trevisan's kitchen to see Signora Amalia wielding a long, skinny loaf of bread like a mallet. "I swear this is the last time I buy bread from that accursed baker in San Marco." She wags the loaf at me as if I too am implicated, then, noticing my hands raised above my head in easy capitulation, she softens.

"Luca, dear one, would you kindly go and fetch some fresh bread for Master Trevisan? If I must stop what I'm doing, I'll never get the pear pie finished in time for dessert!" She presses several coins into my hand, then, with a glance toward the artist's studio, she whispers, "The artist likes his bread crusty on the outside and soft on the inside. If he doesn't get it, he'll be cross for the rest of the evening." She shakes her head and gestures toward the hearth. "I can't leave my stew and my pie." I notice the flour-covered worktable with a rolling pin and half-rolled pie dough. Signora Amalia walks over to stir a large pot that hangs from a chain over the fire, with a delicious aroma emanating from it. "Try Baker Salvini, by San Lorenzo."

My mouth waters, and I smile. "I'll be right back." At the stairwell, I press my hat on my head and jog down the old stone stairs to the boat slip.

I steer Trevisan's gondola from the boathouse into the canal, whistling as I go, my mind anticipating the taste and texture of Signora Amalia's delicious mutton stew. I row to the market where she said the bakery stood. There I find the baker about to close his shop for the day. I pay for a long loaf, squeezing it to make sure it is still soft on the inside but crackles pleasingly on the outside. I emerge from the shop and stop to watch a hawk circling in the air above.

"Hello, there, Trevisan's boatman," a voice says at my ear. Startled, I turn to see a girl standing awkwardly close to me. Her face is familiar. All at once I realize that it is Patrizia, the daughter of Signora Baldi, the costume renter.

"Hello yourself," I say, trying to appear composed.

"Imagine... running into you here by chance. Are you fetching dinner?" she smiles and twirls a lock of hair, cocking her head to the side.

"Yes, among other things," I say. "I was just finishing up."

"A lovely coincidence," she replies. "So was I. I was on my way home. Say, could you give me a ride in your boat?"

I hesitate, thinking that Signora Amalia and Master Trevisan are waiting for me, but, unable to think of an excuse, I reply, "Well, yes, I suppose so."

"Excellent. You never know what a girl may encounter on the evening streets by herself. Safer to be in a boat any day."

"Of course," I say and am surprised when Patrizia loops her hand through my arm and walks in step with me to the place where I have moored Trevisan's boat. With one foot in Trevisan's gondola and one on the quay, I offer my hand to help her into the boat. I open the curtains of the passenger compartment and realize that I have left some of the supplies I was using to clean the boat on the seat.

"I'm sorry, signorina, I left this here by mistake. Allow me to move it out of your way."

She laughs. "Please, I'm not a noblewoman. I've ridden in boats much less accommodating than this one. I do not need to ride in here by myself. All the better, why don't you stay here with me?"

With both hands, Patrizia grabs the collar of my shirt and sinks down on the seat. With all her might, she pulls me down with her. Reeling, I extend my hand and clutch the back of the seat just in time to prevent myself from keeling headlong into the bottom of the gondola. I sit down hard on the seat next to Patrizia, and she tightens her grip on my collar, pulling my face toward hers.

Shocked, I pull my head back, but she persists until I sink back into the seat. I feel completely disoriented, rocking from side to side in the boat with my entire being consumed by the warm taste of this girl's mouth. For a moment, I let myself succumb, then find a way to turn my head to the side and utter, "My goodness, you work quickly."

She smiles, and, still gripping my collar in her fists, she says, "The moment you appeared in the shop, I knew you were the one. Ever since you came to choose the new upholstery for your boat last week, I've been looking for the right moment." She looks at me slyly.

"You mean you've been following me?" I ask incredulously.

"As much as it's possible for a girl without a boat to track a man like yourself," she says. "My mother is trying her best to match me with the son of one of her wealthy patrons. But who wants to be cooped up in a big house with a needle and thread? I'm better suited for someone who can take me places." She laughs and finally lets go of my collar, only to press her torso against me and push my shoulders back against the seat with her hands.

I gather my wits and manage to sit up straight in the seat. I clasp my hand over hers. "Signorina," I say. "I'm very tempted, believe me. But at this moment my master is sitting at his dinner table, waiting for me to arrive with this bread." I gesture to the loaf that now lies toppled over in the bottom of the boat.

She laughs again, then tugs at the leather laces of my vest, making them fall open. "We'll just have to be quick, then," she breathes.

I look earnestly into her face. "If I'm not back in five minutes, Master Trevisan will have my head for dinner instead."

My face must look grim, or at least sincere, for she loosens her grip on my laces and screws up her face in a dramatic pout. The dejected look on the girl's face fills my heart with remorse.

"There will be another time for this—um, for us. Just not now." I make a feeble attempt to reconcile the awkward situation. "Let me take you home, and we'll figure out a time to see each other again. Agreed?"

She begins to cry. Great tears roll down her cheeks, and she muffles a loud sob with the back of her hand.

"No, no, no!" I wave my hand and wish with all my might that the girl would stop crying. How did this happen? I think, my mind racing. I was just on my way to fetch bread, for God's sake. I pull a cloth from my pocket and hand it to her. "Let me take you home," I say.

She sniffs and lifts her head, then assumes an angry face. "Never mind," she spits. "I should have known better than to trust you. I'll get home myself." She shoots out of the seat and climbs out of the gondola, bundling her skirts around her legs as she steps up onto the quay. Then, wiping her nose on her sleeve, she jogs down the alley and out of sight.

Stunned, I huff myself back down on the seat of the passenger compartment. I look down and rearrange my disheveled shirt, then my hair. I pick up the loaf of bread from the bottom of the boat. I emerge from behind the curtain flush-faced and begin rowing as quickly as possible back to Trevisan's house. I tie up the gondola at the dockside, then run up the stairs to the kitchen, where Signora Amalia shoots me an angry glance.

"Where have you been?" she whispers loudly. "He's already on his second course!" She snatches the loaf from my hand. Through a crack in the door, I glimpse flickering candlelight inside Trevisan's dining room, and I hear the clinking of a spoon against a bowl of Signora Amalia's mutton stew.

"Here we are, Master Trevisan!" Signora Amalia pushes the door open with her toe and waltzes into the dining room. "Finally, some fresh bread, crusty on the outside and soft on the inside, just as you like it, sir." Through the open door, I catch sight of the artist's broad shoulders hunched over his bowl, and a large pewter goblet. Several candles pushed into a silver candelabrum illuminate the room with a warm glow, casting shadows onto the fresco paintings that adorn the ceiling and every inch of the walls. The artist dines alone, his whole attention focused on savoring the flavors of his housekeeper's labors in the kitchen.

I exhale and shuffle up the narrow staircase to my room. Ducking under the too-short doorframe, I remove my hat and let my body flop carelessly onto the narrow bed. I turn onto my side, and my eyes fall on the picture of the nude woman, the one I stare at every evening in the candlelight. I heave a heavy sigh and rub my eyes with the forefinger and thumb of my left hand, trying to push the image from my mind. The salty, earthy taste of the costume renter's daughter's mouth lingers on my tongue.

It's not that I did not find myself tempted by the costume renter's daughter, I think. It's only that she caught me completely by surprise, and I realize now how stupid I must have been not to recognize the signs she has communicated to me silently in her shop—the turn of a chin, the twirl of a lock of hair. Now I understand how far away my mind has been. It remains consumed with fantasies of Giuliana Zanchi, a woman who is so far beyond my reach that I must be out of my mind to entertain these illusions. Darkness enshrouds the room and I turn restlessly on my bed.

Finally, I fall into a fitful slumber, my mind flickering with images of Giuliana Zanchi in my boat.

Chapter 33

I am examining the walnut block I plan to use for the new oarlock when I hear the door leading from the boathouse to the kitchen open. Signora Amalia squats down on the landing so that she can address me without walking down the stairs.

"Boatman," she says. "Master Trevisan would like to see you."

"Yes, Signora Amalia. I'll be right there."

I brush the dust from my breeches and do my best to smooth my vest, which is wrinkled and frayed at the shoulders. Ever since the thwarted encounter with the costume renter's daughter in Trevisan's boat, I notice that the quality of my rented costumes has suffered. I lift my hat and smooth my hair, then climb the stairs to the house. My heart begins to pound.

I pass through the kitchen where a wonderful aroma fills the air. Signora Amalia is preparing *nervetti*, pulling boiling calf nerves from a large steel pot then chopping them roughly with a large knife on the wooden block. The translucent organs jiggle as Signora Amalia hacks through them with a sharp blade.

I walk into the artist's studio, but the room stands dark and empty. Beyond the easels, I see flickering candlelight coming from the artist's personal chambers. I approach the threshold and glimpse an enormous, carved wooden bed, which is strewn haphazardly with red silk, a mound of lace ruffles, blue brocade, and emerald satin. The bed stands chest-high off the floor, perched on a carved platform as if it were a throne and reached by a small, wooden stair. Ruby-colored velvet drapes hang from an iron frame around the bed, and a sheer net, normally pulled shut during mosquito season, is tied off to the side by an ornately carved and gilded hook. The air is heavy with the stale aromas of candle wax, paints, varnishes, and sweat.

Finally I notice Trevisan seated in an overstuffed chair, wiggling his bare toes before a roaring fire in the hearth. He holds a stack of what appear to be party invitations and other documents in his lap.

I remove my hat and hold it in my hands. "Signora Amalia said you wanted to see me, Master Trevisan?"

The artist gestures. "Yes, Luca, please come in." I search the artist's face, trying to divine what lies in store for me.

"I am impressed with the progress you've made on that boat," Trevisan begins, then chuckles. "As you know, it's been neglected for a long time, and I would have never believed that that it could be fixed at all."

I breathe a sigh of relief. "Thank you, Master Trevisan."

"The old fittings will not do," he says. "They've seen better days."

"With all due respect, Master Trevisan, I believe I can restore the wooden frame for the *felze*, and the one remaining oarlock. The aft oarlock, of course, will need to be replaced."

The artist lifts his eyebrows. "Very well, then. I wanted to make sure you understand that I will pay for whatever materials you need to do the job."

My jaw drops. I can hardly believe the words coming out of the artist's mouth.

"You know, as a boy I spent many hours in that gondola. My father had me delivered to my arithmetic and Latin tutor six days out of seven in that old boat. Signor Palermo... he was tough, a former cleric." The artist seems lost in the past. "I remember well being ferried to my lessons. In those days, my father kept the gondola in perfect condition, bedecked with a blue silk *felso* and brocade curtains. He was very proud of that boat."

"What happened to it?" I ask.

The artist shifts in his chair. "We had a boatman; I don't recall his name. Even though I was just a boy, I knew there was something rotten about that man. There was something evil behind his smile. One day my father—who was a renowned painter of altar panels in this very studio, you may know—accused his boatman of stealing money that was stored in a drawer in the painting studio. The boatman denied it, naturally, but my father released him from his service. That night, under cover of dark, the man stripped the gondola of its *felso* and oarlocks. But he didn't stop there. He crashed the boat into a stone quayside, leaving a large hole in the bottom of the hull." Trevisan heaves up from his chair and replaces a candle that has burned down to a stub inside an ornate candleholder. He uses another lit candle to ignite the wick.

"The boatman then filled the bottom of the hull with rocks. Surely he meant for the boat to sink. I'll never forget my father's reaction," the artist shakes his head. "I never saw him as angry as he was that day. We managed to save the boat from sinking, but unfortunately it has never been restored. It has lain upside down on trestles—just as you found it—ever since then, more than fifty years now. In some ways I think justice is finally being served. You—my own boatman, repairing the damage caused by my father's rotten one. I only wish my father could see the old boat restored to its original beauty." The artist shakes his head and clucks to himself.

"Master Trevisan, I don't know how to thank you for your generosity," I muster.

"Actually, it gives me pleasure to think about getting that old gondola out into the canal again."

The artist continues. "Not only that but I want to encourage your efforts, as I have a deep respect for good craftsmanship. And you, my dear Luca, are a fine craftsman."

A BOATMAN I HAVE never seen before slows his gondola before Trevisan's mooring. I think nothing of it, since a steady stream of messengers arrives at the artist's land-side and canal-side doors each day. Instead of heading toward the studio door, however, the boatman approaches the door to the boathouse.

"Are you the artist's *gondoliere*?" A young man with a neatly cropped beard and an intelligent face addresses me.

"Yes," I reply, surprised. I wipe my brow with my forearm and rise from where I squat, experimenting with folds in the fabric for the new *felze*.

"I have a message for you," the man says, and he hands me a diminutive parchment envelope.

I take the envelope from the man's hand, thinking there must be some mistake. But there it is: "*Gondolier de xasada*, Casa di Trevisan," scrawled in brown ink across the front of the envelope in an elegant, feminine script. My heart skips a beat.

"Thank you," I say distractedly.

"*Bon lavoro*," the boatman says in a businesslike manner, then plies his strength into his oar and drifts down the canal.

I tear open the envelope and unfold the familiar-looking piece of parchment:

Signor Fabris, if it please you, meet me at the usual place and time this Saturday. Please destroy this note. —GZ

Ignoring her instructions to destroy the note, I instead place it carefully back in the envelope and slip it into my breast pocket.

I APPLY ALL MY force to the sandpaper. The boat is nearly bare, revealing the beautiful grains of various woods my grandfather used to craft it: amber-colored cherry, veined oak, and dark brown walnut planks. I slide my hands slowly down the length of the boat and re-sand a few spots that still feel rough under my fingertips. Black sawdust drifts and collects across my shoes and in the crevices between the cobblestones. The sandpaper swishes beneath my fingers, and I watch the tarnished paint turn to dust.

I return to the prow, where there is one circle of black left on the boat. All that remains of the old boat's original varnish is the mark of the Squero Vianello. The maple-leaf emblem is covered with the shiny, fissured black varnish that once coated the entire gondola. I run my fingertips over the maple leaf. The finish has darkened it into a pleasingly crackled patina that reveals the veins of the rounded leaves.

I cannot find it within myself to sand it away.

Chapter 34

Anyone who happened to pass by the southern chapel inside the dark Church of San Giovanni Battista in Brágora might have perceived a still figure kneeling at one of the benches, deep in prayer, but I know better.

She is waiting for me.

Completely cloaked, her hood covers her face as she kneels, her hands clasped at her chin. I slip into the wooden pew. Her dog shudders and thumps his stumpy tail on the seat, flattening his ears. The dog's trembling catches her attention, and she turns toward me.

"*Bonasera*, signorina," I whisper, kneeling beside her.

"*Salve*," she replies.

"I'm sorry to interrupt your prayers," I remark with a straight face.

She snickers. Briefly, I catch sight of her straight teeth beneath the hood. Making her laugh causes my heart to swell. I smile, too. Overhead, the flutter of pigeon's wings startles us, and we watch a downy feather drift to the large stones on the floor of the church.

"I wasn't praying," she says. "I was wondering about those people at the bottom of that painting." She gestures to a large painting, one of several hanging in the chapel. It shows the Madonna with the Christ Child on her lap surrounded by an assembly of saints. In the bottom corner are three people painted in miniature, kneeling in prayer. "I suppose they must be long-forgotten ancestors of mine. They must have paid a painter to include them praying in perpetuity at the feet of the Virgin."

I nod.

"I wonder what they would think of the great Zanchi family now," she says. We sit together in the stillness of the church, and Giuliana seems lost in her thoughts.

"I sold the bracelet as you asked me, signorina," I say finally, breaking the silence.

"Very good," she says, pushing back her hood. She counts the coins I transfer to her, shifting them from one hand to the other. "Thank you." Then, without a word, she reaches into a small velvet bag in her lap. She pulls out another bracelet, this time with amber-colored gems, and places it in my palm. I turn the bracelet over between my fingers, watching the orange stones shimmer in the candlelight. She remains silent.

I summon my nerve. "Signorina, if you don't mind my asking, why are you doing this?"

She meets my gaze for a moment, then looks at the floor. "It's a complicated story," she says, then falls silent. I nod. My mind searches for a way to keep the conversation going.

"I mean, under the circumstances that you shared with me, I can understand that you wish to raise some money. But why would you not use your family's own gondola, and your own boatman— Giacomo... Beppe?" I pause. "Why me?"

She looks at me cautiously, as if trying to decide how much to reveal. "I am trying to organize a few things for myself." She hesitates. "It has to do with my future. Our junior boatman has already been placed with another family. Beppe and our other servants are loyal to my parents—my mother, I mean—and I cannot risk that one of them will say something to her. Heaven knows Beppe is incapable of keeping a secret. My mother cannot know about this. She is trying to make... other arrangements for me."

"Would she have you betrothed?" I push, then hold my breath as I wait for her response.

"Oh yes," she replies quickly. "It's either I marry or take my vows—as soon as possible. The way my mother sees it, we must pull together enough money to dower me properly or to make a donation suitable to place me in a convent where I will ply my labors for the glory of God." She lifts her palms up subconsciously as if in supplication to the heavens.

"Really? You–in a convent?"

She sighs, then nods. "Why do you look so surprised? What other choice do I have? I was born to a patrician family. My father was a banker, but he was in debt when he died. Now, not even my brother has a chance to save our family. If instead I had been born to a candle maker, a glassblower, a wood carver, a draper, I might have had a path, a chance to work in my father's trade. After all, my father always told me that I was the one with the head for numbers, not my brother Pietro, bless him. But have you ever heard of a daughter taking over her father's position as a banker?" She reads my face. "I thought not."

"And has your mother found you a husband?"

"Actually, I was already betrothed before my father died. As soon as my intended learned that my dowry had been depleted... Well, we haven't seen him since."

"I'm sorry," I manage to say.

She shrugs. "Under the circumstances, I believe my mother will wish for me to join her at Santa Maria della Celestia."

We sit in heavy silence for a few moments.

"What do you want?"

She looks at me squarely in the face now as if surprised that it would occur to anyone to ask that question. Her pale green eyes register concern.

"What do I want?" She hesitates, then takes a deep breath. "I want, well, something other than what my family seems to have planned for me." She laughs nervously then hesitates again, as if framing this thought for the first time. "I do not wish to waste my days with a needle and thread, the wife of an old man with more important things to do." She seems to grow bolder. "I want my own house, my own family. My own boat. It doesn't have to be extravagant. No, not at all. I want..."

"...to be free from what your family expects of you? To make your own way in the world? Not to follow someone else's destiny but to find your own—for yourself?"

Startled, she searches my eyes. "Exactly."

I nod. There is a long pause. "I know what you mean."

Now I understand what selling the jewelry is about, but I still do not understand one thing. "Signorina, what does this have to do with your portrait, the one that Master Trevisan is painting?"

Her smile disappears and she falls silent again. I feel a tingle run up my spine until the hairs on the back of my neck prickle. She produces a cloth bag, heavy with the coins she has counted as my commission, and places it in my hands.

"You ask a lot of questions."

THERE IS THE MATTER of getting the refurbished gondola into the water.

I ponder the problem while I pick up the long-handled *scogolo*, a mop-like brush that I've fashioned from discarded materials in the boathouse and a bundle of sheep's wool I bought in the market. I have reworked the brush a few times, and now I feel it will be perfect for applying varnish along the curve of the gondola's hull. Now that I have stripped the boat of its original varnish, replaced the rotten and split pieces, and added a few personal touches like foot rests on the aft deck and reinforcements under the oak planks along the sides, I feel I have turned a corner. The boat—a new boat, my boat—is beginning to take shape.

My father's workshop, the way it used to be before the fire, was set up so that a gradual ramp led from the studio directly into the canal. Launching boats was as simple as sliding them until the water began to buoy their hulls and they rocked gently under your palms. Trevisan's boathouse, on the other hand, consists of only a boat slip, a sheer drop from the stone floor into the canal. While I apply the first coat of varnish, I consider how I might design a makeshift wooden track that would allow me to launch the gondola gently into the water without damaging its hull. I will need to ask Trevisan's shop assistants to help me slide the boat down the track with the help of several ropes, but I imagine that the solution will work.

The fumes of the varnish are beginning to make me feel light-headed, and I walk out to the dock in front of Trevisan's studio door for a breath of fresh air. The boat slip is not ideally ventilated for such a project, so I have set up a small table on Trevisan's dock, where I have begun to rough out the new oarlock. Now I can alternate between coating the gondola with thin layers of varnish inside the boathouse and stepping outside to work on the oarlock in the fresh air.

I run my hands along the walnut slab I discovered weeks ago in a pile of discarded lumber at the back of Trevisan's boathouse. Its weathered appearance and grainy texture drew my eye immediately. Despite my best carving efforts, however, the piece remains stubbornly block-like, impenetrable. Most oarlocks are in fact relatively straight, with curved notches only in specific places where the oars form a snug fit. The idea strikes me that if I try to elaborate these notches in larger, more curvilinear forms, it might allow the rower to achieve greater precision in handling the gondola. I don't know if my idea will work.

I turn the piece of wood over and try to visualize how such an oarlock might appear in three dimensions. I feel greater respect than ever for my dear *remero* and the skill that goes into forming the intricate nooks and crannies of the oarlocks that have evolved, over centuries, along with the rowing techniques of Venetian boatmen. Taking a deep breath, I pick up my knife and begin to pry away curls of walnut, which drift to the ground. Subconsciously, I begin to follow the curve of the long, blond veins of wood that trail along the block, as if the wood grain itself is showing me a path.

"VALENTIN, LUCA, come please!" Trevisan throws his hands up in a gesture of despair.

"Right away, Master Trevisan." Valentin crosses the studio, wiping a paintbrush with an oily rag. I follow.

Signora Amalia has summoned me from the boathouse to the artist's studio to help the artist move some paintings. "Seems that Trevisan has more work than he has had in a long time. He requires more than the two more apprentices he employs in addition to Valentin. It's a shame we lost Biondino; the timing is terrible," she had clicked her tongue.

Trevisan gives us instructions. "Give Valentin a hand with this painting, would you please, Luca? We must make choices. First, let's move this one out of the way." Valentin and I lift a canvas larger than the two of us together and transport it to a wall on the other side of the room. The painting shows a saint kneeling in a rocky wilderness, wearing only the loincloth of a beast. With a wild expression on his face, he seems to be experiencing a vision in the sky, the details of which are so far only roughly sketched.

His assistants are all listening, but Trevisan seems to mutter mostly to himself. "The priority is to meet our contractual commitments. The others can wait. I am already behind on two deadlines, and a third is looming. And now the Council has charged us with painting three large banners for the Feast of the Ascension." Trevisan sighs. "Banner painting! This type of ephemera is hardly worth our time," he booms. "But how can I say no?" Valentin nods in silent agreement. "I suppose it is the cost of success."

In a corner of the studio, another assistant is painting a land-scape in the background of a picture of an assembly of saints clus-tered around the Madonna with a chubby Christ Child on her lap. The boy furrows his brow, his tongue braced between his teeth in concentration. Impatiently, the artist grabs the easel and thrusts it aside. "This one can wait, too. Father Stefano hasn't even paid me the first deposit." The artist shakes his head in disgust. The boy jumps from his chair with a start, then slithers away and makes himself useful by rearranging pictures stacked against the wall.

Another assistant is stretching canvas in the corner of the studio over a wooden frame, nailing down the cloth to the narrow strips of wood. Valentin has told me that Trevisan borrowed this young apprentice from a painter friend, but the artist now regrets his decision as it takes so much of his time to train this boy that it is hardly worth it. Trevisan snatches the hammer from the boy's hand. "No," he instructs. "The nails must be placed more closely together; otherwise as the canvas shrinks it will come apart and the picture will be ruined. You see? This is very important."

"Yes, Master Trevisan," the boy says with an embarrassed expression.

The artist hands the hammer back to the boy and strides to the other side of the studio where I am helping Valentin wrap a large portrait of a patrician woman in blue paper. The artist delivers his finished paintings wrapped in a particular type of paper that he dispatches Valentin to purchase by the ream at the paint pigments market or the Giudecca. Trevisan has taught Valentin and the other shop apprentices a way to fold and tuck the paper around the four edges of the picture so that it makes a tight, neat package. It is important to give his clients the impression that what is wrapped inside will be more than worth the price they paid, Valentin has explained to me. I watch him carefully so that I can attempt to copy his folding technique.

"Let's get this one out of here today," the artist instructs Valentin, pointing to the picture we are wrapping. "Have Luca ferry you to the silk trader's house. You know that I always personally deliver my paintings, but I do not have the time today. Please convey my apologies to Signor Malatesta." The artist holds up his hands. "What else can I do? I'm just one person."

"Now," he says, taking a deep breath. "First things first. I must finish the portrait of Signorina Zanchi before the Councillor changes his mind about it."

Trevisan strides to the canal-side window where his tufted stool sits before his easel. With a dramatic gesture, he sweeps back the velvet drape that hangs over the portrait of Giuliana Zanchi. The back of the portrait faces the studio, and I see nothing, even though I imagine the picture in my head as I listen to my heart pound.

Trevisan picks up his palette and a fine paintbrush, and begins to paint.

Chapter 35

On the night of the Feast of San Giorgio, fat pellets of rain fall on Our Most Serene City. Cats crouch under the tiled eaves and windowsills, their ears flat. The deluge creates shimmering ponds in the Piazza San Marco, and a dozen state servants are ordered to lay down wooden planks so that the senators of Our Most Excellent Republic may cross the square to the Doge's Palace without soiling the embroidered hems of their robes.

Before putting Trevisan's one serviceable gondola to bed in the evening, I bail out the bottom of the boat with a bucket and a *sessola*, the short-handled wooden shovel that any self-respecting boatman keeps stored in his aft deck for that purpose. I change into dry clothes down to my linen under-layers. Still, by the time I sprint across the square in front of the church of San Giovanni Battista in Brágora, my waist-jacket pulled over my head, water streams from the ends of my hair and sloshes from my shoes.

"You look drowned," says Giuliana when I finally seat myself beside her in the chapel. We both laugh, and I wonder how in the world she has managed to stay dry. In the billowy skirt of her sapphire-colored dress, her lapdog has wound himself into a tight curl where he snores, his tiny wet nose emitting a buzzing noise.

Over the last weeks, my encounters with Giuliana Zanchi in her family chapel have become less about the business of transacting jewels and more about stretching time. Each time, we linger longer. I must work to invent topics of discussion, anything so that I do not have to leave her side. We have covered every aspect of Venetian weather, public events, the price of bread. As if we have all the time in the world. As if neither one of us has anywhere else to go.

Now Giuliana is recounting a story about a mouse that wreaked havoc in her kitchen that morning, scaring the cook half to death until her lapdog prompted the rodent to leap out of the kitchen window into the canal. I smile at her story, even though I am having trouble drawing my attention away from the earthy smell of Giuliana's hair.

An awkward silence falls over us, and, simultaneously, each of us seems to remember the purpose of our meeting.

Giuliana reaches into her pleated sleeve and pulls out a blood-red satin envelope tied with a twisted cord of the same color. She unravels the cord and the envelope falls open. With two fingers, she lifts a piece of lace. Before the flickering flames of the altar candles, I make out fine, web-like patterns of flowers, leaves, and swirls.

I gasp.

"Exquisite, isn't it?" she says. "It's *punto in aria*. Years ago the Spanish ambassador gave it to my grandmother. He went personally to Burano to select it from the lace makers at the convent. She was even engaged to my grandfather at the time. What a scandal!" Giuliana laughs, then her smile fades. She ties the beautiful lace fragment back into its satin package and hands it to me.

"You may entrust this transaction to me with the greatest confidence, signorina," I say.

She nods, then, without a word, Giuliana removes a ring with a large sky-blue square stone from her index finger and presses it into my left palm.

Impulsively, I grasp her hand and pull it close to my torso. Her face turns serious.

"Signorina," I say haltingly. "There is something important that I need for you to know."

She nods and waits for my response. She does not pull her hand away.

"I can imagine... You must think that I am not transferring to you all of the money that I have collected for the sale of your jewels. You have no reason to trust me; after all, boatmen take advantage of people all the time. You must think that I am pocketing some of the *soldi* before handing over the rest to you." I search her eyes to divine if I have made an accurate assessment, but her gaze remains serious and unreadable. "But I want you to know that I have not."

She looks at my face for a few moments in silence. Raindrops splash on the roof tiles of the church, beating a steady rhythm.

"I know," she says finally.

My heart pounds in my chest. "You do? How?"

She shrugs and pulls her hand away. I watch it drop back to the dog in her lap. "Just a feeling, I suppose. An intuition."

I nod, although truthfully, I can hardly believe what she is saying.

"Of course I am not naïve enough to have wondered if you might try to extort me. Also I have not given you anything that is so valuable that I could not afford to lose it, just in case you turned out not to be trustworthy after all. But at the same time somehow I knew that I could feel secure to rely on you," she ventures. "It is difficult to put my finger on it, but I feel certain that there is more to you than people see on the surface."

I squirm in my seat.

"It's just that..." She seems to read my nervousness and jumps to clarify. "Well, please don't take this as an insult, but to me, you seem out of place as a private boatman. You're not like the others. I do not know much about you, but I feel certain that you would not steal from me. You would not extort Master Trevisan. You would not do what so many domestic servants do. I have no rational reason to, but I trust you. In fact, it's as if you were meant for something else, some other kind of trade entirely."

Her eyes scan the floor for a moment, then she looks at me as if struck by a sudden realization. "Luca," she begins. "You were not really destined to be a boatman, were you?"

I take a deep breath. At that moment, I realize that I trust her, too. "No."

I haven't planned to, but I begin at the beginning of my story, all the way back to the day I was born in my family's *squero*. I tell her about the fire, about slipping from the oarmaker's workshop before dawn, about cleaning boats the *traghetto*, about making my way to Trevisan's studio.

I tell her everything.

Chapter 36

I saturate a clean rag in olive oil and, starting at the port side prow, I begin to polish the black varnish to a slick, high sheen. The *ferri* are already gleaming, thanks to my work on them over the course of the last few days. The engraved swirls and coiling metalwork of the forks are old-fashioned, of course, but bring some ornamentation to the boat without the need for carving or gilding, which might appear too ostentatious and bring Trevisan unwanted attention. The green velvet of the *felze*, which Signora Baldi the costume renter has provided and even trimmed with tassels as a personal favor for Master Trevisan, makes for a nice look, too, I think. Even though the curvilinear aft oarlock that I carved with my own hands contrasts with the simpler one at the front, now, with two oarlocks, the boat feels whole.

I am so lost in my polishing that by the time I reach the maple leaf carved on the starboard side, which I have left intact, I can hear church bells heralding the midday meal. I stand back to observe the fully oiled black craft for the first time. A smile crosses my lips.

I bring my palms together and shake them skyward, a silent, heartfelt praise to the heavens. I address myself, my quiet proclamation reverberating off the walls of Trevisan's boathouse: "*Deogràsia!*"

The boat is complete.

Chapter 37

From my position on the aft deck, I examine Master Trevisan's face. I whistle as I row the new-old gondola, carrying my happy tune all the way home from the Scuola Grande, where Trevisan has been inspecting his assistants' work.

I am looking for something, some indication of approval for my work, but my master's face remains unreadable. The new curtains of the passenger compartment are tied open, and I imagine that I see him smile. I wish desperately for my master to be pleased with the restored boat. I do not wish to be guilty of the sin of boastfulness, but Trevisan must admit that the craft is not just utilitarian but a work of great beauty. Surely the artist never imagined that his father's old gondola would be seaworthy again, much less transformed into a work of fine craftsmanship.

Whether or not I read satisfaction on my master's face, I feel nothing but pride for myself. Never have I steered a boat that felt more like it was made for me and me alone. The craft seems an extension of my own body. With the addition of footrests I've nailed to the rowing deck and the curvilinear forms of my oarlock, the boat responds instantly to even the slightest pitch of the oar.

As I row, I wonder how I am going to conjure the nerve to ask Master Trevisan this important question. I no longer whistle but row forward, lost in thought. We arrive at the artist's house, and I pull in close to the dock outside the studio door. I offer my hand to the artist, who waves it aside and alights from the boat without effort. As always, I am amazed at the energy and stamina of this man who must be nearing seventy years old. The artist starts up the stairs to his studio.

"Master Trevisan?" I finally gather the nerve to say.

The artist turns. "Yes, son?"

"I have an important indulgence to ask, sir. Now that the boat is finished... Do you think... Would it be all right..." I swallow hard. "Would it be all right with you, Magnificence, if I take it out this evening to show it to one of my colleagues back at the *traghetto* of Master Giorgio? I promise to be extremely careful with it, of course."

Trevisan chuckles. "If anyone will care for that boat, it's you. Of course you have my permission as well as my blessing."

"Thank you, sir." I bow slightly toward the artist.

"Very well. Plan to ferry me to the house of Costantini the silk merchant tomorrow afternoon. He has asked me to sketch his wife in their ballroom. You are free until then."

"Yes, of course, Master Trevisan."

"Good evening, then, son. And happy boating."

I return to the boat and carefully pull it into the boathouse using two ropes. I have grown accustomed to this maneuver and complete it effortlessly even though it might have presented even an experienced boatman with a challenge. I am especially careful to make sure the craft doesn't bump against the stones. Now, both gondolas are moored side by side in Trevisan's boat slip, and their hulking forms fill the narrow space from one side to the other. I step lightly from one boat to the other and carefully wedge floats between them to prevent the varnish from being scratched.

As evening falls, I climb the stairs to my room and wash my face in a large ceramic bowl that Signora Amalia uncovered for me in the attic. I return to the boathouse and tie down Trevisan's boat, lifting the oarlock and locking it up in its special compartment for the night.

Silently, I pull the new boat out into the canal.

All my instincts lead me to Giuliana Zanchi's house.

I ONLY REALIZE IT NOW, but for months, I have been waiting for this moment.

I sit on the aft deck of my fine new boat, letting it float freely in the Grand Canal within sight of the palace that Giuliana Zanchi calls home. In my time between Trevisan's engagements, I have altered my route to pass by the palace many times, identifying the building thanks to Beppe's description of its location. I am not certain, but I have watched the palace enough times now to surmise that the bedchambers occupy the third floor of the house, facing the canal. From my vantage point, I keep my eye on the third-floor windows, waiting for an opportunity.

The house looks different than it did the first time I glimpsed it. The building now appears nearly empty of its contents, its great windows gaping and hollow like the orifices of a giant skull. The dark, hulking boat slip was designed to house three gondolas; now it holds only one.

When the boat drifts substantially from its post, I stand and row it back to a spot where I have a clear view of the Ca' Zanchi, far enough away from the palace docks not to raise suspicion. As the sun sets beyond the domes of San Marco, candlelight begins to flicker on the canal level of the palace. I see someone—perhaps a servant—light a lantern, then I see the flame move from room to room across the *piano nobile*. I wait an hour, maybe longer. The canal waters turn slick and black, and the air turns cool. I put on a woolen overcoat that I have stored under the gondola's aft deck.

Finally, I make out the flickering of a candle in a window of the third floor. A figure appears. I stand and grasp the oar, then power the gondola silently to the quayside. I light my lantern and place it on the fore deck of the boat. I cup my hands before my mouth and whistle a long, low whistle. I wait. After a few moments, I repeat the whistle. Finally, the figure approaches the windowsill.

"Signorina Zanchi!" I whisper loudly, then stand on the fore deck and hold my lantern high. The figure leans out of the window, and with a sigh of relief, I recognize her now-familiar silhouette.

"Who's there?"

"It's me, Luca."

She leans over the balcony. "Are you out of your mind?" she calls in a frantic whisper. "Don't make another sound!" She disappears from view.

I wait, my heart beating loudly. After a few minutes, I hear footsteps in the alley that skirts the Ca' Zanchi. She appears there, pulling her cloak around her. I row swiftly to the quayside and tie the boat to a mooring post. She furrows her brow and leans down to whisper to me. "What are you doing here? Have you lost your head?" In the distance, we hear the sound of footsteps. To my utter amazement, Giuliana leaps into my boat and disappears into the passenger compartment.

I enter the cabin, and for a moment I suck in my breath. There before me, in real life, is the dream that has obsessed my mind night after night for so long. Giuliana Zanchi is sitting in my boat. In the shadows, she perches on the velvet-upholstered seat, bracing herself as if she imagined she might tip over into the canal. Carefully, I seat myself beside her and reach for her hand.

"Signorina Giuliana, do you remember that I asked you if you had ever seen the moon from the beach at the Lido?"

But she is not paying attention. Her eyes are scanning the shadowy interior of the cabin, taking in the upholstery, the bench, the fittings. "Where did you get this boat?" she whispers.

"I made it."

"What?" she replies in a loud whisper, and I can see that she is genuinely astonished. "Do you take me for a fool?"

"Well, truth be told, signorina, I did not make it; my grandfather did. I just restored it from the ground up. From *felze* to *ferro*." I make an exaggerated sweeping gesture, then grasp one of her wrists with both my hands. "Signorina Giuliana, come for a ride with me to the Lido."

She emits an embarrassed laugh, then stifles it with her free hand. "What? I can't go with you. Not right now." She looks nervously behind her in the direction of her house. "My mother will have every *signore di notte* in town out looking for me. Did you really do all of this yourself?"

"Yes. Don't move." I exit the cabin and pull the aft oarlock from its socket. I return and place the smooth, sculptural piece of walnut in her lap. She runs her fingers along its curved surfaces, and turns it over in her hands.

"My God..." She shakes her head. "You told me your story, and I did believe it was true. But I had no idea that you could do this."

"I didn't know that I could either. This is the first oarlock I've ever tried to make." I lean toward her. "Signorina, if not tonight, tomorrow. Come with me," I insist, emboldened by her fascination with my boat.

She shakes her head, looking nervous. "I cannot."

"Wednesday." I grasp both of her hands, which feel small and cold between my palms. I begin to hum a tune that surely she must recognize, a popular madrigal I've heard performers sing thousands of times during Carnival and other feast day celebrations. My serenade grows louder with each note, and my voice begins to carry outside the passenger compartment, I am sure of it.

"Sssshhhh!" She pulls one hand away and puts her finger to her lips, then looks nervously around her. "You're blackmailing me!" she complains in a loud whisper that ends in a whine.

"Agree to come with me to the Lido on Wednesday, signorina, or I will put the entire work of Petrarch to music." I smile, realizing that my persistence is beginning to pay off.

Giuliana sighs. "*Santa Maria*! You have succeeded. Wednesday—yes. Yes, I will go with you to the Lido. I will have to invent an excuse to be away from home. Pick me up at the quayside that abuts the rio dei Scoacamini on Wednesday at dusk in your new boat. Hold your lantern up for me so that I know it's you."

For a moment, she gazes directly into my face. "Now please, please, before anyone catches us, before I change my mind, I beg you to leave this dock at once!"

She gathers her skirts in her arms, clambers out of the boat and runs down the alley alongside her house.

I MAKE MY WAY down the stairs from my room and encounter Valentin having breakfast in Trevisan's kitchen.

"Your timing is perfect," he greets me, biting into an apricot. "I believe that Master Trevisan is sending us out momentarily." He stands and gestures for me to follow. The two of us step into the artist's studio, quietly opening the door.

Before his easel, Master Trevisan paces nervously back and forth. I recognize the back of the portrait of Giuliana Zanchi with its drape cast over the back of the canvas. The artist makes several silent hand gestures, as if he were conversing with the picture. He steps forward, then back. I watch him swirl the hairs of his brush against the wooden palette. Grimacing, the artist makes two small swipes with his paintbrush, then takes a few steps backward, looking at the small picture with a furrowed brow and a frown. Beads of perspiration appear at his brow. He scratches his gray beard vigorously and fluffs his hair.

At a corner table, one of Trevisan's assistants is mixing paints. Another is working on a tree in the background of an enormous religious painting propped on the other side of the studio, and wiping paint from a fistful of brushes with a dirty rag. Signora Amalia is straightening a stack of books and dusting the shelves. Out of respect for our master, all of us remain silent. As quietly as possible, Valentin makes his way to a table and begins rubbing a collection of paintbrushes with a rag soaked in oil. He places each oiled brush on top of a clean cloth spread out on the table before him. I wait by the kitchen door, observing the artist as he continues his peculiar pacing, murmuring, and beard-scratching before his easel.

Finally, Trevisan picks up a fine brush from a nearby table, dips it into a small pot of black paint, and, tongue between his teeth, signs the lower right corner of the canvas. He catches the eye of Valentin, who looks up from his work and studies his master's face. Finally, the artist wipes a few beads of sweat from his forehead and smiles. His entire body seems to deflate as he exhales.

Trevisan scrawls a note on a piece of parchment, then rolls it up and addresses me. "Luca, please ferry Valentin to the Scuola Grande. In my absence I need for him to make good progress on the Saint Anthony frescoes today."

"Of course, Master Trevisan."

He hands me the scroll. "Then as soon as you are finished, deliver this message to the His Most Excellent Councillor at the Ca' Leoncino, as soon as possible please."

With a tinge of sarcasm, the artist murmurs to himself, "His little picture is finally done."

Chapter 38

Valentin waits for me on the rear deck of the gondola while I unlock the gates and propel the new boat into the canal.

"Is that the first time you've ever seen Master Trevisan do that strange dance?" Valentin asks. "I've seen it a thousand times. He does it every time he finishes a picture."

"So Master Trevisan has completed the picture of Signorina Zanchi, it seems?" I ask, hoping that I've succeeded in concealing my anxiety.

"Yes," says Valentin. "The latest of many the artist has painted for the Councillor."

"Is the Councillor a... collector... of some sort?"

"Mostly he's known for torturing criminals, at least according to what I've heard," says Valentin. "But yes, he also has one of the finest paintings collections in the Republic of Venice. He has commissioned many of our city's best painters, but I think he likes Master Trevisian's work in particular. I've helped with some of the pictures. Recently we finished a very fine Venus and Cupid, and he also commissioned an allegory of Justice for one of the halls where The Ten hold their meetings. His private painting collection is notorious," Valentin tells me. "Especially certain parts of it."

"What do you mean?" I ask.

"He keeps one part of his paintings collection hidden away in a small room of his palace. He only shares it with a select group of his friends. I'm sure the portrait of Signorina Zanchi will end up there."

"And why is that?"

Valentin snorts. "Let's just say that they are private. His Girls."

"His Girls?" I feel desperation rising from somewhere deep inside. My tongue feels dry.

I realize that we are approaching the *scuola*, and I turn the oar to slow the gondola so that I can pry for more information, but Valentin is already standing and waiting to disembark.

"Yes. Trophies of his conquests." Valentin shakes his head. "He seems to prefer the daughters of the most powerful men he can find. Usually the father receives a hefty sum in exchange for his daughter's virginity instead of having to hand over a large dowry to marry her off instead. After that, the father can pack away his daughter to a convent along with a donation to ensure the family's spiritual salvation, and the Councillor goes away with a memorable portrait to share with his closest friends. Usually that's how the story ends." Valentin places a finger to his lips, seeming momentarily confused. "In this case, though, I'm not sure. Signorina Zanchi's father is dead."

I hear a throbbing sound, seemingly audible panic that stretches from my bowels and rises through my chest and finally between my ears. I feel that I can hear every ounce of blood coursing through my veins.

Valentin does not seem to notice. He looks at me and shrugs. "To tell you the truth, I don't understand any of it, but I suppose that Master Trevisan and I don't need to understand the story behind everything we are paid to paint."

Valentin picks up his bag of horsehair brushes and exits the boat. I watch him disappear through a small door inconspicuously tucked into the bottom of a gigantic façade of colored marble patterns.

AT THE THRESHOLD to my room, I stop and listen. The house stands dark and silent except for the regular rasp I hear coming from the bedroom door of two of Trevisan's assistants. Surely they must all be asleep by now. I pick up the candlestick from my desk and tiptoe from the room. I make my way down the narrow stairway, keeping to one side to avoid stepping down the worn, creaky troughs in the middle of each tread.

The kitchen is as dark as a cave except for the flicker of sparks in the hearth, but my eyes have already adjusted to the darkness. The room smells of smoke and Signora Amalia's sweetbread piecrust. My mouth waters and I swallow hard. I creep to the door of the artist's studio and silently lift the latch. I cross Trevisan's studio on my toes, passing the now-familiar table crowded with plaster casts of once-important, long-forgotten men. I pass alongside a second table stacked high with books and pencil drawings. Suddenly, the floor creaks under my weight. I cringe and freeze.

No sound from upstairs.

More carefully, I tiptoe to Trevisan's easel and raise my candle.

My jaw drops.

The painting is a portrait of Giuliana Zanchi, it is true. She reclines on a rich, emerald sofa with gold trim, similar to the one in Trevisan's studio but more ornate. At her mistress' feet, her little brown dog curls into a knot. A female servant in the background of the picture kneels before a large chest, the sort of *cassone* that rich people commission as part of their daughter's dowries.

I am drawn to the face again—I have been observing it for months, both in the painting and in person—the alluring gaze, the soft green eyes, the full, slightly parted lips. But now I realize that Trevisan has painted the girl fully nude, her hand resting calmly at the V-shaped spot of her groin, her breasts emerging with pink nipples from white flesh.

This painting is clearly intended for only one pair of eyes. Is this what it's been about all along?

I huff loudly in disbelief. The sudden rush of my breath extinguishes my candle's flame, and the room falls into darkness.

Chapter 39

"Madonna mia!"

From a dead sleep, the Councillor shoots straight up in bed. Disoriented, he is not certain if it was a knock on the door that he heard or just the pounding of his own heart.

There it is again—a rapping at his bedchamber door. This time he is sure of it.

The Councillor scrambles to a standing position, now fully awake. His linen nightshirt flaps as he strides to his bedchamber door, which is, as always, locked.

"Si?" he demands, his hand on the door latch. He does not open the door.

"I am very sorry to disturb you, Magnificence, but your boatman has just reported to me an important incident. I thought that you should hear about it right away." The Councillor recognizes his valet's voice, and he opens the door a crack to a sliver of candlelight. His valet Alberto bows subserviently. Behind him the Councillor spies his private boatman, the leather-skinned Algerian the Councillor had brokered out of slavery in order to ensure his loyalty. The boatman's real name is unpronounceable, so the Councillor calls him Gabriel.

"Gabriel? Well?"

The boatman, nearly invisible in the darkness, steps forward and begins speaking with a heavy accent. "Magnificence, the woman you

*have been having me follow, Signorina Zanchi..." He hesitates. Even
in the pitch darkness, the Councillor notices that the man's hands are
trembling and his eyes search the floor.*

"Yes, yes, what is it?"

*"Last evening, as the sun was setting, I saw her board a boat I've
never seen before. It was a very peculiar, old-style gondola. The boatman
approached the house and called out to Signorina Zanchi. There did
not appear to be anyone else in the boat except for the man rowing it."*

*"And?" The Councillor begins to breathe audibly, his chest puffing
out and in.*

*Alberto holds the candle before the boatman's face. The Councillor
scrutinizes his features. The whites of the man's eyes glow like orbs in
the candlelight. The boatman wrings his hands, trying to stop them
from shaking. He swallows, then continues.*

*"And, Sir, I watched him lure her into the gondola. But I must
report, Magnificence, that it seemed that she boarded the boat willingly."*

*The valet watches a shadow cover his master's face. His eyes re-
semble two coals, turning blacker by the moment.*

"What else?"

*"Magnificence, then the boatman and Signorina Zanchi disap-
peared inside the passenger compartment. I could not see anything else.
I could not hear anything they said, but I did hear singing. And laughing. They were there for... a while. Then, after a bit she got out of the
boat and ran back inside of her family's house."*

*The boatman and valet observe the scowl on their master's face
grow deeper.*

"Who is it?" he hisses.

The boatman swallows audibly. No one speaks.

*"Who is it?!" the Councillor demands again. The boatman flinches.
Finally, Alberto answers on behalf of the quivering Algerian.*

*"Your Eminence, it's the boatman in the service of the artist
Trevisan."*

Chapter 40

The *pozzi*, the prison cells that lie beneath the Doge's palace, prove even more squalid than their notorious reputation.

My ankles shackled, I shuffle along the stone floor, observing moss growing on the damp stones of the wall. The dank corridor is punctuated at regular intervals with wooden doors and reeks of urine and sweat. Two hulking bailiffs tighten their grip on my elbows. In the distance, I hear water dripping... *tink, tink, tink.*

As I pass, eyes peer out at me from the squares covered by iron grilles that lend access to each cell. Each dank receptacle holds a handful of poor souls. In the first, behind the pair of prisoners who approach the grille to look at me, I spy a woman cowering in a fetal position in the corner of the room, her body resembling a heap of rubbish in a burlap sack. At another grille, a man with a smudged face, his clothes in tatters, seems to look at me without really seeing. He mumbles a low, disturbing, and unintelligible string of words that sound like moaning.

I flinch as I perceive the face of another man pressed against the grille, leering as I pass. The man's brow and cheeks are lined, and the sallow skin below his eyes hangs in bags. The old man's eyes are strangely shiny, enormous reflective orbs. His mouth screws into an exaggerated smile, then lapses into a straight line.

"Is that you, Grimaldi?" he screeches.

"You're dreaming again, Padia," says one of the bailiffs, smirking. The bailiff unlocks the door to the cell occupied by the man with the shiny eyes. He shoves me forward, and I stumble, then catch myself from falling headlong onto the cold stone floor. The door clangs shut behind me, and I hear the footsteps of the two men recede.

"That is no way to speak to the Duke d'Este!" the man shouts at the bailiff through the grille, his voice crackling with hysteria. "I'll have you drawn and quartered before a cheering crowd. Ha! You think I won't do it? Just wait till I get out of this miserable place!" The man's mouth twitches uncontrollably. "This is my second-in-command, you know! He fought with me on the battlefield in Lepanto!"

"At last, you're here, Grimaldi!" the man whispers loudly at me as he turns and grasps my arm. "Grimaldi! I've been waiting for you! You and I together again—ha! Finally! We can devise a plan to get out of here!"

The cell stands completely bare, except for four wooden planks along the wall. The stench that arises from a cesspool in the corner is so vile that I feel I will vomit. I swallow hard.

"Grimaldi! I've been waiting so long." My cellmate smiles raggedly at me again. He sits on one of the planks and appears to address someone I cannot see. "You see? I told you he would find me after all this time! Grimaldi, my dear Grimaldi, all the way from across the sea." The man finally settles into mumbling, humming, and giggling to himself as he addresses the invisible person on the nearby plank. I pace the cell.

"Grimaldi!" the crazy man's voice scratches again, now in a loud whisper. "Now, we must make our plan. I tell you, we must go to the aid of our compatriots in Famagusta. They've all been taken prisoner!"

I sink myself down on a wooden plank and put my head in my hands.

"Grimaldi, don't you recognize me?"

"The name's Luca," I state loudly to my neighbor. Quietly to myself, I add, "Luca Vianello. Son of the gondola maker."

Chapter 41

The official charge is attempted rape, but that is not what excites my prison mates the most. Soon enough they get word that I stand charged for the attempted rape of one of Our Most Serene Republic's most inaccessible patrician women. The prison guards have done their job—chiding me, demeaning me, wearing down my resolve hour by hour. With every insult they hurl at me through the iron grate, the more titillated they become. Soon my fellow inmates in the neighboring cells have been stirred into a frenzy.

"Out with it, *sior*!" One of the bailiffs demands, his sour breath reeking through the air. "We want to hear all the details."

I do not respond.

"Come, now is not the time to be bashful! Tell us what magic words you used to make the lady jump into your boat!" He flashes a twisted grin, and his colleague emits an evil chuckle.

"*Tuxi*, have you already forgotten about me? I am accused of rape, too!" A small man with a high-pitched voice presses his dirty face against an iron grate.

A prisoner two cells away answers. "Bonaldo, you screwed the baker's wife behind some straw bales in the hay market. Where is the *xixolàda* in that? Lieutenant Grimaldi there lured one of Our Most Serene City's most celebrated virgins into his boat. He cannot be called a criminal, only a hero!"

The adjoining cells erupt into cheers and howls. Two men in a cell across from me collapse from laughter, their loud cackling echoing down the dank hallway. Only my cellmate, usually talkative, abstains from commenting. Instead, Padia sits on his wooden plank and hugs his knees to his chin, rocking aggressively forward and back, seemingly oblivious to the carnival of jeers around him.

From the relentless heckling, I learn that there will be no trial, no questioning. At any moment, I could be taken to the upper floors of the Doge's Palace, where I will be hoisted onto a platform and hung by my wrists on the rope, writhing in pain until my hands turn purple, my breath comes in ragged bursts, and I confess. If I admit to the charges, I may be left on the rope and branded with fire, then eventually returned to my cell. If I deny it, well, surely there is something worse to come.

That is nothing, though, compared to what they tell me will happen to my grandfather's gondola, my gondola, the boat I returned to the water through the labor of my own heart and hands. My jailers have left nothing out of the story. It took seven servants of the state, they tell me, to build the great pyre on which the gondola will burn, and a sizable crowd has already assembled to watch the spectacle. In my mind's eye, I see the flames lick the fresh varnish I slicked along the bottom of the gondola with my own hands.

I struggle to imagine if Giuliana Zanchi is there to witness the burning. I wonder if she herself is the one who has accused me, whispering in the ear of her black-eyed patron, her future lover, the man whose money will pay for her freedom in exchange for her innocence and her likeness in paint. With some hope I cling to the idea that we are both victims of the Councillor's passions, and that she is somewhere out there wishing for my deliverance as much as for her own.

Then I face the truth that I do not know Giuliana Zanchi well enough to anticipate her thoughts or her actions. In fact I hardly know her at all, and I cannot begin to imagine what is coursing through her head. All I know is that I was a fool to believe that I held her heart, a fool to risk my own, a fool to imagine that I would have a sliver of a chance in this world with such a woman as she.

Only one thing is certain. I have ruined my life completely, not only once but two times. I deserve the fate that awaits me now. Whatever my destiny, I am resigned to it.

Chapter 42

*From the viewing platform erected across the square from the pyre,
the Councillor scans the crowd. So far, so good, he thinks to himself,
nothing out of the ordinary. All that matters is that this public burning
proceed as smoothly and normally as any public act of justice. There
must be no reason for one of his colleagues to go digging into this matter
in greater detail. It would get too personal, too fast.*

*In the crowd, people whisper to one another that the criminal is
named Luca Fabris,* gondolier de xasada *to the painter Gianluca
Trevisan. The impudent boatman had the gall to attempt to rob the
innocence of one of the city's most upstanding patrician women and
disrupt the order of Our Most Serene Republic. Justifiably, he has been
thrown into the* pozzi, *where he is awaiting transport to the slave galleys. The boat in which the crime was committed will burn.*

*The whole affair has become too complicated, too confusing, the
Councillor observes. First, there is the matter of the identity of the boatman. Two witnesses have already attested that the man held in quar-
antine in the* pozzi *is not Trevisan's boatman at all, but the son of a
gondola maker from Cannaregio. With two witnesses, under Venetian
law the Councillor sees no way to pursue the matter further without
involving his colleagues on the Council of Ten, and at all costs, he
cannot afford to call any more attention to this case. Let the gondola
burn and let everyone think Trevisan's boatman was exiled to the slave
galleys; who will know the difference?*

And as for Signorina Zanchi, quite simply it is time to forget about her, the Councillor thinks. As great as his obsession had grown—and it had grown to uncharted heights for this young woman—she is no longer what he originally perceived. She is no longer the beautiful heiress of one of the richest banking families in Venice. She is no longer an innocent girl. She is probably no longer even a virgin, thanks to that boatman, whoever he is. The Councillor now realizes that he should have trusted his instincts when she first approached him with her proposal; something was bound to go wrong. As he observes the crowd, the Councillor vows never to negotiate directly with a woman again, especially one without a father.

Moreover, the Councillor decides, he will not accept delivery of the portrait that the artist Trevisan has completed. The artist will not receive payment in exchange for the hours he spent observing the woman's flesh and replicating it in paint. Instead, the sum the Councillor secretly pays Trevisan will serve as compensation for the artist's gondola, which must be sacrificed in order to provide a semblance of public justice.

The Councillor sighs. Yes, the neater this act of justice appears, the sooner the whole affair will disappear from public view. As soon as he returns to his chambers, he must summon the court scribe. The Councillor will dictate an account of today's act of justice, using a particular type of language he reserves for such matters, a sanitized recounting of the facts, no more. The scribe will record the dictated words in a graceful and immaculate script, and the case will be recorded for posterity in the Doge's archive. After that the matter will be put to rest.

The Councillor watches a servant approach the boat with a torch. The crowd grows still, and the servant ignites the tender tucked into the bottom of the pyre. With a roar, the wood catches fire, and the flames reach upward toward the keel of the shiny boat. The fire casts the elegant curve of the gondola into silhouette, and dark curls of smoke begin to rise into the air.

Chapter 43

Eventually, I lose track of time.

Has it been days since my arrest? Weeks? My mind struggles to make sense of the seemingly endless cycle of singing, arguing, jeering, moaning, cursing. Water drips relentlessly down one wall of our cell, collecting and slurping into the floor drain. One of the large jailers pushes two bowls of tepid soup through a small opening in the door. I take a spoonful then spit out the disgusting liquid as the bowl rattles to the floor. My stomach rumbles. The relentless nothingness is interrupted only by the serving of inedible food and weak beer diluted with fishy-tasting water, which could only have been drawn from the canal.

I lie on my wooden plank, my eyes closed. I drift in and out of sleep—what else am I to do—while my mind torments me with visions. I see my mother laughing, my baby brother's transparent skin. I feel the chisel in my hand as I work in my family boatyard overlooking the canal. I imagine myself loading crates onto a gondola at Giorgio's *traghetto*. I see myself sanding the prow of my grandfather's gondola, varnishing the keel, carving and smoothing the new oarlock. I see Trevisan sitting in his chair with his feet before the fire, contemplating the stream of unreliable boatmen that have darkened his doorway over decades.

Over and over, I see the image of Giuliana Zanchi in my boat. My mind shuffles through images of her straight teeth, of her walk, of her laughing in a church pew. I imagine burying my face in her neck, feeling her breath against my face, sitting with her in the sand at the Lido. What is real and what is imagined? I no longer know the difference.

Around me, my fellow inmates chat aimlessly, cursing and annoying one another. They talk about the only thing they share in common: whatever infraction has landed them in the *pozzi*. A man in the cell next to us says that he is guilty as charged for stealing a small collection of silver implements from the master of the house where he was employed. His master had beaten him repeatedly, he tells us; he would rather stay here in prison than return. His cellmate stands accused of poisoning his parish priest. A man everyone calls Little Lion says he was arrested for allowing the clockmaker's apprentice into his master's house for a series of clandestine meetings with the master's young daughter. When he insists that he's innocent, his neighbors collapse from laughter.

My insane cellmate Padia launches into unexpected outbursts, most directed at me: "Don't you understand, Grimaldi? They are coming after us, those cowards! It's a conspiracy, don't you see? Our compatriots—all held for ransom! Upon my life, I swear to you that you and I will be vindicated!"

Not only do I not wish to participate in these interactions; I no longer care at all. I stare blankly into the darkness, or close my eyes and pray for the abyss of slumber.

No sooner does the mercy of sleep overtake me that I am haunted by the same dream that has appeared again and again since I landed in prison. In the dream I am a small boy, bracing myself between my father's knees and reaching my hand high above my head for the oar. From our post on the aft deck of the gondola, I feel my father propel the boat forward, the wind in our faces. The muscles of his thighs tighten and release as he rows, right leg forward, left leg back. I feel the polished wood of the oar slip in my palms as it works hard at the beginning then becomes effortless as the craft gains speed. When the waves chop in the widest part of the canal and the boat bucks, I let go of the oar with my left hand and squeeze my father's thigh. Even though I lead with my left hand, from my father's rhythmic rowing I intuit how to push with my right. He places his right hand over my small one, and I feel the callouses on his palm as he presses my hand to steer the boat.

I awake with a start, drenched in sweat. My linen shirt sticks to my back and turns the wooden planks under my body dark. I open my eyes to see the shiny, reflective eyes of Padia, his face just a finger's length from my own. I peer into the bottomless pits of his dark irises and notice the ashy lines that streak his teeth.

"Grimaldi..." His rancid breath spreads across my face as he emits a long, slow hiss. "They have come for you."

THE SOUND OF SCRAPING metal rouses me out of my stupor, and someone fumbles with the great lock of our cell. The door opens, and the figures of two hulking men fill the doorway. Unceremoniously, the men enter. Each man grasps me under an arm and thrusts me through the doorway of the cell.

I know that my punishment is near, and I feel an incongruous sense of relief as I accept my fate. The men drag me down a long hallway past a dozen cells. From them come a stream of catcalls, cursing, and cheering. I do not see their faces because my head hangs so low that I cannot see anything beyond my bound feet. I stumble forward in my shackles, barely able to keep pace with the long strides of the two guards.

At the end of the hallway, the larger bailiff steps forward to unlock a large wooden door, and we fumble up a short flight of stone stairs. Then, the two, each with a hand under my arms, cast me forward with all their might. I feel myself airborne for a moment, then I crash onto the pavement, my shackles rattling on the great cobblestones outside the prison. My cheek scrapes against their cold, hard dampness. Stark sunlight blinds me, and all I see are the hulking shadows of the men against the white light.

"What in God's name?" I gasp, incredulously.

"You got a second witness—your pass out of here. Now disappear."

One of the bailiffs pushes me roughly onto my stomach and unlocks my ankle shackles with an iron key. The man spits a wad of saliva at me, then turns back to the prisons and locks the great wooden door behind him.

There is silence.

For a moment, I lie still, face down on the cold stones, stunned.

I turn my head to the side. As my eyes began to adjust to the light, a pair of leather shoes comes into focus within an arm's reach of my nose. I scramble to a standing position as quickly as I can manage on shaky legs, which feel strangely uncontrollable after being freed from their shackles.

For the first time nearly a year, I find myself standing face to face with the oarmaker.

Chapter 44

I can hardly believe how quickly the oarmaker has wasted away since the last time I saw him, nearly a year ago now.

The man has been scrawny for as long as I have known him, yet there has always been something solid, strong about him. Now Anton Fumagalli seems little more than a bag of bones. The oarmaker's kneecaps protrude beneath the thin cover of his stockings. Loose skin hangs from his neck in bags. His eyes have grown dark and sunken into his skull. His walk is unsteady, and he grasps his workbench for support.

The *remero's* poor physical state has taken its toll on his workshop. Dust collects in the corners, and the workbenches stand cluttered and neglected. "*Cavolo,*" the oarmaker says, scratching his forehead and surveying the mess that his youngest apprentice has left behind. A chisel, two hammers, and the core of a gnawed apple lie strewn across one of the workbenches. A stack of boat plans drawn on parchment lies unfurled across the design table in the back of the room. "I instructed the boy that he was to roll them and tie them neatly, then stack them on the shelves. He was too big of a rush to finish for the day and flee to his mother down the street." He makes a fist. "It's not that I expect perfection from my apprentices, especially brand new ones. It's just that I feel I should not have to supervise every step involved in cleaning my studio."

"*Remer*, please, sit. You are not well." I lead him to a chair before a crackling fire in the hearth that warms the oarmaker's workshop. Cool night air rushes in from under the door and swirls around our feet. With a skeletal hand, the oarmaker clutches a woolen blanket tightly around his shoulders. Under a worktable, I spy a pile of wood shavings and sawdust that litter the floor. I find a dustpan and broom hanging on the wall and squat to fill the dustpan with the shavings.

"I have been a fool, *remer*," I say, breaking the silence as I stab at the floor with the broom.

He looks up at me from his chair and raises his eyebrows. "Luca, you do not owe me explanations. You are young. You make mistakes. I made them too, when I was your age. I have never told you this, but I left my father's studio as a young man, just like you. I thought I was meant for something else." He chuckles. "I even served my time as a rower of the galleys."

"You? Really?" I struggle to imagine the oarmaker seated on a bench in the belly of a great merchant galley, rowing in unison with several dozen others as the great ship propels them far away from whatever they felt compelled to leave behind in Our Most Serene City.

The oarmaker shrugs. "Eventually I came back to the house where I was born. It is true that my own father was a more benevolent fellow than yours, but still, what else was I to do? My studio was here waiting for me." He looks into the fire. "It is no matter. It's all in the past. I do not have much time left now. This malady takes a little more of me each day."

"Don't say such things, *remer*. I am more likely to go to my grave before you are." I lean on my broom handle and smile, but the oarmaker waves his hand at me in a gesture of dismissal.

"I cannot waste a moment talking about what's already been done. We have work ahead of us, you and I." The man who seems to be dying a little more every moment, before my very eyes, is prepared to hand over his workshop to me.

"Master Fumagalli, I am honored beyond words. I don't feel worthy, I don't feel ready to take over your work."

He raises both hands now, then slaps them on his knees. "It's already settled. I have already told you that you are the *only* one worthy to be my successor. This idea did not just appear in my head yesterday. I started thinking about it even before you left the *squero*, truth be told. After the fire, well, I saw my opportunity but then you vanished. You had better not even think of doing that again." He wags a finger at me.

I continue sweeping, my eyes cast to the floor.

"At first I tried to find you," the *remero* says. "Annalisa Bonfante is the only one of us who laid eyes on you after the morning you left my workshop. We all questioned her at length, of course, but I believe that she was honest about not knowing what became of you. Truth be told, I am not sure that she wanted to find you as much as we did after that anyway, poor girl."

I shake my head and continue sweeping.

"Your father had enough on his hands, I suppose, but your brother and sister pled with me to find where you had gone, and I did my best," he continues. "I inquired through my contacts at the Arsenale state shipyard and even the docks where the slave galleys embark. I lay in bed wondering about it every night; I just could not understand how you disappeared so completely. Finally, I had to convince everyone that we needed to wait for you to make your own way back. I was beginning to doubt that you would, but I held out hope, trusting that you would reappear one day and that you would be willing to accept the life I have described to you, the life that I myself have lived."

I know as well as anyone what it takes to pull the master oarmaker away from his workshop, his place in the world. I feel humbled and ashamed that he has gone to all this trouble for me. I move to where the oarmaker sits before the fire. I sink into the chair beside him, hang my head in my hands and shake it in disbelief.

"Your training begins first thing tomorrow morning," he says. "Of course, it's not something you can learn overnight. But you will learn quickly. I am sure of it. I promise you that I will teach you everything I know until I take my last breath." His face softens. "And you thought that you were supposed to make gondolas," the oarmaker teases me, chuckling to himself. For a fleeting moment, I glimpse the man I remember, full of vigor and eager to poke fun at me. "Son, sometimes your destiny turns out to be not precisely what you thought it would be."

"Not according to my father," I say with a hint of sarcasm.

The oarmaker's face turns serious, and his voice lowers to nearly a whisper. "Your father accepted it even before you did, my son." He looks at my face. "You will see."

We sit in silence, and I contemplate this possibility as I watch blue veins dance inside the flames that consume the charred wood. I feel a draft across my feet, and I rise to stoke the fire with a long wrought-iron poker that Master Fumagalli has told me was made by Giuseppe Pontarin, the city's best blacksmith, unfortunately struck down by the last outbreak of plague. I replace the implement in its iron holder next to the hearth, then watch the flames leap anew.

"*Remer*, there is one thing I don't understand," I say, breaking the silence. "They told me that I was released from the Doge's prison because I had not one but two witnesses who could vouch for my true identity. Who was the second witness?"

"I was," he says.

"What do you mean?"

The oarmaker remains silent for a moment while he studies my face. "Bring me that box on the workbench." I notice a large, black wooden container with a metal latch sitting in the shadows at the back of the workshop. I bring it to the oarmaker and place it on the floor. The old man reaches over to unhook the latch. He lifts out a beautifully carved oarlock. He turns it over in his hands, examining it closely through his round spectacles.

I stand up with a start, a shock rending its way through my body. It's the one I made in Master Trevisan's boathouse with my own hands, the one that I assumed had gone up in flames with the rest of the old gondola. There is no doubt that the oarlock is mine; I would recognize its peculiar curvilinear silhouette anywhere. Indeed, there is not another one like it in the world.

"Clearly an oarlock made not only for a left-handed rower, but by a left-handed carver, too." The *remero* smirks and shakes his head. "I should have known it was you the moment I saw it."

I am nearly speechless. "How? How did this get to you?!"

The oarmaker focuses his gaze on my face. "The first witness delivered it to me: a young woman escorted here in a fine gondola, a striking lady with green eyes and a dog. That is how I learned what became of you." The *remero* runs his hand over my oarlock, tracing one of the blond grains in the wood with a crooked finger. "It was she who brought me this box."

It is only then that I notice there is more inside the box, a parchment folio with elegant script, and a flat parcel wrapped in blue paper. As I lift the parcel out of the box, I immediately recognize the familiar paper wrapping that the artist Trevisan uses to package his finished paintings, and I feel the hard edge of the rectangular frame. I do not have to tear open the paper to know what's inside. I feel the heat rise to my face, and I wonder if the *remero* can see my cheeks turn red.

The oarmaker peers at me over the top of his spectacles. "I've been wondering how long it was going to take you to tell me who she is."

MY DEAR LUCA,

You may find it unusual to receive this package, under the present circumstances.

When Signorina Zanchi came to me to ask for my help with your situation, I must admit that I was more than a bit surprised, not only by the unexpected turn of events but also, of course, by the fact that I had been completely unaware of your rapport with the banker's daughter.

After some reflection, however, I believe I better understand the motives that led to this most curious set of circumstances. Moreover, some of the unresolved questions that had occupied me about your talents as a boat maker have now been answered. As much as I regret no longer having you in my service as a gondolier de xasada, *I consider that business arrangements are now settled between us. You should not bear any burden of obligation toward me or toward my studio.*

What became of the old gondola is of course regrettable, but you must understand that it was the price of putting this matter to rest. I did manage to salvage the oarlock, which of course no one else noticed was missing from the boat. I hope that it will bring you not only some measure of consolation but of pride, as it is the mark of a fine craftsman.

Rest assured that I shall refer my patrons to your workshop for the repair and replacement of their gondola fittings.

Gianluca Trevisan

Painter

IN VENICE, THINGS ARE not always as they first appear. I contemplate this observation from my post on the aft deck of one of Master Fumagalli's gondolas, taking in the panorama of bridges, domes, bell towers, and quaysides of my native city. I row into the neck of the Grand Canal, and, one by one, the reflection of each colorful façade appears, only to dissipate into wavering, shimmering shards under my oar.

As I head in the direction of the Convent of Santa Maria della Celestia, I try to imagine Giuliana Zanchi cloistered behind its stark walls. Has she traded her elegant gowns for the drab gray habit of the Dominicans, her opulent palace bedroom for a bare cell? I try to imagine her intoning hymns in the choir stalls for decades to come, but I fail to picture the image.

I pass the façade of the Ca' Zanchi, the residence I have been watching at a distance for months. Her palace now stands empty, a cold, inhospitable mass of stone, marble, and wood, stripped bare, its black windows no more than gaping holes. An image of Giuliana Zanchi leaping into Trevisan's old gondola from its quay-side crosses my mind, and I feel the familiar pang of loss stab me under my ribs.

If the Councillor does not possess her portrait, it must mean that neither does he possess her innocence, nor she the money that would buy her freedom. Surely the sale of her jewels would not be sufficient to sustain her for years to come or provide a dowry worthy of a nobleman's hand in marriage. A life in the convent is the natural solution, as much as she—and I—might wish for her a different fate.

I ring the brass bell outside the canal-side door to the convent, and a servant answers the door. Of course I know that they will not accept an unknown visitor, especially a man rowing a gondola, so I use the excuse I've prepared:

"I have been instructed to hand-deliver an important message to Signorina Zanchi," I say.

"Wait here, please," she says, latching the door back into position. I hear the murmuring of two female voices behind the door.

A nun in a gray habit cracks open the door, setting her clear, blue eyes on me. "You have a message for the Widow Zanchi?" she asks.

"No, I refer to her daughter, Giuliana Zanchi. I understand that she has taken her vows here."

"I'm afraid you are mistaken, *missier*," she says. "Signorina Zanchi has not taken her vows. She is not among us."

I am stunned. "Where is she?"

"I am told that Signorina Zanchi has left the city. I understand that she is lodged with her cousins on terra firma while the family awaits the settlement of her father's affairs."

"When is she to return to Venice?" I ask.

"Of that I cannot say, *missier*," says the woman. "I do not know more than what I have just told you. May I convey a message to her mother?"

"No," I say. "Thank you for your assistance."

"May God bless you, *missier*," she says, then latches the convent door.

I row back to the studio, feeling a wave of relief followed by another pang below my ribs. Will Giuliana Zanchi return to Our Most Serene Republic, and if she does, will I find her before another man claims her as his own, or before she resolves to take her vows at Santa Maria della Celestia after all? Is there a chance in the world that she, in her reversal of fortune, might consider a life as the wife of an oarmaker?

For now, I hold onto a speck of hope, a collection of memories, and a painted souvenir.

Chapter 45

Little Antonio is barely old enough to walk, but I can already tell that he is cut from the same cloth as my mother and me. Our brother, Daniele, stands next to me at my workbench, balancing the wiggly toddler on his hip. The little boy buries his face in Daniele's shoulder, then dares to peek at me with amber-colored eyes that are replicas of my own. A shock of dark hair falls over his forehead. I stick out my tongue at him. He giggles and mashes his face against Daniele's shirt again. I feel my heart surge.

For two days my brother Daniele has not left my side. He confides that he is afraid I will disappear again, and he won't stand for it. While I work, he talks of many things—Antonio's love for the mallet, the squash that Mariangela now has growing in the garden, our Uncle Tino's strange illness in the winter from which he has now recovered. Gingerly, he tells me of Annalisa's betrothal to the goldsmith's son following her father's wishes, a turn of events for which I feel satisfied. Daniele does his best to talk to me about the boatyard, but on that subject I am a reluctant listener.

"We were able to start building boats again quickly thanks to Uncle Tino's friendship with Master Enrico of the Squero Rosmarin, and of course the help of the guild. Last month we finished roofing the new *téza*," he tells me. "There is still much to do, but for now we stay dry when it rains. Even Mariangela visits us in the boatyard sometimes," he laughs.

I harden my expression and raise my palm toward my brother. "Daniele, I have told you. I am not ready."

"Yes, I know. I can understand that you are not ready to see the *squero* or even hear about it. It stands to reason," he says. "But you cannot delay seeing our father, Luca. It is only right."

I lay down my file and walk to the front of the oarmaker's shop, where the old *remero* has placed my oarlock in a prominent window facing the street. I run my hand over its smooth, polished arc. Behind it stands a cluster of two dozen oarlocks carved in a more old-fashioned manner, each beautiful piece wrought with the master's collection of rasps, saws, blades, and sanding blocks. Daniele sets our little brother down on the floor, where he races under a table on his hands and knees. He picks up a scrap of sandpaper that has fallen to the floor and waves it in the air.

"Antonio will make a fine replacement for me in the *squero*." I laugh nervously and return to my worktable. I have begun to block out a new oarlock—a copy of the one in the window—that the old oarmaker insists I begin right away. At the guildhouse, our fellow *remeri* have begun to whisper about my new way of fashioning the arc and proportions of the oarlock. Gondolas carrying a few of our more curious colleagues have already begun to appear at our ramp.

"Surely you are kidding?" Daniele replies. "Together the Vianello brothers will make the most beautiful boats—and oarlocks—Our Most Serene Republic has ever seen!" My brother laughs too, then his expression hardens. "Luca, he will be here soon. I will admit, it took some convincing, but Father agreed to walk here from the *squero* after the midday meal. You must understand; you cannot postpone the inevitable."

I turn the newly shaped oarlock over in my hands as I let my brother's words settle into my heart, then I lay the oarlock gently on the table. I walk to the door of the oarmaker's studio and rest my forehead against its wooden planks. I close my eyes and lift my left hand—my "correct" hand—the one I was always meant to use. The wood of the oarmaker's door feels cool and smooth against my palm. My brother comes to stand behind me. I feel his strong hands press on my shoulders. For the first time in my life, I feel peace wash over me.

In my mind's eye, I see our father walking up the alley to the oarmaker's studio—my studio. I imagine his familiar, purposeful stride carrying him toward me, toward this moment that must be as inevitable as my brother has said. I feel I can almost hear him breathe, his chest heaving from the trek.

My father stands on the other side of the door now, lifting his right hand. On either side of this narrow barrier my father and I stand like reflected images. Our hands are the same: large knuckles, flat, smooth nails, his skin more lined, mine smoother but worn now from labor. We are separated by the hardness of the oak planks, the hardness of life, the hardness in our hearts. We are mirror images nonetheless.

I am so lost in my vision that when the knock comes, I doubt that it is real, but my heart, which skips a beat, confirms it. I open my eyes and take a deep breath.

Gently, I open the door.

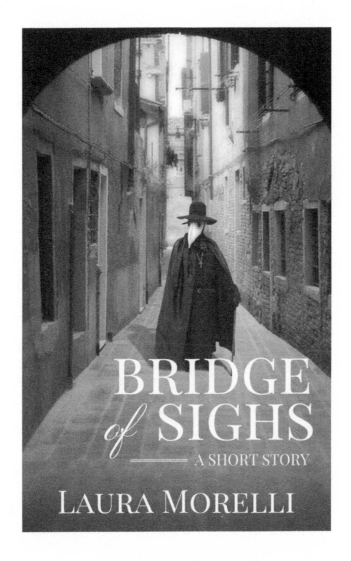

Download your free copy of
"Bridge of Sighs: A Short Story of the Bubonic Plague."

www.lauramorelli.com/bridge-of-sighs/

Author's Note

The story of *The Gondola Maker* germinated inside my head while I was busy researching another book called *Made in Italy*. The contemporary Italian artisans I interviewed, one after another, told me how important it was to them to pass on the torch of tradition to the next generation. I began to wonder what would happen if the successor were not able or willing to take on that duty. The characters of the gondola maker and his heirs began to take shape.

Luca Vianello and the other characters in this novel are figments of my imagination. Still, it was essential to me to portray them inside a world that was as authentic and historically faithful as I could make it; any shortcomings in this area are mine alone.

Constructing the backdrop for *The Gondola Maker* was a joy thanks to the wealth of historical sources from which to draw. Renaissance Venetians were well aware of their position in the world, and their culture is voluminously documented in primary sources. David Chambers and Brian Pullan assemble one of the most valuable compilations of these sources in their *Venice: A Documentary History 1450-1630*. Primary sources for a handful of Venetian painters are collected in the now-dated but excellent *Sources & Documents of the History of Art* series edited by my former teacher at Yale, Creighton Gilbert and his co-authors, Robert Klein and Henri Zerner. The artists' contracts, conflicts, lawsuits, and

incidental reports shaped my understanding of the complex rela-
tionships between Venetian painters, their patrons, and the public.
My depiction of the artist Gianluca Trevisan and his workshop is
set within this transitional period in the history of art when the
status of a handful of artists rose from that of mere laborers to reach
unprecedented heights.

Even though Venetian boatmen once numbered in the tens
of thousands, because they were members of the lower class they
remain relatively silent in historical documents except for random
incidental accounts. I am grateful for the scholarship of Dennis
Romano, whose work shaped my understanding of the private lives
of domestic servants and other members of the Venetian lower class.
Patricia Fortini-Brown's work immersed me in the material world
that Giuliana Zanchi would have occupied, with its infinite variety
of fine objects from paintings to tableware and platform shoes.

The sixteenth-century gondola was a simpler contraption than
the elaborate boats now synonymous with Venice. To my knowledge no complete Venetian gondola made prior to the mid-1800s
survives intact; only a handful of iron prows from the Renaissance
era have endured the humid Venetian climate that destroys anything made of wood, even of the highest order of craftsmanship.

As an art historian I am trained to view every work of art, even
a photograph, as a "re-presentation" rather than a faithful record-
ing of actuality. Nonetheless the earliest depictions of the Venetian
gondola let us imagine what the craft that Luca Vianello restored
in *The Gondola Maker* could have looked like. A sketchy carving on
an altarpiece erected by gondola makers in 1628 inside the Church
of San Trovaso depicts the familiar arc of the gondola with its spiky
iron prow decorations, the *ferri*, on either end, and a covered passenger compartment, or *felze*.

Still, these boats must have remained relatively somber thanks
to sumptuary laws that decreed that all gondolas be painted black.
We can envision these dark, elegant boats with the help of a series

of beautiful wall paintings executed by Vittore Carpaccio in the 1490s for the Church of Saint Ursula, now preserved in the Accademia in Venice. Not only Venetians but also foreign visitors must have been impressed by these distinctive boats, since printmakers such as the Swiss artist Joseph Heinz the Younger and the Dutch author and statesman Nicolaes Witsens disseminated views of the gondola in woodcut prints and engravings that made their way across Europe. A woodcut by the Swiss artist Jost Amman portrays a gondola with a fore and aft oarlock, rowed by two oarsmen, in "Grand Procession of the Doge of Venice," published in Frankfurt in 1597. More elaborate oarlocks, upholstery, carving, and the peculiar asymmetrical form of modern gondolas that allow for more effective rowing, all developed from the 1700s onward.

I am grateful to the handful of modern historians, mostly Venetians, who have chronicled the development of the gondola through the centuries. Carlo Donatelli describes the boats' technical, engineering, and hydrodynamic evolution. Giovanni Caniato and Gianfranco Munerotto have made significant documentary contributions to the history of Venetian boats, including the gondola. Caniato has also pulled together comprehensive documentation of the history of Venetian oarmakers, and I am grateful for this important and unique contribution. Guglielmo Zanelli has chronicled the history of Venetian ferry stations, or *traghetti*, like the one where Luca found his first gainful employment after fleeing the boatyard fire. I am grateful to the Museo Arzanà in Venice for their efforts to assemble the remaining fragments—oarlocks, tools, seats, and other pieces—of historical Venetian boats.

The famous "Barbari map," an enormous woodcut by Jacopo de Barbari dating from 1500, shows an aerial view of Venice that gives us an appreciation of the huge number of gondola boatyards, or *squeri*, in the city at that time. Today vestiges of only a few historic *squeri* survive. The most well-known of these is the Tramontin boatyard still in operation today in the Dorsoduro quarter, but there are others that are not as well-known or no longer used for their original purpose. The organization and inner workings of the historical Venetian *squeri* are well-understood thanks to the rule books, or *mariregole,* that each Venetian trade guild was required by law to maintain. From these important documents, we learn intricate details about the making of gondolas in centuries past. Giovanni Caniato and Guglielmo Zanelli have published important work on the Venetian *squero* that helps us understand what daily life in a gondola boatyard for a journeyman like Luca Vianello would have been like.

Scholars have paid surprisingly little attention to the late medieval church of San Giovanni Battista in Brágora, where Luca and Giuliana meet on several occasions. The composer Antonio Vivaldi was baptized there, an event noted in the church record book in 1678. The church also houses important works by Venetian painters Cima da Conegliano, Bartolomeo Vivarini, and Palma the Younger. If I were to choose a spot for a clandestine meeting at dusk, I can hardly think of a more perfect setting than this quiet, beautiful gem of a church.

The Gondola Maker begins with an incident in which a gondolier hurls a stone at another gondola ferrying the French ambassador, resulting in a distinctly Venetian act of justice: the public boat-burning that Luca witnesses. This incident, along with many others that play a role in this story, are based on specific events documented in the Venetian historical record. My hat is off to the historian Dennis Romano for extracting these juicy morsels from the Venetian archives—from boatmen punching a hole in the bottom of a boat and filling it with rocks, to the stealing of oarlocks and jewelry, to the arrangement of complicated associations with tavern owners and courtesans, to gondoliers' notoriously foul language. These fascinating glimpses underline not only the checkered history of the Venetian gondola, but also the consequences of pride and the universal passions that drive our human nature.

As always, truth is stranger than fiction.

Would you like to delve deeper into the research behind
The Gondola Maker?

Would your book club like additional resources to support
your discussion of *The Gondola Maker*?

Visit the bonus section of my web site for videos, pictures
of gondola-making and the sites mentioned in this book,
and more bonus material available exclusively to my readers:

http://lauramorelli.com/gondolamaker-bonus

Want to know what happened before *The Gondola Maker*?
Read *The Painter's Apprentice*

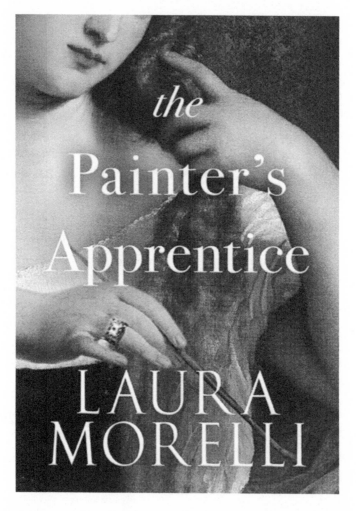

Would you rather sacrifice your livelihood, your lover, or your
life? When the Black Death comes knocking on your door,
you'd better decide quickly.

The Painter's Apprentice by Laura Morelli

www.books2read.com/PaintersApprentice

Acknowledgements

I have dreamt of writing a novel since I was a little girl, but it took me forty-six years and a giant leap of faith to actually write one. My parents and their previous generation taught me the value of stories, and for that I am ever grateful. I thank my husband, my children, and my extended family for tolerating my flights of fancy with patience and support.

Special thanks go to those who commented on early drafts: Lisa Andoni, Don Bell, Wendy Beasley, Karla Bole, Matteo Casini, Dan Cicora, Elisabeth de'Ath, Ann Fisher, Jessica Hatch, Therese Keelaghan, Sophia Khan, Faith Lusted, Frances Mayes, Danielle and Holly Pisano, Pamela Sheldon Johns, Mark Spencer, Ellen Tener, and Bridget Weber. With their eager and surprising questions, my art history students pressed me to see my work in a new light.

Most of all, I owe my deepest respect and thanks to the Italian artisans who have endured my questions and disruptions over the years with patience and generosity, especially Daniele Bonaldo, Franco Furlanetto, Gilberto Penzo, and Saverio Pastor. In particular, I am grateful to Roberto Tramontin and his colleagues. My hat is off to these last *squerarioli* in Venice—just a handful of men who hold the grand tradition of Venetian gondola-making in their hands.

I HOPE YOU ENJOYED READING THIS BOOK.

Would you consider leaving a review to help other readers?
Thank you! Visit www.books2read.com/GondolaMaker
to leave your review.

Sign up to receive news and information about my new projects:
www.lauramorelli.com

Thank you and happy reading!
—Laura Morelli

About the Author

LAURA MORELLI holds a Ph.D. in art history from Yale University, has taught college students in the U.S. and in Italy, and produces art history lessons for TED-Ed. She authored a column for *National Geographic Traveler* called "The Genuine Article" and has contributed pieces about art and authentic travel to *CNN Radio*, *The Frommers Travel Show*, and in *USA TODAY*, *Departures*, and other media. Laura is the author of the Authentic Arts guidebook series that includes the popular book *Made in Italy*. Her fiction brings the stories of art history to life. *The Gondola Maker* is her debut novel, and won an IPPY for Best Historical Fiction and a Benjamin Franklin Award.

Made in the USA
Monee, IL
27 January 2021

58873960R00173